Mary

Call Me Blessed

PATTY FROESE NTIHEMUKA

Published by Autumn House® Publishing, a division of Review and Herald® Publishing, Hagerstown, MD 21741-1119

Autumn House® titles may be purchased in bulk for educational, business, fund-raising, or sales promotional use. For information, e-mail SpecialMarkets@reviewandherald.com.

Autumn House® Publishing publishes biblically based materials for spiritual, physical, and mental growth and Christian discipleship.

The author assumes full responsibility for the accuracy of all facts and quotations as cited in this book.

This book was
Edited by Gerald Wheeler
Designed by Ron J. Pride
Cover photos by Joel D. Springer
Interior designed by Heather Rogers
Typeset: Bembo 11.5/13.5

PRINTED IN U.S.A.

12 11 10 09 08 5 4 3 2 1

Library of Congress Cataloging-in-Publication Data
Ntihemuka, Patty Froese, 1978- .
Mary : call me blessed : the story of an unwed mother / Patty Froese Ntihemuka.
p. cm.
1. Mary, Blessed Virgin, Saint—Fiction. 2. Bible. N.T.—History of Biblical events—Fiction. 3. Christian women saints—Fiction. 4. Women in the Bible—Fiction. I. Title.

PR9199.4.N825M39 2008
813'.6—dc22

2008031884

ISBN 978-0-8127-0484-6

Dedication

To my husband, Jean,
my love and my life,
and to our beautiful new boy,
Jean Claude

Preface

Two thousand years ago in the land of Judea what the modern world would consider an unwed mother gave birth to a prophesied baby.

It doesn't matter if the girl lived in ancient Judea or in modern North America—an unwed mother attracts attention! Who was she? Who was her family? And how did her community react? Because everybody knows that a baby changes everything.

As I worked on this story—researching the writings of Josephus, an ancient historian, and looking into the social customs of ancient Judea—I discovered that I myself was pregnant. And as I write this, I am still pregnant—experiencing the miracle of a baby's development for the first time. I also realize, in a very real way, that a baby changes everything.

My body is changing. My emotions are reeling. My husband is ecstatic! And suddenly I feel that I understand Mary just a little bit better. She wasn't a saint—she was terrified! Nor was she perfect—she was vulnerable. And she wasn't an icon—she was an unwed mother in a society that would kill her because of that fact.

You see, a baby changes everything.

Two thousand years ago a baby did change everything! And it is because of that baby born to an unwed mother in Judea that I am not afraid to face bringing my child into the world. Because I am not alone. Neither is the baby inside of me.

Glory to God in the highest! And peace and good will on the earth!

Chapter 1

Rather any sickness than sickness of the bowels; rather any pain than pain of the heart; rather any disorder than a disorder in the head; rather any evil than a bad wife.

—*From the Mishnah*

Nasim pried her son's sticky hands off her hair and flipped him around to face the kitchen. An oven stood just outside the door in the courtyard, but for the time being she was finished baking and cooking. That could not be said for many hours out of the day. Tall clay jars lined the walls, and her son reached out to grab at some herbs that were drying near the window, but instead managed to snag another handful of her hair.

She felt irritated. This was not what the family needed, and she felt more annoyed than anything with the entire situation. It was an embarrassment—that's what it was!

"Oh, stop it!" she said, tugging her hair free from the baby's grasp a second time. Her son screwed up his face and tensed his body as if to wail, then, thankfully seemed to change his mind.

"I don't know what our father is thinking," her brother James grumbled, shaking his head. Arms crossed over his chest, he leaned against the wall.

"She's only two years older than you are," Nasim pointed out. "Why couldn't he have found a sensible widow?"

James fingered some of the herbs hanging nearby. He still got the same expressions on his face that he had sported as a small boy. Seeing him chew the inside of his cheek made her smile, and she shook her head. At least he had come when the home was neat as a water-polished stone. She wouldn't have him believe that her housekeeping was not as good as their mother's had been! But keeping up with a baby was harder than she'd ever imagined. Caring for her younger cousins had never been like this.

The house had two stories. The bottom level consisted of one room, segmented off into two sections—a kitchen storage area and a living area. The cooking fire was outside in the courtyard facing the neighboring homes, and unless Nasim wanted the entire community to hear about their family issues, discussions were best held indoors. The upper level was more of a loft, with a ladder for access. It was where the family slept, with straw pushed under their sleeping mats for comfort. Her husband was a younger son, and since his father's house was filled to overflowing with his eldest son's family and his unmarried daughters, his father had helped him to settle in a small home of their own close by.

Nasim found it lonely being separated this way. She was used to a bustling house with brothers and sisters, two parents, two grandmothers, and a cousin all under one roof. Time moved on, however, and after the death of her mother, both grandmothers also passed away. Then she and her sister had married and moved out of the family home, leaving their father and her newly married brother in the old family quarters.

"What does your wife think of it?" Nasim asked.

"Hannah thinks that it would be *fun* to have a younger woman about the house with her," James replied with a pained expression. "Obviously her interests are not with this family, but her own. If it were her father doing this, she'd have other opinions, I'm sure."

Shrugging, Nasim couldn't blame the girl. A daughter-in-law was always on the outside, something that she had learned firsthand. She acutely felt the slight of not being included in her father-in-law's household.

"I suppose he wants her for her beauty," James said after a moment. "Mary is beautiful, you have to admit."

"I have to admit nothing of the sort!" Nasim said with a sniff. "She's pretty, I'll give you, but to call her beautiful is a stretch."

"She has nothing on you, of course," he said, giving his sister an amused smile. "You have Mother's well-bred looks."

Wrinkling her nose at her brother, Nasim deposited her son at her feet, where he stretched his fingers toward the bristles of a nearby broom.

"Father has always been so sound in his judgment," Nasim continued. "Maybe it is the grief that has affected him. We can't be angry at him for wanting to remarry . . ."

"No, of course not," her brother agreed, but his tone betrayed the lie in his words.

Nasim brought another plate of dried dates and sat down next to her brother. They were silent for a few moments, both lost in their own thoughts.

"It seems like a betrayal to Mother," she finally broke the silence.

"It does," he agreed quickly, looking at her with an expression of relief.

"Do you remember how she used to sing that song to us when we had bad dreams? How did it go?"

"God bless you, God keep you, God grant you sweet rest," James sang softly. "God hold you, God love you, for you are His blessed . . ."

"It always made everything better, somehow," she commented, glancing fondly down at her son. "I sing it for him sometimes, too."

"Mother always used to tell me that a good wife was the daughter of a good woman. And one day, when I was a small boy, she pointed out Hannah, and said, 'That would be a good wife for you, son.'"

"You two were betrothed before she died. Perhaps the families were already discussing your marriage then."

"I wouldn't doubt it," he said with a wry smile. "But she was right about Hannah."

Nasim nodded. "Mother taught us well. I was ready to care for a home of my own at the age of 12. Of course, there are too many things in marriage that I was not prepared for . . ."

"You always have us. Don't let your in-laws make you too upset."

His sister just smiled. It was not her problems with her in-laws that she was thinking of. No, she was considering the difficulty of getting to know this man she must live beside. A brother was easy to deal with in comparison to a husband! Even a teasing, difficult brother! Someone you had known from childhood and shared memories with. It provided an established relationship already there to help cushion the bumps along the way. With a husband, the only cushion was the role she must perform . . . a new role that she had only watched from the outside. And now there was the baby . . .

"I have to get back to help Father in the shop," James said, pushing himself to his feet. "But I wanted to see you."

"Have you seen Yafit? I think she looks pregnant."

"Praise God!" he exclaimed. "Be sure to tell me as soon as she tells you."

"Of course," Nasim said with a wink. What was family if not an intricate network of gossip? Besides, Yafit was their sister and being informed about her life was not gossip so much as their right. Her other brothers would be glad for the news, too, and she could only hope that she could be the first to relay it.

James kissed his sister's cheek and ruffled his nephew's sparse hair.

"God be with you, brother," Nasim said affectionately.

"And with you," he replied as he walked to the door.

"Don't worry. Father will realize that this betrothal with Mary is not a good plan."

James didn't answer, but as he turned away, she felt that surge of frustration. If she were a man, she would find something to beat until she had exhausted her irritation. But she was a woman. She chose the next best thing—she kneaded the bread with the ferocity of a warrior in battle.

Joseph ran a work toughened thumb over the edge of a plank he was planing. It was straight and smooth, and he made a satisfied sound in the back of his throat. As his son worked behind him, the sharp sound of hammer on nail rang cheerfully through the air. James was a good craftsman. He always measured twice and cut once—the golden rule of their trade.

The perfume of shaved wood and the breeze carrying the scent of the white blossoms of myrtle trees filled the small shop. It was actually one room of the lower part of his house, and on fine, hot summer days such as today, they opened the door wide and moved the work outside under a tarp for shade.

It was hard not to be in a good mood on a day like this. Joseph tucked his thumbs into his leather belt and looked back at his son's work. He felt younger than his 35 years. Married at 17 and five children in quick succession—he'd done well for himself. He had an heir to take over the business. His daughters were both advantageously married. The community recognized him for his skill in carpentry, and with all the building that Rome was doing in the surrounding cities, his business was thriving. And he was about to be married again.

"Fine work, son," he commented.

James wiped his moist forehead with the back of his hand and shot his father a smile that reminded Joseph of the young man's mother. Joseph's wife, Hadas, had died two years earlier from a fever.

"Thanks," James said absently, his attention still focused on the work in front of him.

"You're looking more and more like your mother, son," Joseph said in a low voice that the rasping sound of James' saw drowned out.

Hadas . . . she'd been a good woman. Joseph remembered the day that he married her. He'd never seen her before in his life and he'd been sweaty-palmed and dry-mouthed wondering what kind of woman his father had provided for him. Only 16 at the time, Hadas had not, like most girls, arrived crying at her wedding. The groom and the male members of his family collected the bride during the night, and it was very rare for a girl not to be sobbing her heart out as she was carried to the house that her new husband had provided for her. But Hadas had been dry-eyed and solemn, as if approaching her doom.

Joseph chuckled now at the memory. Both of them had been so young, without a pinch of foresight or experience. They had been utter strangers to each other, and in the course of one honeymoon week were expected to get to know each other to a tolerable degree that would allow them to put a good face forward to the village. Practical and a good homemaker, Hadas cooked well, but tended to overspice the stew, something that drove Joseph's own mother up the plastered wall of their house and down the other side. Hadas would always manage to add more spice behind his mother's back, and there was no end to that struggle.

Luckily, Joseph's parents had been still alive, and the family lived together in one house. His parents provided both a buffer for the new couple and an example of how to behave in a marriage. He learned to behave correctly toward his new wife, something that consisted of what felt like exaggerated politeness. But his father was right—the overdone civility did cushion many bumps. Hadas learned what to expect and what not to. Joseph admired her. Brave and resolute, she would rise to every challenge. She was a loving mother. But she always did overspice the stew . . .

Yes, Joseph could not complain about Hadas. A good wife, she had known her duties and performed them well as she cared for her family. She had raised her children to be well-mannered and obedient. Although neither quarrelsome nor a nag, she did have a way of fixing him with a look, though, that still made him squirm to think about! His father had chosen well for him.

When Hadas died after 20 years of marriage, he felt the loss of her acutely. He missed her pragmatic approach to problems. He missed her presence in the home. He missed her kind words. If children were the blossoms of life, then a wife was the root and branch.

And now, two years after the death of his wife, Joseph planned to marry again. But it was different this time. No one else was arranging his marriage for him. He was a grown man, widowed, and remarrying for himself. Furthermore, he was not selecting a young woman based on dowry, the status of the family that she came from, or in a strategic attempt to amass more land. Rather, he was choosing Mary for a reason that seemed ridiculous even to him—he had fallen in love with her.

Love before marriage was unheard-of, though love after marriage was hoped for. If a bride was chosen judiciously, and she had a gentle temperament and a submissive attitude, it was conceivable that the husband would grow to feel tender toward her through time. But love was equivalent to marriage, was it not? When Isaac married Rebekah, the Torah said that he loved her. A good match in which both parties received what was their due was love, wasn't it? It was what he had always believed. That is, until he saw Mary and spoke briefly with her one morning in the market. . . . Then everything that he had always believed about love seemed to melt away like morning frost.

It was terrifying—something that a man did not like to admit. Joseph struggled to turn his attention back to his work.

The beams that Joseph and James were adzing into shape would support an upper addition to a villager's home. Joseph examined those they had finished. He did not like to submit poor-quality work to anyone. What did a man have when he lost his good name?

Houses were constructed mostly of stone and mortar with wooden support beams in the walls and across the roofs. A good carpenter also knew how to make the supports secure for the upper story.

"Father, you seem distracted."

Joseph shrugged and looked down at a beam that he had been holding in his rough hands for several minutes. He put it down with a self-conscious laugh.

"I'm to be married soon. You remember how preoccupied you got when your wedding approached, son. It's strange for your father now to be in the same position, but here I am."

"Are you concerned?"

"I'm feeling things that I have not felt before," his father said carefully.

James nodded, but a wounded look lurked in his eyes that saddened Joseph. His children did not understand.

Joseph realized that they still carried the memories of their dead mother with them. He knew that a part of them felt betrayed by his decision to remarry. And he also recognized that his betrothed was younger than they were. So he couldn't blame his grown children for feeling what they did. They missed their mother. They resented change. They were human. His precious children . . .

"How did you choose my wife?" James asked suddenly.

"I thought and prayed about what kind of woman would complement you. We looked at all the eligible girls in the area and chose the one with the most suitable temperament and the best family business connections."

"And how did you choose your new wife?"

Joseph did not answer for a moment.

"She is a good woman, son," he said finally, his voice controlled and signaling the end of the conversation.

Mary was a good choice, but his method for choosing a wife was different from the way he had used to select mates for his children. Mary came from a respectable family. Hard working, religious, and sweet tempered, she had a sparkle in her eye that betrayed her own humorous view of life. She had a reputation for being virtuous and kind and seemed a perfect choice. But all these things were not enough for him to decide on her. No, there was something else . . . and it was Joseph's perplexing secret.

It was the way she stopped his breath when he saw her. It was the way he wanted to protect her from anything that might cause her pain. It was the way his heart sped up at the mention of her name and the way his palms began to sweat when she flicked her veil down over her shoulder before she hoisted her water jar. It was that hammering of his heart, his loss of speech around her, his constantly preoccupied mind. This was why he must marry her.

He had never felt this way before. Not even with Hadas. And Hadas had been a good woman. Yes, he could marry another good woman like Hadas and find equal happiness, he was sure. But could he ever find another woman to make his heart beat faster in his chest?

The strange thing was that the more he prayed for God's guidance, the more his heart seemed to flutter at the very thought of her and the less he could think of eating. . . .

This was what he could not explain to his son. It was something that he could barely admit to himself! No, it was not a reason to marry. Men married for other reasons entirely. They married for family alignment and enhanced social reputations—not for a feeling.

But apparently, Joseph did.

Foolishness! The collective village opinion resounded through his mind. They would think that the sun had finally touched him. That he needed to rest and gather his fleeting senses. Perhaps a poultice might help, or a change in diet . . .

But no, he did not need those things. He needed her. He needed Mary to be his wife.

And then perhaps his appetite would return.

CHAPTER 2

If a man happens to meet in a town a virgin pledged to be married and he sleeps with her, you shall take both of them to the gate of that town and stone them to death.

—*Deuteronomy 22:23, 24*

Esther crossed her arms, her fingers leaving floury marks on her forearms. Her kitchen was her pride, and she watched as her two eldest daughters ground meal and sifted the newly made flour. Mary and Naomi were both beautiful girls. Taken more after their grandmother than herself, Esther thought ruefully. They had finer features than she had. Even as a young woman, her features had been large and her figure described as "solid." But Mary and Naomi were both more slender and delicate, with fine hair and large eyes. But they had their mother's generous lips—that much Esther could say came from her!

"It will not be long before your husbands come for you," Esther said. "I heard Ruth mention to your aunt that Ashi has been purchasing large quantities of fabric. I'm sure it is the last step before he comes for you, Naomi! Any day now, I'm sure of it!"

"Oh."

It was all Naomi said, and her mother frowned, wondering at her daughter's meaning.

"Ashi will be a good husband, Naomi," Esther continued. "You cannot stay at home forever. You must have a home of your own. A husband. Children."

"Of course," Naomi replied, an unconvincing smile on her face.

"Mary, put some sense into your sister," their mother sighed. She turned back some dough she was kneading in a stone trough.

"Father knows his family well," Mary said tentatively. "Father says he is a good young man with a strong character."

"I'm sure he is," Naomi echoed with the same vague implication.

"You will get out of your home only what you put into it, Naomi," Esther advised. "And with an attitude like that, I'll be surprised if Ashi doesn't send you back for me to finish raising you! Should that happen, girl, so help me . . ."

The unfinished threat hung in the air.

Esther pounded the dough harder, squeezing it flat with the heel of her hand. In her day a girl would not have been so ungrateful about having a good marriage arranged for her! In her day a girl would have worked her heart out to make her new husband happy. And in her day a girl would have spent every day trying to learn how to please her husband. What had gone wrong with this generation? They were afraid of hard work, that's what!

"Have you heard from Joseph?" Mary asked, her voice sounding slightly breathless.

"Joseph has finished the addition put onto his house," Esther replied. "I also took it upon myself to suggest a beautiful bracelet that would fit your wrist perfectly . . ."

"Oh, mother!" Mary sighed. "I hope he didn't find it too forward of you!"

Esther clucked her tongue in exasperation.

"Girl, a man's choice in adornment is best to be molded early if you don't want to be weighted down with some heinous but expensive contraption the merchant insisted was sure to delight. You should thank me!"

"I do, Mother!" Mary said quickly.

"There is so much I wanted to tell you girls before you left me," Esther said, tears coming to her eyes. "I dreamed of the day that you would marry, but now I think that when you leave you will tear out my heart and take it with you!"

"Oh, Mother!" Naomi said, her voice quivering. "Maybe we could postpone it, just for a little while. I'm not ready to be away from you!"

"That's enough from you!" Esther snapped, sentiment evaporating. "And as for you, young man," she added, turning to see one of her younger sons standing in the doorway of the kitchen courtyard, "out, out, out!"

She flapped a cloth at him, sending a cloud of flour in his direction.

"This is woman's talk!" she declared with a shake of her head. "Boys . . ." she muttered to herself.

With a sigh Esther noticed her two eldest daughters exchange a glance, and she softened a little. It was always hard to let go of your children. Part of her wanted to shelter them and keep them by her skirts, and another part of her wanted to shoo them away into lives and homes of their own. The greatest gift she could give them now was advice.

"I am going to tell you how to have a successful marriage," Esther began slowly, measuring her words. "The success of your marriage and the happiness you find in it reflect on your family here at home. If you do not follow my advice and fall into a bitter situation, the village will think that I did not teach you properly, so open your ears and listen, girls."

Mary's gaze had fastened on her mother's face with an expression of strange anxiety while Naomi stared resolutely at her hands. Their veils were down around their shoulders, ready to flip up over their hair in case an unexpected visitor should arrive, and their dark hair shone in the dim light of the courtyard. How many more days would she see them here in the kitchen with her?

"The first secret of a happy marriage is to think twice and speak once. No man can stand to live with a nag. A woman's place is to support her husband, not criticize him. But there are times she must speak. When those times arrive, think hard before you speak. Time your words well—after he has eaten and has relaxed. Never speak in the presence of any other person. Be certain before you say a word, because you can never repeat yourself again.

"The second secret is the most obvious," she went on. "You must work hard. Solomon spoke of the wife who worked hard, and it was because of her own work that her home was happy and safe. Don't waste your time in gossip and fashion. It will drain your resources and weaken your home."

How many girls had heard such advice before marriage? It was the same speech her own mother had given her, and too many times she had forgotten it herself! She had been born with a too inquisitive mind—especially when it involved dealing with anything outside the home. Her mother had called it her biggest weakness, but Esther had always secretly disagreed. Such things were not part of a woman's world, that was true, but if she could understand them, perhaps she could give her husband well-timed hints without him noticing too much . . . Perhaps she could save them both from too much financial loss. That balance had been a painful one to find, however. Like all men, Ebenezer resented a meddling woman.

With a sigh Esther remembered the setting down he had given her the first time she had tried to suggest a way to deal with a troublesome neighbor. Clamping her mouth shut had been the hardest lesson she'd even learned! Biting back words had been easier in her father's house, but once she was in the house of her husband's family, she seemed to be overflowing with opinions that seemed to have bubbled up out of nowhere. It was then that she had learned the third rule of a happy marriage . . .

"Third," she continued, "everything you say must be cushioned in kindness. For each remark that might be negative, you must surround it with kind, uplifting things. It will get you much further."

"How?" Naomi asked.

"Oh, dear Naomi," Esther said, putting a calloused hand onto her daughter's soft cheek. "You are just as lovely as a flower! I can see why Ashi's family asked for you. And so sweetly naive of the ways of the world . . . But you see, a good wife is more than pretty eyes and sweet smelling hair like you have. A good wife is intelligent and wise."

When Mary laughed, Naomi looked up sharply.

"Don't you see what she did?" Mary asked, her eyes sparkling with humor.

A petulant expression crossed her sister's face.

"Kind words take you much further than a sharp tongue," Esther reiterated. "Remember that in your dealings with your husband and his family, as well. It will not be easy adjusting to a new home where you are on the outside."

Both girls sobered at this. They would not have the same coddling in their new homes that they had here with their mother, and they knew it. Instead, they would have to prove their value and their worth with their hard work. Besides having to live up to their dowries, they would have to please both a husband and his mother at the same time.

"Marriage is not a Sabbath rest, girls," their mother said with a sigh. "It is a week of work. But just as during the week we do our work with our minds in the Sabbath, during your marriage look always to God and He will guide you. No matter how hard a week may be, the Sabbath always comes at last."

Mary stretched her arms out in front of her, trying to relieve an ache forming between her shoulder blades. No one ever said that a woman's work was easy! In a way, though, she would be lucky. She would not have a mother-in-law, as Joseph's parents were already dead. However, she would be sole mistress of the home, and that meant that everything—every scrap of work that needed done—would fall to her.

"Did Joseph say anything else?" Mary asked tentatively.

"To your mother?" Esther laughed. "I certainly hope not! Sweet nothings can wait until after the wedding, my girl!"

Her daughter felt the heat rise in her cheeks. It wasn't quite what she'd meant, but she was hoping for some shred of conversation that she might be able to scrutinize for signs of his affection. If there were no affection, he certainly wouldn't want to marry her after he discovered the truth.

"You are a mystery, Mary," her mother said with a chuckle. "There are few women who sigh and moon about like you do before her wedding!"

"Perhaps because she actually knows him!" Naomi cut in, tears welling up in her eyes. "I don't even know Ashi!"

"I can see that I've babied you too much!" their mother replied tersely. "Since when do you need to know a man to marry him? You have the rest of your life to get to know him! A good wife knows her work and puts her heart into the children."

"Being too familiar with Ashi before the wedding might ruin your reputation," Mary added. "People would talk."

Then Mary abruptly sighed. It was difficult to keep up her obedient, happy exterior. "People's talk" was a threat that every girl felt keenly, and it wasn't her younger sister who should be worrying about it! She adjusted her position. Her body was slowly changing, and kneeling on a mat was not as comfortable as it used to be. So far she had hidden the signs. But for how much longer could she?

"You're familiar with Joseph!" Naomi blurted out. "He talks to you on the street, and you at least know what he's like! You know that he likes to laugh and that he works hard. And you love him already!"

"Love him?" their mother said, a look of mild surprise registering on her face. "Really?"

Glaring at her sister, Mary tried valiantly to stop the blush that burned across her face. Love him? Maybe she did! But it was not her sister's place to bark it out like a scavenger dog howling at the moon!

"And what does our Mary know of love?" their mother asked.

"I didn't say I loved him!" she defended herself. "I said that he was handsome and kind. I said that he worked hard, and that he had strong hands. I said that he makes me feel weak when he looks at me so directly . . ."

Both her mother and her sister stared at her without saying anything until Mary's voice trailed away and she lapsed into silence.

"Well," her mother said finally, turning toward the younger Naomi. "See what a good choice your father makes? You should trust him instead of pulling away like a stubborn donkey!"

Joseph—he liked to laugh, but he didn't talk very much, Mary thought to herself. She thought she could read more in his gestures and expressions than she could ever glean from his words. Very kind and incredibly gentle, despite his obvious strength, he worked with stone and wood. His labors had hardened and defined his muscles. A girl would expect him to be rough as well, but she'd seen the gentle way he handled a goat that had broken its leg, and she knew she had nothing to fear from him. He made her stomach feel empty and sick all at once . . .

Or perhaps that was something else. She'd heard from some village women that a sick stomach was one of the signs of pregnancy, and her stomach had been upset now for some time.

"Do you think that Joseph will come for me soon?" Mary asked.

"Soon enough" was the reply.

"This week?" she pressed. "Maybe next?"

Her mother looked at her with a confused expression.

"How can I know? A man doesn't ask a woman's opinion before he acts! He will come when he comes, Mary. You will have to learn how to wait for your husband's decisions!"

Would he take her to his home before anyone knew about her condition—that was what she wanted to know! Would he marry her before it became obvious to everyone? And even when he did come, would he accept her once he knew? After all, he had children of his own and would recognize a pregnant woman when he saw one. Joseph would know immediately! Would he send her back to her father to be punished? Or would he understand?

But could anyone understand? It was a dream, they'd say. She'd eaten too late at night. Or a lie. They'd say that she was making up stories to protect herself. And what girl wouldn't? Who wanted to be stoned to death? Who wouldn't lie and scream and run away—anything to stay alive?

But it wasn't a lie. One night several months ago, when she lay in her bed trying to sleep, a light had entered the room like a glow bug. It was soft at first, but then grew brighter and brighter until she had to cover her eyes and pulled her blankets over her head in terror. Why was no one else waking up?

"Don't be afraid, Mary," a musical voice had said. "You will be the mother of the Messiah. You are the most blessed among women. You will give birth to a little boy, and you must name Him Jesus. He will be great, and He will be called Son of the Most High. God Himself will give Him the throne of His father, David, and He will reign over Israel forever. His kingdom will never end."

Slowly she uncovered her face, squinting against the brightness. She couldn't make out the one speaking to her, but she could sense his presence the way that you feel your family sleeping around you in the dark.

"I don't understand," she had said, her voice barely above a whisper. "I don't understand how this can happen! I'm not married. I'm still a virgin, sir."

"The Holy Spirit will come upon you," came the reply. "This child will be the Son of the Most High. The power of God will overshadow you."

Mary was silent, taking in the words like someone who had drunk too much wine. What was this? How could it be? What did it mean? Would she truly be pregnant, or was there another meaning behind the words? Who was this speaking to her? It all seemed so unreal and strange, like a dream, except too vivid.

"Even your old cousin, Elizabeth, is going to have a baby in her old age," the voice went on. "She has been barren her whole life, but she is in her sixth month of pregnancy! Nothing is impossible with God!"

Nothing was impossible with God . . . that was true. But what did this mean in her case? What was the significance of this message?

"I am God's servant," Mary had said, swallowing hard. "Let it happen as you have said!"

Unable to sleep that night, she had lain awake, her eyes wide as serving bowls, the words echoing through her mind. As the mother of the Messiah, she would have a little boy, and He would save the Jews from the Romans. That was what the Messiah would do, wasn't it? Wasn't that what the rabbis said? A mother . . . a baby inside of her . . .

Her mind whirling, she felt her belly. Was the baby there now? Had it begun already? A mother? No fear of barrenness for her! No terror of never having children to care for her in her old age!

But who would ever believe her? Ever since that night she had prayed every waking moment—begging God to show her the way through her desperate situation. But the angel had told her that the power of God would be over her, hadn't he? God was with her, no matter how frightened she was.

Now, as she knelt on a mat in the kitchen with her mother and sister, the vision seemed very, very far away. Even the comfort that she found from her prayers seemed to have evaporated like dew on a hot morning. What seemed closer than anything was that her body was changing ever so subtly, and faster than she had imagined that such things happened.

"Mary," her mother said. "Fetch me some water from the jar, would you?"

Her daughter gave what she hoped was an ordinary smile and pushed herself to her feet. As did so, her mother stood also, heading toward a tall jar filled with grain.

"You're a good girl, Mary," Esther said fondly, patting her daughter's hip as she squeezed past her. Mary tried to pull her body away from her mother's, but her mother's ample bulk pushed against Mary's growing stomach as she tried to squeeze by.

Mary dropped her gaze, and she felt her mother freeze. When Mary slowly raised her panic-stricken eyes to meet her mother's, all she saw was shock registering on Esther's square face. She put her hand out and touched Mary's stomach, then pulled away as if she had burned herself on a glowing coal. Her mother's lips were open and her eyes were wide. Then, after an eternal moment, the shocked expression melted into a look of crushing disappointment.

Chapter 3

If all the seas were ink, if all the swamps were producing pens, if the whole expanse of the horizon were parchment, and all the men were scribes, the (thoughts that fill the) void of a ruler's heart could not be written in full. Whence is this deduced? . . . "The heavens as to height and the earth as to depth, and the hearts of kings cannot be fathomed."

—*From the Mishnah*

Carefully Simak rolled a scroll in his palms, listening to the dry rasp of his skin against tanned animal hide. He held the roll in his hands, his eyes focused on the green and white tiled floor. A golden tray of fresh fruit lay untouched on an elaborately carved table not far from him, and next to the tray stood a bronze water jug, beading with condensation. The ceiling above him was lofty, and painted over the arching supports were the scenes of battles won by Persia and of victories celebrated. The room was light and airy, and the tiles and the bubbling fountain in the center cooled the hot afternoon.

Simak pulled his mind out of his reverie and slid the scroll into a silver etched tube, the rounded ends encrusted in sapphires. The document was a rarity even in his own learned realm. This scroll came from the Jews.

As he held it out a servant swept forward to take it from his fingers, then vanished again as quickly as a shadow. His brow furrowed in thought, Simak stood motionless.

"Nadr," he said, his voice breaking the stillness. There was a silence that stretched several moments, and then a small, bald man entered the room. One of his advisors, Nadr had served his father before him, and Simak found him to be invaluable as well as trustworthy.

"You interpreted my father's dreams, did you not?" he asked.

"Yes, my lord," Nadr replied, inclining his head downward in a respectful gesture. He wore a tunic of clean white and his head was shaved smooth so that it shone like a polished stone.

"And what kinds of dreams did my father have?"

Nadr frowned slightly and pursed his lips, folding his hands in front of him.

"That was many years ago, my lord," he answered slowly. "I remember one dream that he had about fruit falling from a tree, overripe and bruised . . ."

"And the meaning?"

"It was a warning from Ahura Mazda about the years of plenty to come. We are experiencing those years now, when life is easy and we forget about our duties to Ahura because we have no trials to remind us."

"Yes, yes," Simak said, nodding and recalling his father's dream about the fruit tree. He had been only 10 or 11 at the time, but he remembered how it had disturbed his father. The dream had motivated his father to open the schools for boys. Higher learning was necessary to shape young minds in the ways of Ahura, the uncreated Creator.

"Did he dream about kings?" Simak continued.

"Not that I recall, my lord," the little man replied after a moment's pause.

"I have dreamed about a king." Simak's words came slowly, as if reluctantly. "It was not an ordinary dream. It was not made up of my mind's fancies from the day's events. It was as clear and real as you are in front of me. I remember it as well as I can the events of yesterday."

"The dream held power?" Nadr narrowed his eyes in thought. "A dream sent by Ahura Mazda is known by its clarity—like a jewel among ordinary stones."

"I would like to tell you this dream." Simak began to walk slowly toward a tall window with billowing silk curtains. "And I would like you to advise me."

Nadr gave silent consent.

"There was a star rising up in the sky. It ascended higher and higher, and then exploded, and when it did, the night vanished and it was day. I saw caravans of camels and linen clad servants as far as the eye could see. They were crossing the desert in an endless procession. When one of the servants passed by me, I called to him and asked, 'What is this? Where are you being taken?'

" 'To Judea,' the servant replied. And he smiled, his entire face lighting up. 'Don't you know that the king of the Jews has been born? Haven't you seen his star?' "

Suddenly silent, Simak crossed his arms and stared out across a garden. He could hear the bustling of the city on the other side of his palace wall, and he smiled as he heard the laughter of children spilling over it. It was the time of day for the school to be let out, and he did not need to see the scampering boys and the ambling young men to know the scene in the streets.

"A king, you say?" Nadr questioned with a frown.

"A king. And I could not help feeling that this foreign king had come for us . . ."

"As a threat? To enslave us?"

"No, as a blessing."

"Perhaps an ally?"

"I don't think so. In my dream, when I looked down at myself, I was dressed in the same white linen of a servant. I was expected to follow . . . to go in search of this newborn king."

"It is an omen, my lord. Something magnificent is about to occur, and Ahura has given you knowledge of it."

"That is my belief as well." Simak stroked his beard with one hand. "Not that I am worthy to hear the secret plans of Ahura. To gain knowledge of the future from the stars is one thing, but to be pointed toward them so directly is . . . disconcerting."

Simak continued to face the window. He didn't turn as he heard the soft slapping sound of Nadr's sandals as the servant left the room. Birds twittered outside, and Simak could feel the hot breeze brushing against his ornately embroidered robes.

He hadn't spoken yet of what he had read in another scroll from Judea. It was one written by a prophet named Moses—a Jewish prophet who spoke under the guidance of the Jewish God. "There shall come a star out of Jacob, and a scepter shall rise out of Israel."

Was it heresy to trust the words of a Jew?

Simak had a royal education. He had to be wiser and more learned than his people. While true wisdom came only from Ahura, he must be a faithful steward of all that Ahura had blessed him with. His wealth brought responsibility for the people he led. It was his duty to study everything he could . . . to decipher this strange dream about the star and the baby king. Perhaps Ahura had given some light to the Jews. The stars were in the heavens, there for all to see—were they not? Perhaps the Jews had deciphered something there that the Magi had missed.

The idea worried him. But something about the dream nagged at his mind and would not give him peace.

In distant Judea the sound of celebration clattered out beyond the fortified walls of a palace high on a cliff side. There was laughter and shouting, the sound of drunken excitement. Music wove through the babble of voices, the jangle of bells from dancer's ankles, and a woman's sharp scream. A party at the palace of Herod was not a safe place to be. Too many people had disappeared during such occasions. Too many unmentionable things happened at them.

The palace was more of a military fortress than a traditional royal residence. Archers stood along the walls, watching down the cliff side, their bows always strung. Armor clattered as soldiers made their rounds around the walls, and no less than a squadron stood guard at the one gate that allowed access to the fortress.

Herod sat at the front of a banquet hall, mentally reviewing his security precautions. The soldiers were handpicked. The archers had orders to shoot at the slightest disturbance. A secret passage waited just to his left, behind his back, if anyone made any attempt on his life. Only his most trusted servants knew the alarm signal—a certain tune to be played on a flute, which would warn him that he was not safe.

The jingle of the bells on the dancer's ankles drew Herod's mind back to the feast. He sat in his white toga of nobility, his curly black hair oiled away from his face. Silver streaked his temples, and his eyes had lines around them. His face was handsome still, but it had gained the plumpness of middle age, as had the rest of his body.

The palace may have been a fortress, but it was also fit for a king. Herod was not ashamed to have his guests visit him here. His wealth was immense, and people feared his military and political prowess. He had the most elaborate banquets—the finest the world had to offer. The world could offer much to a kingdom with strategic ports! And he had the most beautiful wife in the known world—Mariamne was his, and he adored her.

Where was she?

"Where is my wife?" Herod asked a steward standing nearby.

"She was not invited to this party, Your Majesty," the man replied, his expression blank. "At Your Majesty's request . . ."

"I did?" The king shook his head. "I may have. Find her! I want her here!"

"Yes, Your Majesty."

The steward melted away. Herod did not recall denying his wife permission to enjoy this banquet. Was the steward lying? As he stared in the direction that the man had vanished, his eyes narrowed. What was his name? He'd be dead by morning.

Laughter came from a pool of water across the room. Men were lounging around the water's edge, and some sat in the water itself, allowing serving girls to drop bits of meat and other food into their open mouths. Yes, this was a party that people would speak of for years to come! No one would ever forget the entertainment that Herod the Great had provided for his guests . . .

"Is that Aristobulus?" Herod said suddenly, grabbing at a nearby noble's sleeve.

The young man looked in the direction of the pool with exaggerated attention.

"I don't believe so, Your Majesty," he said softly, lowering his eyes.

"It is . . ." The king stared at one of the men in the pool. Yes, it looked like him. The same curls. The same hooked nose. The same way of holding himself.

"I'd know my brother-in-law anywhere, friend," Herod said with a low laugh. "I appointed him high priest myself!"

The young man paused for a moment before responding.

"Of course, Your Majesty," the noble said smoothly. "But of what importance is such a worm as he at this elegant party?"

"I like you, friend!" Herod said, barking out a laugh. "You see who has power and who does not!"

"No one has the influence that you wield, Your Majesty . . ."

Herod eyed the man warily. Was he being sincere or slyly making fun of him? But that was his young brother-in-law in the pool. He knew it! And no one could convince him otherwise.

"Tell me of Aristobulus," Herod said, forcing a smile onto his face. "He is well-liked, I know. So tell me what people say of him."

A hint of anxiety flickered across the noble's face, and he licked at his lips like a serpent, the end of his tongue twitching as if to smell danger.

It didn't matter what the young man might have said. Herod turned his attention away from him in disgust. His words would have no truth in them, only oil and spice to cover the stink of the lie.

Aristobulus was his beautiful wife's younger brother. To please Mariamne, he had appointed him high priest. It was a lofty position in Judea, but Herod had never dreamed that the boy would be popular or influential in any way. He had hoped that a mere pup would weaken the position itself, but he had been wrong. Aristobulus was much more politically savvy than Herod had given him credit for. The young man knew how to curry favor. Herod's lips curled down in distaste.

"He is a beautiful young man," Herod said, his voice light and wistful, in direct contrast to his sour expression. "He is entertaining and knowledgeable."

Much like his wife. . . Ah, Mariamne! She was divine! She was delicate and beautiful, with a wit and intelligence that was staggering in a woman! And she could drive him wild with a mere glance in his direction. Mariamne was tall and slender, and her voice was deep and mysterious. Where was she? Why was she not here? He looked around peevishly.

"Where is my wife?" he demanded of no one in particular.

"Your brother-in-law, Your Majesty," the young noble murmured. "Has he always been so . . . forward?"

Herod shot the young man a suspicious glare and turned his attention back to the individual lounging in the pool. What was the man saying? What was he telling people?

As Herod leaned forward, his belly squeezed into three solid rolls. When he wiped at his mouth with the back of his hand, his jewel-encrusted rings scratched gently against his smoothly shaven face. Aristobulus was a threat. He'd known it for some time now, but he was loath to act. His wife would not like it. Stupid women! Why could they not see how vulnerable a ruler really was?

"It would be unfortunate for any of my guests to . . ." Herod glanced in the direction of a man who seemed almost invisible. Dressed in a simple black robe, he wore an expression as blank as the wall behind him. But Herod's personal assassin was not someone to ignore.

"To what, Your Majesty?" the young royal pressed.

"To have an accident," the king replied in a low tone. "What is your name?"

"I am your servant Penxius" came the reply.

Penxius. Herod did not trust the young sap. No, he must remember that name.

"I'm sure many accidents happen, Your Majesty," Penxius said suggestively. "Many, many accidents that were simply the will of God."

With a grunt of annoyance Herod turned away. Many accidents happened, but Mariamne was no fool! She would know, and would be angry! Protective of her younger brother, she would not take well to having him turn up dead. She would stop letting him touch her . . . No, he could not risk the love of his wife. His heart could not survive an ugly glare from her!

The king felt like a caged animal. He was not safe! Someone was planning something—he could sense it! It was Aristobulus—he was almost certain. But he was trapped! He could not act!

Sinking down into an angry slump, he glared across the room at the young man lounging in the pool. He did not notice when the young noble beside him got up and walked away.

Leaning back against the richly embroidered pillows, Penxius interlaced his fingers behind his head. He was in his own private quarters, and he lounged easily, a smile toying at the corners of his lips.

"You look like a cat who has just eaten a mouse," his wife said with a giggle. "What have you done now, my husband?"

"It isn't done yet, woman," he said with a shake of his head. "And I should not tell you anything."

"Not tell me?" Her eyebrows raised questioningly. "Am I not the one who informs you of what I see in the palace? If I ceased doing that, dear husband, I would be a widow in a short time!"

He sighed and eyed her for a moment. She was right, of course. His wife was just as conniving as he was, if not more so! But she was a good ally in the silent intrigues of the palace. Penxius rubbed his hands over his bloodshot eyes. It had been a long evening, and, as usual, too much wine had flowed.

"The king was in one of his moods again tonight."

"Living in the past, was he?" she asked eagerly.

"It seems that Herod's son Antipater looks very much like his uncle Aristobulus did at the same age," he said with a wink. "I hadn't realized, being too young to have ever known the man!"

His wife froze for a moment, then her eyes lit up with malicious glee.

"Is it so? Herod had his brother-in-law Aristobulus killed years ago, didn't he?"

"Yes, many years ago, when you, my dear, were only a baby," her husband said with a chuckle. "But to Herod tonight, the event had not yet happened."

"He's insane," she whispered.

"Undeniably! And tonight he couldn't take his eyes off of Antipater. I simply encouraged the idea that his son was really his late brother-in-law. If all goes well and God favors me, Antipater will be dead by morning, and I will never have touched him!"

"Antipater, the direct heir of Herod," his wife breathed. "You are a conniving and dangerous man, husband!"

"I am," he said with a satisfied smile.

"And Herod . . . you did not call any undue attention to yourself, did you?"

"Well . . ." His face darkened.

"What happened?" she demanded sharply.

"He asked my name, and I told him. It could be in my favor."

"Or it could sign your assassination order." Her eyes widened with fear. "Why didn't you lie?"

Penxius didn't answer. He didn't know why he hadn't lied. Lying was his first nature, yet when it mattered, he came out with the truth like an infant! As he slumped against the pillows he felt a shiver slide slowly down his spine like a trickle of icy water.

"Why didn't you lie?" his wife repeated, her voice tense and frightened, tears welling up in her eyes. She turned away from him.

Suppressing a shudder, Penxius eyed the entrance to their quarters warily. He would have to bribe the guards a veritable fortune to stop one of Herod's assassins!

CHAPTER 4

Let him kiss me with the kisses of his mouth—for your love is more delightful than wine.

—Song of Solomon 1:2

Ebenezer could feel his honor draining away like sand from a clenched fist. This could not be happening. Strangely enough, he would have been less shocked had it been his younger daughter, Naomi. Obstinate and bullheaded, she was the one that he would expect to ruin him with her fiery beauty. Not Mary!

Lips compressed into a thin, angry line, he rose to his feet. Who would be the man to pay for this? Joseph, no doubt. Not young. And deceptively religious, it would seem. But unable to wait a matter of weeks before the girl would be his? What was happening to this generation? No self-restraint at all.

"Get her in here," Ebenezer ordered, his voice low and menacing. His wife's face was a sealed scroll to him—it was impossible to read her thoughts from her expressions. When she didn't move, he struggled to control his fury.

"Husband, I beg of you to calm yourself first," she said softly. "Don't talk to her when you are enraged. You might do more damage than you wish."

He shook his head in exasperation. Disobedience from his wife, too? Esther, it seemed, was trying to protect the girl from the punishment that she had coming. Mary should be beaten within an inch of her life, that's what she deserved! She had single-handedly stripped him of his honor.

"Is this where her disobedience began?" he shouted.

His wife remained immobile, though, her solid girth standing between him and the door. He would not strike her, and she knew it. Even if he did, Esther was a strong woman, as unbending as a tree lodged in a crevice. She would not wither like a wildflower in the desert wind. Once she stood her ground, God help the man who tried to push her.

Ebenezer sat down on a stool, covering his face in his hands. His rage had begun to seep away, and in its place he felt the throb of fresh pain.

"Oh, Esther," he sighed, tears choking his voice. "Where did I go wrong?"

"You didn't, my husband." He sensed her relax her protective stance and approach him, her sandals whispering against the packed dirt floor. "If anyone failed, it was I."

"Not you," he said, but a part of him deep inside silently agreed with her. A girl was her mother's responsibility to raise and mold into a good woman. When had Esther relaxed her vigilant watch?

It was his honor that was at stake. His daughter's actions and sins reflected on him as if they were his own. He carried her dishonor like a burden on his shoulders, stooping him under the weight of it. The only way to put it down was to cast her to the village . . . but that was unthinkable! Their hearts would not break at the thought of her tiny form as a baby. They would not recall her big, black, adoring eyes staring up at him as a little girl. Nor would they feel the pride that he had always felt in the beautiful young woman she had become. No, they would only share his rage and injury. But they would feel it as their own, and would express it in the only way they knew how—stoning. The people of the village would hurl sharp stones at her until their collective rage subsided and her breath ceased. Only then would they stop. And only then would he be able to set his dishonor down beside the broken body of his baby girl.

"She insists that she is innocent," his wife said quietly.

Ebenezer looked at her in shock. "Innocent?" he said incredulously. "In her state?"

"She says she is still a virgin."

"A liar, too," he muttered. It was a stupid lie—huge and obvious.

"She says that an angel visited her and told her that she would conceive and give birth to the Messiah."

He struggled to make sense of it all. What girl in danger of being stoned to death would not tell ludicrous lies in order to save herself? But to add lying to the sins that she had already obviously committed was even more disgraceful.

"Disgusting," he muttered, his lips curling in distaste.

"And what if she isn't lying?"

Surprised at the firmness of her voice, he stared at his wife, who stared back at him evenly. Her gray hair was pulled away from her face in a tight twist, and some hair had escaped in a frizzy halo around her face. Her eyes were small and direct, and her lips were generous and set in a determined line.

"To use God as an excuse for fornication is blasphemy," he snapped.

"To disregard a direct message from God is equally blasphemous."

"And you believe this . . . story?" he demanded, frowning.

"When has she lied in the past?"

"How do we know? We missed the signs of this!"

"All I say is that there is a possibility of her telling the truth. And if she does not lie, then you, my husband, will be grandfather of the Messiah."

Ebenezer looked down and shook his head.

"I don't know what to think right now, wife," he finally said in a low voice. "I don't know what to think . . ."

But he did know what he was thinking. His mind was furiously trying to figure how he would deal with all this. How long could they hide the terrible truth? Where could he send Mary to, away from the unforgiving village, someplace where they might believe her to be a young widow . . . or choose to believe . . . ? Could an old man use his body to protect his daughter when they came at her with stones . . . ?

Mary was his. His little girl. She was his responsibility to protect and care for. She was his responsibility to raise to be a good wife for her future husband. She was his child. His.

And she was now his burden.

"Esther," he finally spoke in a subdued voice.

His wife looked up at him, her own expression bleak and sad, her earlier optimism seeming to have evaporated under the pressure of reality.

"Send her in."

Naomi chewed nervously at her fingernail, her dark eyes silently following her sister as she walked into the main room where their father waited. It all seemed so unreal! Such things didn't happen to their family. They happened to only poor people with immoral daughters! In homes in which the father drank or the mother was lazy. Never to *good* people!

The courtyard was silent, and Naomi looked up at a fly droning through the air. What were they saying? The voices did not carry. Obviously their father was not shouting at her sister. Naomi crept back into the house and put her ear closer to the woolen curtain that separated the rooms.

". . . I swear I am innocent, Father. I swear it!"

"Is it Joseph then? Did he do this?"

"No, Joseph is a good man. No man did this."

"A man did do it, girl! Now which one?"

"None, I swear it!"

"Do you not know what kind of trouble you are in? How long can we hide it? How long before the village demands justice? If you will tell me the man who did this, I can speak to him, or his family . . . I may be able to work out some sort of deal with them."

There was silence then, and Naomi pressed closer, holding her breath. Suddenly the curtain snapped back, and Naomi faced the livid face of her mother.

"Out!" Esther ordered, and Naomi melted back. The curtain fell back into place.

No, this did not happen to *good* people. Good people planned marriages and had babies afterward. Good people took care of their parents when they got old. Good people celebrated together and prayed to God for blessings. Good people followed the laws given by Moses and those received through tradition. Good people did not have unwed mothers in their homes! It still seemed so unreal. Mary, of all people, to be pregnant! It was shocking! Mary had always seemed so *good*.

Naomi's younger brothers, Adam and Japheth, entered the courtyard, looking uncertainly at their sister.

"What's happening?" Japheth asked quietly. "Father wouldn't let us come inside!"

"Shhh," Naomi said with a frown. "It is nothing that you should be concerned with. Now be quiet!"

"Let's listen!" Japheth said, his eyes lighting up. Naomi shot him a warning look.

"This is something serious," she reprimanded him in an angry whisper. "Now hush up, both of you! Go back outside to play."

"I don't want to play," Adam protested, his eyes clouding with worry. "I want to know what's happening!"

Japheth seemed to see the wisdom in his sister's command, and he tugged at his brother's sleeve. Naomi watched them nervously as they left. Boys were not to be trusted with a secret of such magnitude! They might tell their friends about it, or talk about it together in public where others might overhear them.

Poor Mary! She must be terrified, Naomi realized. Even she was terrified! What did it mean? How would it affect her? It would in some way—that much was obvious. Nothing happened in a family that didn't touch everyone. Perhaps Naomi's betrothed would no longer want to marry her.

The thought sat in her mind for a few moments, causing no emotional reaction at all. Then slowly she began to feel a mixture of fear and relief. On the one hand she was afraid, because to be cast off was a humiliation. It would be embarrassing for her and for her whole family. But she felt a sense of relief, too. Perhaps she wouldn't have to marry Ashi after all! Maybe he would go away and his family would stop demanding her, allowing her to spend a few more months with her mother . . . or even a year or more! Then her father could arrange for a different marriage for her . . .

Would Ashi still want her? That didn't matter, really. He had never met her, either. What mattered was what Ashi's family wanted. Would his father still think Naomi was a girl to be taken into their home and called daughter? She didn't know. But then she'd never known a family with this problem before. Probably they would think she was unclean now and want nothing to do with her.

It was all rather confusing. And it couldn't be hid forever, either. Mary's body would only get bigger and rounder. Things would start to happen because of it. There would be no stopping that. Life would change.

Naomi looked around the courtyard. The flour they had been grinding sat in the trough, still course and filled with broken grain fragments. The lid was off the oil jar, and some spilled flour hadn't been swept up. It was strange to see the courtyard so empty and haphazard like this. As if life had just stopped and no one remained to see it.

Thaddaeus understood how the world worked. After all, he'd traveled with his father to Jerusalem! Even more than that, he'd gone there alone with his cousins, too, when they had to help some family complete a large job that Herod had commissioned. It had given him glimpses of city life and people in new situations, and he understood how it all came together. She felt like a silly girl next to Thaddaeus. Probably he would laugh at her, his eyes crinkling up the way they did when he was having fun. He'd tell her that she hadn't seen anything till she'd seen Jerusalem!

With a sigh she looked out the doorway of the courtyard at the scruffy grass and fig trees that grew along the path beside the house, offering some welcome shade in the later summer heat with their wide, leathery leaves.

Thaddaeus . . . So kind and worldly, he was everything she'd ever wanted! And he loved her. He said it all the time. Maybe Ashi's family wouldn't want her anymore.

And maybe Thaddaeus's family would!

In a blacksmith's shop not far away, Thaddaeus paused in his work to wipe the sweat that kept dripping into his eyes. A strong young man, tall and bronzed from the sun, his muscles had become well defined from his heavy work. Putting down his hammer and iron pincers, he headed toward the water jug. The heat and labor made him thirsty.

Nazareth was boring. He didn't want to stay here. No, he wanted to find his own fortune! He wanted to go to Jerusalem and set up shop with his cousins. Jerusalem was a bustling metropolis. It was exciting. People everywhere . . . important people! Not like this hole in the ground. Nazareth was nothing but a watering stop for merchants who had lost their way. One day he'd leave this town and never look back.

"We have to get these plows finished, son," his father said. "No time for daydreaming!"

"One day I won't be making plows, Father," he said, returning to the hearth. "I'll be making swords for soldiers . . . and breastplates that will cost a fortune!"

"If they cost a fortune to buy, son, they will cost a fortune to make," his father replied pragmatically. "Besides, the only ones who are buying war gear are the Romans."

Thaddaeus shut his mouth, knowing when the subject would get too heated. Why couldn't they just make money off the occupiers? The ones who had all the money would pay someone to make their armor . . . Restricting his skill to the Jews wouldn't let him tap into the Roman treasury. Sometimes he thought his father was too small-minded. Too caught up in old ways of thinking. Herod had expanded the Jewish Temple, hadn't he? That had to count for something . . .

The only thing that seemed bright in this little hole of a town was Naomi. A pretty girl—plump and sweet—she had eyes that could trap him like a fly in honey! She was the only part of Nazareth that he enjoyed. He liked the way she looked up at him and drank in every story he told her. He liked the way she got bashful when he slipped close beside her to kiss her cheek or touch her hands. And he liked the way she laughed—and even the way she pouted!

Her mother seemed a bit hostile, but what was he to expect? Esther was solid and large. She had a face as square as a soldier's and an iron grip to match—a force to be feared, that was for sure! But Naomi . . . no, she could never age into that brick her mother was. Naomi would stay pretty and sweet. She would remain delicate. He couldn't imagine her hands rough with calluses. Not Naomi . . .

"Thaddaeus! Careful with that!"

He blushed, or would have, if his heat-reddened skin would have allowed it. His mind was wandering again. But Naomi had a way of doing that to him. If he got the chance, he'd take her away from here. He'd bring her to Jerusalem where life was . . . where excitement was . . . where the money was!

CHAPTER 5

Like a gold ring in a pig's snout is a beautiful woman who shows no discretion.

—*Proverbs 11:22*

Lydia let her gaze wander over the merchant's wares. Bracelets sparkled in the sunlight . . . earrings lay in jagged piles, enticing in their sparkling disarray . . . silk scarves were spread out to display the fineness of their weaves. The merchants also had some more sensible fabrics and some plainer scarves, but her eyes slid over those like rain off a stone. Any girl could have some coarse woolen veil. But to have a fine linen veil—as light and delicate as silk, she imagined—that was something the other girls would covet!

She picked up one soft veil, embroidered elegantly along the edges in a water pattern. It was lovely! Would her father buy it for her? Probably not. That kind of expense was not common in her family. They had growing boys to feed and provide for. A good husband would buy her the pretty things she wanted, though. He would give her jewels and veils of silk. He would let her ride a donkey wherever she went. And he would give her money to buy ointments for her skin . . . perfumes and dyes . . .

Very few men could afford such luxury, she thought peevishly. She would even settle for less if she could get a husband who could give her a nice home and a few luxuries when she pouted.

"Too much for you, miss," the merchant said, plucking the delicate scarf from her fingers. "Look at these bracelets here . . . or this veil—much thicker to hold out the dust. Still very pretty, eh?"

Lydia cast a cool eye over the merchant before turning regally and sweeping away. He would get no sales from her! No better than a shepherd, he was! And with the discerning eye of a camel! May fleas infest him, the lout!

As she looked over the crowd she could see her aunt Esther buying some herbs, but not putting the attention into her task that she ought to. Also she could see several cousins and uncles talking in a group, gesturing and raising their voices as men were apt to do. Having grown up here, she knew every face in town. This village was her life.

Her gaze slid over her relatives and family associates and stopped on the form of a tall man with dark curls and a trimmed beard. Pursing his lips as he listened, he was nodding and discussing something with another village man. His arms were crossed over his chest, and she could not ignore the bulge of his muscles. He was a carpenter, and physical strength was part of the job. If a man did not have it naturally, he would acquire it quickly enough! Sighing, she watched him from the shadows of her veil.

Joseph! He was much too old for her! Or was he? Certainly he didn't consider himself too old for her cousin Mary. He was betrothed to her, but the marriage was not finalized yet. It wasn't over till the wheat was in the barn, her mother always said. Marriages fell through before the actual joining often enough . . .

"Lydia!" someone called, and she blushed, turning her attention toward the approaching young woman. Round and plump, she moved like a rolling wheel, her strong legs propelling her forward with surprising grace.

"Shali!" she said, forcing a smile to her lips.

"You have heard about the butcher's wife, haven't you?" Shali asked, her eyes alight. She plowed on without waiting for a response. "Her brother lost two crops in a row in good weather! If you can believe that . . . what kind of sins he must be hiding I have no idea, but God punished him in the most obvious way. Well, he lost both crops and asked his sister, the butcher's wife, if she would convince her husband to go into business with him—put up some money, you know. Well, the butcher would have nothing of it! Smart man, if you ask me! He said that if God was punishing him, he wouldn't be trying to ease his pain! And his wife got in such a rage that she refused to give him more children, saying that with that kind of regard to family, she didn't know if he would provide for them when they were grown. Well . . ."

Lydia ignored the tale, instead watching Shali's expressions of delight, disgust, alarm, and general enjoyment as they crossed the girl's sun-reddened features. How much would she give to hear Shali announcing that Joseph and Mary's betrothal had fallen through! Then she would listen like a child to a rabbi, begging for details and passing them along with the speed of the wind!

Mary was her cousin. Some people said that Mary and Naomi got the good looks for the whole clan, but that was just stupidity talking. Not prettier at all, they just acted more pious and religious, and it fooled people into thinking that those awkward features added up to anything at all! As if piety were worth more than tinkling bracelets . . . They'd grow into women just like Aunt Esther—square and large like the wall of a house. Just give it time!

". . . so the butcher struck her, and she went to her father, who took his kinsmen to the butcher's kinsmen. But when her father heard how she had spoken to her husband, he apologized for her behavior to all of them and then took her home to punish her himself!"

Shali's rush of words stopped all at once, and she looked at Lydia with horrified delight in the story she had just relayed.

"Shocking!" Lydia said. "She deserved to be beaten!"

"Or did she?" Shali whispered. "She was standing up for her brother! And the families were joined in marriage. Did the butcher not owe his own brother-in-law something?"

"Even if he was hiding sins?"

"Well, there is that!" Shali threw her hands up. "But it is still wrong when men don't treat their in-laws with the same respect as their own families. It is shameful. What is a wedding for, if not to join two families into one?"

Lydia made some appropriate noises of sympathy that seemed to appease her friend's indignation. As Shali prattled on, Lydia's eyes strayed back toward Joseph. He was a very handsome man. And his business was successful—more so than he let on through any sort of ostentation, but very successful nonetheless. What he needed was a young wife to show him how to display his wealth to his friends! Yes, he needed a young woman like her to wear just the right clothes and to display just the proper amount of jewels to hint at even more wealth than he really had. And to have his children, of course . . . And to support him . . . She wasn't a selfish woman after all. Most assuredly, she would take care of her man.

Just as there appeared to be a break in Shali's steady stream of words, Joseph seemed to have concluded his business with the man he had been speaking to and was moving in her direction.

"Excuse me, please. I haven't much time, really!"

Shali accepted the excuses and turned her attention toward another young woman further away. Now was Lydia's chance to speak to Joseph! It was her chance . . . but how? A young woman didn't simply address a man. No, there had to be some reason for the conversation.

But Joseph was approaching—his attention elsewhere—and Lydia had only a moment to make her decision. She'd bump into him and spill the basket of figs she had just purchased, forcing him, if he felt anything for her at all, to bend and help her pick them up. It was perfect! She couldn't believe that the genius of the plan had come to her all at once.

As he came closer she could almost smell the scent of wood on his clothes. Pretending to look elsewhere, she smoothly stepped into his path. The basket splintered with a crunch as they collided, and Joseph let out a sound of surprise. Lydia opened her eyes wide and turned her face toward him with a schooled expression of shy alarm.

"Pardon me, miss."

Lydia stood motionless. The figs had not fallen. Instead, one fig that had a rotten side she hadn't noticed had crushed against her chest, its acrid juices seeping into her robes.

"I'm sorry, sir," she said, a moment too late. "Dear me! How silly of me!"

"Don't worry. I was not looking either. God be with you."

And as his eyes slid over her, he did not even pause for a moment to regard her beauty or take notice of her hair that she had so artfully allowed to slip out of her veil. Instead, he moved easily on through the crowd, leaving Lydia standing there with her hair exposed and a rotten fig pressed against her chest. Her lips curling in displeasure, she flung the fig away and shuddered in disgust. A crimson blush had risen in her face, and with a struggle she resisted the urge to stamp her feet in rage.

"Stupid! Stupid!" she muttered to herself. If only the figs had fallen! That would have made the difference. But they hadn't. And now she had a foul-smelling stain on her robe and tunic, and a solid bruise where the basket had jabbed into her ribs.

Raising her chin in an expression that she hoped did not betray her shame, she headed for home.

Joseph glanced back at the young woman standing there with the basket of figs. She had a petulant look on her face, and he sighed. Young women made little more sense now than they did when he was young himself. It was a world that a man never truly fathomed, even after years of marriage. But he recognized a sour expression when he saw one, and he chuckled to himself. One day soon that girl would be his own relative. She was Mary's cousin, wasn't she?

But he didn't have time to be wondering about strange girls in the village, relatives of his intended or not! He wanted to choose some fabric for Mary, something that she could make herself a beautiful robe out of. She wouldn't want anything too expensive, but his young wife would be dressed in quality, that was for sure!

Stopping at a stall with some samples of fabric draped over a wooden frame, he fingered one fine orange weave, only to pull his hands away uncertainly as he felt his rough fingers snagging on the delicate threads.

"Yes, getting ready for a wedding, I hear!" the man said with a low chuckle. "And every bride loves beautiful clothing."

Joseph shrugged uncomfortably. How many times had he teased young men about to be married? And here he was facing his own wedding and feeling just as bashful! He had to hold back the urge to describe his betrothed—every last detail he knew of her—to get some meaningful advice on what sort of fabric she might like. And one he could hold her in without leaving it snagged and rough.

"The orange, then?" the merchant pressed.

"No, no, not that one," he said, shaking his head. He looked at a rust-colored woolen blend, still high quality. For a moment he fingered the fabric, then studied a pale-blue linen. It was exquisite, but doubtlessly more than he could reasonably afford.

"Ah, the blue!" the merchant was saying. "Truly beautiful! A woman would love this."

Joseph turned away from the stall, and the merchant, seeing his customer losing interest, grew restless.

"Think about it, then." Turning his attention to some approaching women, he exclaimed, "Ladies! Come see the beginning of the most beautiful robe you've ever worn!"

With a sigh of relief, Joseph glanced at a few more samples. None were as beautiful as the blue, but he was not sure he would be able to bargain the price down to a feasible level.

". . . it's hard to tell, of course . . ."

Joseph glanced in the direction of the voices. Two old women were talking eagerly, their cracked voices carrying farther than they realized, he was sure. They were bent over, leaning heavily on walking sticks and wrinkled like the shell of an old nut.

"Not so hard to tell this far along!" the other said, shaking her head. "How many pregnancies have we seen over these years? Not to mention our own!"

"Not so many before the wedding . . ."

"But enough of them! The wedding just came quick enough! When a big, bouncing baby is born three months shy of nine, the questions tend to fly!"

"If those big babies had been born at the proper time according to the mothers, they would have emerged walking and memorizing the Torah already!"

They cackled together in laughter, and Joseph had to conceal a smile. So it seemed there was another unwed mother in the village. It was sad. In fact, it was disgusting, really, that a man could not wait until the girl was his, but had to shame her! If the man had any good sense, he would marry her first. He knew as well as any man how hard it was to wait . . . he had a bride waiting for him! But he had respected her. Soon, though, all the waiting would pay off. And he couldn't help feeling resentful of anyone who would disregard God's law and so dishonor a woman.

Joseph tried to pull his attention away from the gossiping old women. It was embarrassing to be so interested in their conversation! But he knew as well as other men that there were things that women discussed that men would never in their lives know about.

"But she was the last I would have expected," the first woman said. "A good girl, that one. Or, I always thought, at least . . ."

"A good family!" the other agreed. "Some others wouldn't surprise me. What's happening to this generation, I'll never know!"

"But she's as pure as the girls of our day," she with a sigh. "Well, she seemed to be at least! Always so proper and good!"

"Not so good as we thought!" the other said, sucking at her teeth and spitting onto the ground. "Ebenezer raised a good family. I'd hate to see him shamed this way."

Joseph froze. Ebenezer? Not his father-in-law-to-be! Certainly a different man? Could Naomi have been so disgraced? He's always known she was not as good a woman as Mary, but to be with child in her own father's house?

"The younger sister, I might have guessed," the woman went on. "But Mary? It's sad, that one."

"Could we be wrong?"

"Eh? Wrong?"

They exchanged a glance and shook their heads in exasperation at the very thought.

Joseph was stunned. Pregnant? Not Mary! He'd never touched her! That he could swear to heaven above! God knew his innocence. And what conniving old donkeys to tell such far-fetched stories as truth. It was impossible for Mary to be pregnant if he had never been with her!

Rage bubbled up in his veins, and his narrowed, fury-filled eyes met those of the merchant as the man turned his attention back to his soon-to-be-married customer. The merchant opened his mouth in shock and took a step back. Joseph did not say a word, but turned away from the stall and toward the old women. How dare they tarnish the name of a good woman!

But as he started toward them, the old women looked up together and saw him. They were the age his own mother might have been. And they pursed their lips in the same way she used to, their shrewd eyes evaluating him.

It was disgust he saw in their eyes. They knew who he was. And they believed that he had taken what was not his before marriage. So why was he stopping and fumbling like a guilty boy?

The women moved on through the crowd, their sticks clattering out an offbeat rhythm as they went, and Joseph stared after them with a mixture of confused feelings boiling through him. The most prominent was shock.

Old women knew a pregnancy when they saw it. Why did they think Mary was with child?

CHAPTER 6

Our principal care of all is this, to educate our children well; and we think it to be the most necessary business of our whole life to observe the laws that have been given us, and to keep those rules of piety that have been delivered down to us.

—Flavius Josephus, Against Apion, *Book 1*

Elias placed one coin carefully on top of another, balancing them precisely before adding a third. Then, exhaling, he looked up at the man who sat across the table from him.

"It's all I have. I'm sorry, my friend, I know I promised more, but I am not a wealthy man. With a daughter to be made marriageable, and an inn that keeps draining my purse before it is filled . . ." He spread his hands in a gesture of defeat.

"The inn has been prosperous, *friend,*" the man said, exaggerating the word with a twist to his lips. "Bethlehem is not a poor place. You promised full payment. Now you give me only three drachmas instead of four? That is a large deficit!"

"I do apologize, sir," Elias said, licking his lips nervously. "Here! Look!" He dumped out his purse, four kodrantes, or Roman copper pennies, spinning across the tabletop. Slapping his hand down over the coins, he then slid them toward the pile.

"Take them! It is all I have to feed my family, but I am sure that God will provide for us somehow."

"Do you think I do not have any financial pressure?" the other man demanded. "I leant you this money in good faith that it would be returned! Now, I get only four pennies more . . . I have men coming to my door with payment due to them, as well!"

"Friend—and we are friends, are we not?" Elias responded. "Let us not quarrel about money! Here, eat at my inn for free. Take your payment from the services I can offer you. Nona is a fine cook, isn't she?"

"A friend would not be made to pay for his meal like a common traveler," the other pointed out grimly. "But if this is what you offer, despite the deep insult I feel, I will accept it."

"Thank you!" Elias sighed, holding out his hands. "Take my hands in friendship! You have saved a poor man from great hardship, and you are a fine person to put our longstanding relationship ahead of these hard financial times."

The man pushed his chair back with a scrape and rose to his feet. He fixed Elias with a grimace and sucked his teeth in dissatisfaction. Elias spread his hands again and shrugged.

"Have mercy, friend," Elias said. When he heard the rustle of someone close to the door, he tried to hide his anger. It was Nona, no doubt, spying on things that were none of her business. He was the man of this house, and he would take care of things without her input!

After letting his guest out the front door and offering a few more pathetic gestures of poverty, he returned to the table and sat down cheerfully.

"Husband, this is not right," his wife said, entering the room.

"Isn't it? We've faired rather well, I'd say!"

"He agreed to help you only because he was a dear friend of my father's!" she said, her voice rising to an unattractive pitch. He winced at the sound of it and looked at her out of one eye.

"And he would hate to see the daughter of his dear friend imprisoned with her husband for failure to pay a debt, wouldn't he?" Elias asked with good humor. "We are quite safe, dear wife."

"By not repaying him in full, you have sullied my father's honor!" Her face grew pinker as her voice got even louder. "Do you think my father will take kindly to this?"

"Bah!" He swatted at the air in a dismissive gesture. "And lower your voice, woman. I don't want the neighbors to listen to our marital bliss, do you?"

Elias knew how to make her angry, and he was succeeding. It could be fun to needle her, especially when she went on about her father's honor and seemed to care little for his own. But this was not the time.

Going to one corner of the room, he pried a stone from the wall. Behind it was a purse, and he pulled it out, feeling the satisfactory weight of it in his hands. Bringing it to the table, he opened it, pulling out one coin at a time and piling them carefully by denominations. As he sensed his wife's anger dissipating, he glanced up to see her eyeing the coins as hungrily as he did. This was the wife he knew! She recognized the value of a coin just as well as he . . .

"It still isn't right, husband," she said, but the conviction seemed to have left her voice.

"Stay out of men's business, Nona," he said warningly. "I know what I'm doing more than you imagine you do! Look to our daughter . . . she's your concern!"

"Orli is a good girl," Nona said defensively. "She's a good cook. And she's got some muscle to put into the cleaning, too."

"Lazy," he muttered.

His wife sniffed and turned her back on him, heading out of the room. He gave her back a wry smile. Life with Nona was far from boring! But she didn't do her job as she should. That was his complaint. Their daughter was less than an accomplishment, at least to his view. They had been able to have only one child, and it was regrettably a girl. At the very least he had hoped for a pretty daughter, one whose beauty made up for her deficiencies in gender. Instead, he had gotten Orli—a sullen girl with a tendency to get lazy and doe-eyed. Not even worth a hard day's work! And that could not be blamed on him. It was his wife's fault. Raising the girls was a woman's role, and Orli was not much of an achievement, especially considering that Nona hadn't given him any other children!

If he weren't so . . . economical . . . Elias might have considered taking a second wife. But women cost money, and money was something he didn't like to part with. Nona's sovereignty in the home was quite secure.

Just then he heard a rustling near the door.

"Nona?"

Silence.

"Orli! Come in here!"

The girl slipped around the corner, her face downcast, stopping one step inside the door.

"What do you want?" he barked.

"You called me, Father," she replied simply.

"You were outside the door."

"I was only passing by, Father."

"Hmmph."

She stood stock-still, looking downward, a petulant set to her mouth that he didn't like. Orli was older than he remembered. It always shocked him to realize that she was becoming a young woman and was no longer the little girl who used to run and play. Now she was this . . . this foreign thing he didn't understand. Short and stocky with firm muscles and a reluctant way about her, she tended to be silent and sullen unless he asked her a direct question. Never did she offer anything on her own.

His daughter did not like him. He knew that very well.

"Go on your way, then," he said, turning away from her. She was too confusing for him. Let her mother deal with her! The best thing he could do was to get her married off to some strong-willed fellow who could make something out of her.

But even as she walked away, a small part of his heart wanted to fix everything for her . . . to put it all straight again . . . to hold her in his arms as he used to do, and tell her stories. But he didn't know how to fix it, so he put it out of his mind.

On a hillside quite far outside the town of Bethlehem the sun slipped down toward the horizon and a soft, red glow crept along the grassy slopes. A large herd of sheep was grazing, milling about and bleating contentedly. From time to time a sheep on the edge of the flock would venture away from the others. If another started to follow it, then the entire flock would move as well, shifting to engulf the fugitives once more. Safety was in numbers. The animals were freshly crutched, in which the wool on the heads and bellies had been sheared away, leaving them looking strangely small-headed in comparison to their woolly bodies. Crutching was necessary, though, to keep the flies from laying eggs in the wool and then biting the sheep and tormenting them. It also kept the wool clean from feces and urine—a health precaution for the flock as well as a financial decision to protect the quality of the wool.

Several small fires crackled, and the shepherds' evening meals sizzled on the coals. The men clustered around the fires kept an eye on the sheep, and from time to time would call out an order and the spreading flock would regroup. The wind was blowing a cool relief over the men, and they leaned back, enjoying the scent of sheep, cooking supper, and evening calm.

"Long day," Nathaniel muttered. "Crutching the whole herd in one day was rather ambitious."

"But we finished, didn't we?" Tenin asked, stretching his arms above his head.

"Finished with sore backs and aching limbs!" Nathaniel replied, but he looked up over at the herd and nodded in appreciation.

"Better now than when the flies bed down," another shepherd said in a gravelly voice. "Nothing worse than sheep going fly crazy."

"That one will have three," Tenin observed, nodding toward a pregnant ewe. "Mark my words!"

"Care to make that more interesting?" Nathaniel asked, his small eyes twinkling. "Care to put a penny on it?"

"You're saying less than three?" Tenin responded.

"Two big ones, that's all."

Shaking his head, Tenin turned back to the food on the fire. A pot of beans bubbled over the flames, and he poked at them with a long-handled stick, testing their softness.

Amichai watched his kinsmen as they moved about performing their duties. They were the single men of the clan. Their people were nomadic by nature, but the men who herded sheep were the ones with no womenfolk. Rubbing his callused hands together, he worked off some of the dirt. It was a life of outdoors in all weather. But he couldn't say that he minded. With no women around, he wasn't constantly reminded of what he was missing.

"Another eight weeks, and we'll be crutching again!" another shepherd muttered, then belted out a laugh when a man close by tossed some water at him from his small cup.

"Enjoy success for an evening!" Amichai laughed. "Just because the night will come again does not mean you don't enjoy the morning!"

"And that Raold will be doing the majority of the work, mark my words!" Nathaniel spat out. "Slipping off when we're about to do the heavy work is not to be quickly forgotten, am I wrong?"

Murmurs of agreement spread among the men.

"Too young for brains and too old for his mother's milk," Amichai said, shaking his head. "Where'd he go off to?"

"Where?" Tenin laughed. "Where else? To town!"

"Which girl this time?" Nathaniel asked, dipping some beans out of the pot into his clay bowl. "Stupid boy needs to be taught how to behave himself."

"Marry him off, I say," another man retorted. "Can't wait for a woman, then he should get one to provide for and keep. That'll cool his heels."

"Learn from his example, kid," Amichai said to the young Tenin. "Nothing but trouble will come to him, I warrant you that much."

"Hey!" Tenin said, raising his hands in denial. His hair was curly and long, and his cheeks were only downy with the beginning of a beard. "I may be young, but I'm not empty-headed!"

The men around him laughed, and one rapped on the top of his head in good humor.

Amichai bit into a bean and sucked his breath through his teeth to cool the hot food in his mouth. Raold worried him. It wasn't unheard-of for a young shepherd to go into town after some diversion, but the result was never good. And Raold was his distant cousin. The boy needed some straightening up. If he wanted a woman, his family could provide a wife from his own clan, from his own people. A village could stone a shepherd for nosing around where the townsmen didn't want him! Besides the fact that what the boy was up to was a sin against God.

Or probably up to. Amichai remembered being young himself. Although he hadn't quite known how to get himself into trouble, his father had always assumed the worst. He'd received enough beatings for his father's past sins instead of his own recent ones! His father always concluded that young Amichai had been doing much worse than he'd been able to think up on his own. And it could be the same with young Raold . . .

"Someone needs to take a stick to that boy," a shepherd grumbled in disgust. "Correct the boy before it's too late."

A round of hearty agreement greeted his words.

"I'll talk to him," Amichai said in his quiet voice.

"Talk?" Nathaniel bellowed. "Let the stick do the talking!"

"Talk first, Nat," Amichai said.

Nathaniel spat into the fire and muttered something Amichai was pretty sure that he didn't want to hear. What the whole lot of them collectively knew about parenting, Amichai had no idea. A couple of them were widowers, but the vast majority of their lot had no women or children. At least no legitimate children to bother about. An illegitimate child was a shame worse than no children at all. And here they were trying to correct a youngster as if they were his parents.

Amichai's own father had been a tyrant, but that wasn't so unusual. Everyone expected men to be tough on their sons so that they wouldn't be spoiled. Men did not spare the rod. And Amichai's father was as manly as they came. But Amichai had been from a different mold . . . he had been more sensitive. And each time his father beat him for real or imagined sins, Amichai's heart became a little bit harder and a little more brittle. Even now, as a grown man, as he thought back on the whippings and berating his father had showered on him, he felt his blood begin to boil.

Stupid. Womanish. Ugly little runt. Sinful buck. He could recall all of the words his father had hurled at him. Still did. But now his father was a feeble old man who could no longer walk on his own. Now he was bony, with skin as transparent as a garlic skin. And he'd look up at Amichai defiantly through his watery eyes, and the streams of words would still burst out. But he had no power anymore. Amichai respected him as his father, but Jonah could no longer punish. No longer able to beat anyone, he was an impotent as a wether—the male sheep castrated so as not to be competition for the virile rams.

But some things didn't seem to change. Amichai had never married. He hadn't taken a woman or had his own family. Instead, he'd turned to caring for the sheep, and he had felt safe here. His father was back at the camp, and as much distance as two leagues could separate him from those words . . . from whom his father said he was. Out here on the hills, Amichai was someone else. He was a protector, a provider, a man, out here with the sheep.

But he was a quiet man. A gentle man who kept mostly to himself. He would watch the younger men marry and see them have children. And still Amichai would stay out here on these hills, where his father's words could dissipate harmless into the big night sky.

CHAPTER 7

As for her, she was in most respects sensible and faithful to him; yet in her nature she had something that was as feminine as it was cruel, for she treated him contemptuously, as befitting the enslavement he was under by passion for her. She did not appropriately consider herself as living under a monarchy and that she was subject to a master, and accordingly would behave insolently toward him; on his part he pretended to ignore this and bore it steadfastly.

—*Josephus, on Mariamne, wife of Herod*

Herod turned away from the commotion. Most of those present were well past tipsy. Silver-fringed panels hung from the high ceiling, dipping down like waves in the sea. Servants wearing sheaths entirely made of tiny shells waved huge fans, cooling the guests as they lounged. Several men lounged in a large pool as serving women waded through the water to bring them platters of food and pitchers of wine balanced on their bare shoulders. The pool, normally a site of playful frivolity, was now the site of shouts and splashing. One dangerous-looking man who moved like a shadow was holding something under the water with one hand while bubbles and splashing ensued. The female slaves leaped from the water with shrieks of fear, and there came the bass shouts of men's voices. The splashing in the pool reverberated against the walls of the palace, and Herod looked away from the excitement and allowed his gaze to rest on his wife's beautiful face.

Mariamne's mouth was open, and her eyes were wide with an expression of shock. Her face was as pale as sand, and she pushed herself shakily to her feet, her golden plate with some remnants of food on it clattering to the ground, ringing out a clear note. She was lovely, his wife. Her lips were scarlet and her hair a long, lustrous black that fell away from her face in waves. Slender hands rose slowly to her throat, and a thin, high sound started to come out of her mouth as she stared.

"Sit down, wife," Herod said. "It is nothing, I'm sure."

But she ignored him, the same high noise still issuing from her mouth, and strangely, it was not louder than that ominous splashing.

"Aristobulus!" she suddenly gasped, the sound stopping abruptly. "Aristobulus!"

Mariamne was poised as if ready for flight, all of her muscles tensed, and Herod would not have been unduly shocked if she had launched herself into the air. Instead she sprang forward, dashing down the marble stairs, her scarlet silk robes flowing out behind her like a wave of blood. Her sandals clattered against the tiles as she elbowed her way through the people.

"Move!" she shouted, her voice ringing with authority. "Move, you swine, move!"

Herod stood to get a better view of her as she dropped to the dripping side of a young man who lay motionless on the floor. His companions had pulled him out after the strange man of shadows had finished with him. Several times she pushed futilely at him, slamming her fists against his chest. Then she let out a loud wail and buried her face in his wet clothing.

"My brother!" her cracked voice moaned. "Oh, my brother!"

Herod lowered himself back to his seat and made a motion with his finger toward the musicians. Silence. When he turned a threatening gaze toward them, they fumbled to begin playing again. It was painful, those dropped notes and missed beats. He closed his eyes against the ugliness of it all. Ugliness had no place here. What he required was tranquillity and loveliness. He focused on the sound of the music, letting it flow over him like a warm bath. And he allowed himself to feel the breeze coming from the fan of a nearby slave, stirring the curls that lay on his forehead and tickling his lips.

"You monster!" her voice shattered through his forced calm.

Opening his eyes, Herod stared at his wife in shock. What was this?

"You brutal, evil wretch!"

Shaking with rage, she stood, her fists clenched at her side and her eyes wild with fury. Her hair hung in front of her face in disarray, and foam began to trickle at the corners of her lips. All Herod wanted to do was to hold her close and calm her down into the beautiful creature that he knew she was.

"It was you!" she said, her voice beginning to calm, but the venom remaining. "You killed him, you coward! Scared of a boy! What kind of man do you think you are?"

His bodyguards edged toward her, but Herod stopped them with a gesture. No, that would not do. Mariamne was his wife, and he would not let another man touch her.

"Darling," he said softly. "Come back and listen to the music with me. We will have more wine, and I will tell you how beautiful you are . . ."

She shook her head in disbelief, her expression incredulous as if he were something foreign and vile. Something like fear slithered down his spine, and he swallowed quickly. Was she really blaming him? Did she really hate him for protecting his throne? But he was only protecting his life—protecting their love! Because what love could survive after death? The lovers must live!

"I hate you!" she whispered hoarsely. "I despise you. May God curse you!"

Herod sucked in his breath at these words and eyed her nervously. This was not going as planned. He had expected tears, but he had meant to dry those tears. Grief, yes, but he would assuage that grief. But this hatred was something that he had not counted on. Her previous indifference to him was supposed to become a need for him without her brother in the court! Instead it had turned into something quite ugly and uncontrollable.

"Oh, dearest!" Panic began to pump through his veins. "I adore you! I worship you! What am I without you, my love? No, don't say such things. I know you love me. I know you do!"

The image of her . . . the images of the royal feast . . . the fumbling music of the musicians . . . all seemed to fade into a smoky darkness.

"Oh, darling, I love you!" he shouted through the mist. But she was gone. All of it was gone. And he suddenly sat up in bed, his heart pounding and his face drenched with sweat.

"Mariamne!" he shouted.

Silence. He looked around the room, his heart threatening to stop in his chest. Tears choked his throat shut, and he felt as if he could not breathe. His bedroom was as it always was . . . the curtains around his bed draped delicately to protect from night insects. The embroidered bedclothes were wrapped around his legs like seaweed, and the lamps that were always lit cast their orange glow over the gold and glittering jewels. Elaborately carved tables held ornaments from across the known world . . . carvings of ivory. The smell of bath salts and fragrant oil overpowered him in a sickening rush.

"Mariamne?" he whispered.

Silence.

"Mariamne?" His voice grew more agitated.

"Yes, darling."

Her voice was smoky and low. She sat in a shadow so that he could not see her as he liked. But he could see the silver that now glittered through her raven-black hair. Her slender hands folded in her lap, she looked at him gently. The dress she wore was a simple white one with a belt of silver at her waist. Looking tired, she held a bone comb suspended as if she had forgotten what she was to use it for and had simply put it in her lap until she remembered.

"Oh, darling!" he sighed. "I hate to sleep. Sleep is a torture."

"But you must rest, sweetness. A man must rest or go mad!"

"You care for my comfort," he said, smiling at her. "You do care!"

"I want you to be comfortable," she said, moving closer to the bed. Her eyes were older now, and the lines at the corners of her lips betrayed her age. The comb remained in one hand.

"You remind me of my nurse sometimes. I don't remember my mother, but I remember my nurse. She loved me. She would hold me and tell me stories. She would comb my hair."

"I am not your nurse," she said, putting a cold hand against his forehead. "I am your wife! Your own true love . . ."

"I knew it!" he laughed softly. "I knew you loved me! I knew it always. Even though you always pretended to hate me so, I knew it wasn't true. How could you deny our love?"

"Hate you?" Her eyes were wide and innocent. "I have never hated you!"

"Oh, my darling!" he sighed, holding out his arms to her. "Come to me!"

And as he pulled her toward him, her hands melted in his and her body became nothing but a cold, chilling mist. She evaporated like smoke, slipping through his fingers, and vanished.

"Mariamne!" he shrieked. "Mariamne, come back!"

He kicked savagely at the bedclothes, entangling his legs, and tore at the curtains around his bed. Finally, pulling himself free, he staggered out into the room, circling several times before dashing for the door.

"Mariamne?" he called more softly. "Sweetness?"

Opening the door, he tiptoed out, calling her name as gently as he could.

"Where is my wife?" he asked a soldier standing duty near by. "Did she come this way?"

The man shook his head, something strange in his eyes that Herod did not like. If he weren't so intent on finding where his wife had scampered off to, he would have pursued the issue.

"Mariamne!" he repeated.

Ravi slipped back into the shadows, holding his breath, not trusting himself even to breathe. Herod was creeping down the hallway in front of him, his glittering eyes peering this way and that.

"Where is my girl?" the king said quietly. "Hiding, is she? Come now, come out!"

Remaining motionless, Ravi slowly exhaled and tried to control every muscle in his body. He knew the stories of what happened at night in this palace. Some claimed that ghosts haunted the king. Others said he was simply a raving lunatic. The king was out of his mind—that much Ravi knew. And Herod was a brutal, bloodthirsty man. Too many servants had died, too much blood had flowed, during the king's strange nightly excursions.

Everyone had heard of the king's wife Mariamne. She had been a Maccabean, and Herod had needed a Jewish wife to legitimize his half-Jewish status as he tried to rule a reluctant nation Mariamne was beautiful, but it was very much a political marriage. Who would have guessed that Herod would fall desperately in love with her?

Mariamne, it was said, had hated Herod with as much passion as he had loved her. She would cringe at his touch and stiffen at the sound of his voice. While she bore him five children, the women servants claimed that their mistress did not do so willingly.

But this was all rumor. Ravi did not have time for such things. He did, however, have time to listen to the sound advice offered by his superiors.

"Avoid him at night," his supervisor had warned him. "I cannot protect you if the king demands your execution because he has seen you during one of his delusions."

"What kind of delusions?" Ravi had asked.

"It depends on the night," the official had said with a shrug. "But it always remains constant. They always involve his late wife Mariamne."

"He loved her," Ravi said softly.

His supervisor gave a short barking laugh.

"Better to be a dog in the street than loved by the king! It is safer!"

"So avoid him?"

"At all costs. I have lost an entire staff of servants who were too eager to please the king, not realizing that he would not reward them the way they had hoped. He can be full of promises of wealth, but his moods change more quickly than desert winds."

"And if he requires my service?"

"Keep your head down. Do not let him know your name. And do not seek advancement."

The rules of survival in the palace of Herod. Ravi had taken the advice to heart, and he had stayed carefully out of Herod's sight during the night hours. He wanted to live long enough to see his grandchildren. And he wanted to live to see the Messiah come, God willing.

Now Ravi watched as the king moved further down the long hallway, creeping along like a boy sneaking out at night if it hadn't been for his grizzled mop of gray hair. He was wearing his short night tunic, and his thin legs protruded out from underneath it like hairy sticks. Something close to pity filled Ravi's heart. But a healthy fear tempered that pity.

CHAPTER 8

A time to embrace and a time to refrain, . . . a time to keep and a time to throw away.

—Ecclesiastes 3:5, 6

Ebenezer stood with his back to the room, staring out the small window. On the windowsill was a collection of dust and grit from the day's wind. His wife would wipe it off, and tomorrow it would again be there. Rolled above the window was an animal hide tied with a thong, ready to be dropped over the opening for privacy or to keep out the ever driving dust and sand. Outside the window he saw the myrtle trees—tall and regal, with their dark shiny leaves offering shade. The sun had settled low in the sky, lengthening shadows and softening the bright sun to a golden glow. It was the time for a man to come home to his family . . . to feel the pleasures of domesticity and to play with his children. Instead, he was standing in this room awaiting something that he never thought he would ever have to face.

Tugging at the thong, he let the animal hide drop over the window. Then, taking a deep breath, he faced the young man standing before him. The room became suddenly dim and the oil lamps seemed insufficient.

"I am grieved, Joseph," he said in a low voice.

Joseph frowned, but met his future father-in-law's eyes evenly. Ebenezer saw that he looked worried, but frustratingly not guilty. Here was a good man to bring into their family! Why did it all have to go so wrong?

"Things are not as they should be," Mary's father began slowly. "I wish you had told me that you were dissatisfied with the wedding plans. You could have come for my daughter at an earlier time, and I would never have stopped you."

"Has someone told you that I spoke against you, sir?" Joseph asked directly. "Because I have not. When we discussed this betrothal, I understood how hard it was for a father to let his daughter go. I have experienced the same conflicting feeling with my own daughter when she married. I am a patient man, and still am. Another month or even several months is better if it allows Mary . . . if it allows you, sir, time to grow accustomed to the change."

Why was the man being so obtuse? He must know by now what his actions had caused! Why force an old man to declare it openly?

"Young man!" Ebenezer said, his voice raising. "You know what I'm speaking of!"

"I'm afraid I do not."

Ebenezer scrubbed a hand over his face. Having married late in life, he was now an old man. But if he had been younger, would he have been any more able to deal with this kind of situation?

"You've ruined her, Joseph," he said, his voice shaking with emotion. "You've ruined her. My beautiful daughter . . ."

Joseph opened his mouth to speak, then closed it, an expression of hurt evident on his features. He clenched his jaw and seemed to be organizing his thoughts before speaking.

"How can you say that?" Joseph asked finally. "I have treated her only with respect and dignity. I have prepared tirelessly to give your daughter a home worthy of her." He paused, clenching his jaw. "How could you say that I have ruined her in any way?"

"You have lain with her before the wedding!" Ebenezer burst out. "And now you must make it right!"

Ebenezer could feel himself shaking with rage, and he struggled to control his breathing, aware that if he shouted, he would only be declaring his daughter's guilt to all the neighbors.

"I have not lain with her, and I will personally deal with any man who tells you differently!"

"No man needed to tell me," Ebenezer said, struggling to control his voice. "She is with child."

An ominous silence filled the room while Ebenezer gauged the effect of his words on Joseph's face. The younger man looked stunned; his mouth moved, but words did not come out. Then he cleared his throat, and seemed to think twice about speaking. Finally he put his head down and turned away.

"Her condition is obvious by now," Ebenezer explained quietly. "I, as her father, would choose to believe otherwise, but it is already too obvious. The girl is pregnant, Joseph. And as her father who loves her, I am asking you to do what is right by her."

"I have not lain with her," Joseph repeated.

"No one need know!" Ebenezer persisted, feeling the panic rising in his voice. "All can be mended! Come for her in a few days. Send her away to some family before she has the child, and no one will know the difference in the timing!"

"I have not lain with her," Joseph said a third time with a frown. "It is impossible that she is pregnant. There must be some other explanation."

"You still deny it? You would not set her aside, would you? She is a good girl! You know that she will work hard and be a virtuous wife!"

The words almost stuck in his throat. Virtue. His daughter had no more claim to that attribute anymore. How could this man know that Mary would be virtuous if she consented to lay with him before her marriage? Ebenezer felt the heat of humiliation rising in his face.

"You say that there is no other possibility, sir?" Joseph asked slowly. "That she is indeed pregnant, and there is no mistaking it?"

"Would her own father call her down?" Ebenezer could feel the tears welling up in his eyes. "Would her own father bring her chastity into question? There is no doubt!"

Putting a hand over his lips to hide their quivering, Ebenezer squeezed his eyes shut against the tears. His daughter. His little girl. His Mary . . .

"Then some other man is the father of this child," Joseph said woodenly. "It is not I . . ."

Despair filled Joseph's voice, and as Ebenezer looked into the younger man's eyes he saw tears there as well. Unwilling to speak, Joseph shook his head several times in frustration.

"It is not I, sir," he stated again, his voice choked.

The two men faced each other in silence.

"You could come for her," Ebenezer said futilely. "I would not stop you."

Joseph shook his head sadly. "I will not answer you yet, sir. Let me leave now. I must think alone."

Ebenezer nodded and watched as Joseph walked heavily toward the door. He believed him. It would be easier if he did not! If he believed that Joseph were lying, he could at least find some comfort and release through feelings of rage and indignation. But it was obvious that this man was as crestfallen as any betrayed man could be. Joseph was telling the truth. He had not lain with her. In some illogical part of his mind, that realization was a relief. He did not have to think of Joseph demeaning his little girl that way.

But Mary was pregnant. And someone was the father of her child! *Someone* had lain with her!

Once again he stood facing the window covering, his head down, his beard brushing against his chest. He did not want to move, nor could he speak. Sadness pressed down on him like heavy boulders. He longed to go lie down—to sleep and never face this thought again. But he knew he could not. Whom did Mary have now but her father?

The only answer was to get the girl to admit who had done this to her. Better for her to be married to the snake who had raped her than have her stoned by the village.

Two weeks had now gone by since Mary had seen Joseph. The last time, she had passed him in the market and he had whispered to her that she was beautiful, his gentle smile tugging at her heart like nothing else could. Two weeks ago he was still planning their wedding. Two weeks ago he was still allowing her to see him purchasing beautiful things in the market . . . a tiny taste of the gifts waiting for her when he came to take her back to his home. Two weeks ago he would still watch her as she went by, his expression so tender that she longed to run to his arms, even though she knew she could not . . . not yet . . .

Two weeks ago she was still naively hoping that her betrothed would come that night . . . that he would take her back to his home before anyone knew. But that was two weeks ago. And she had not seen him since.

Mary sat silently in the sleeping quarters she shared with her siblings, her hand on her belly. Every passing week seemed to make it a little bigger. Bending was no longer as easy as it had been. Her mother treated her more coldly, and her father would not even speak to her.

Perhaps Joseph would return today! Perhaps he would try to see her alone. Perhaps he would love her still. But would she forget so easily if Joseph had made another woman pregnant? Would she be so willing to forgive?

How could he believe her claim that she was pregnant through a miracle? Yet it was the truth. Despite the opinion of her family and the spreading rumors, she was still a virgin. She was innocent. Not that it seemed to matter. The proof was in the broth, as they said. After all, she was pregnant. How else could she have gotten that way?

"Mary?"

As her little brother came into the room, his eyes wide and his lips pressed into a thin line, she glanced up.

"Hello, David," she said softly.

Approaching her, he looked at her curiously, putting one pudgy finger into his mouth.

"Were you bad?" he asked in all seriousness.

"No, honey," she said with a sad smile. "I wasn't bad. But Mommy and Daddy think I was bad."

"Oh." He seemed to absorb the information and nodded to himself.

"I don't think you are bad," he said after a moment, coming closer and crawling into her lap.

Tears filled Mary's eyes, and she pulled him into a hug. He nestled comfortably against the fullness of her stomach. Anyone else, she realized wryly, would have pushed away from this evidence of her "sin."

One of the older boys poked his head into the room.

"Come on, David," he said gruffly. "Let's go out and play. I'll take you to the spring."

"Don't want to."

Mary looked at Japheth, watching the thoughts swirling around his mind. He assumed that he hid them so well! It made her smile. All men thought they could carefully mask their feelings. But Japheth was only a boy.

"Are you mad at me, Japheth?" she asked him.

"Yeah, I guess," he said, frowning and looking away. "Yeah."

She didn't have an answer for that. Although she had claimed her innocence endlessly, no one believed her. It felt pointless to continue.

"They say you are a sinner!" Japheth said, spitting out the words. "They say you are a sinner and a liar!"

"They do say that," his sister said, nodding. "I know."

"So that's why you're getting fat like that, right?" Confusion filled his words. "You're having a baby even though you aren't married!"

"Yes, I will have a baby. I know that is hard to understand."

Japheth looked at the floor, digging his toe into the dirt. He sniffed loudly and wiped his nose with the back of his hand.

"You should use a handkerchief," she said before she could catch herself.

"Well, you shouldn't have . . ." he started to say, his eyes dark and defiant, then turned and left the room, leaving Mary and little David staring after him.

"Why is he so angry?" his brother asked.

Mary smoothed his hair with her hand, put her cheek against his soft curls, and sighed. She felt as if she'd even betrayed the children!

"Go play, David," she said, hoisting him to his feet.

"I don't want to."

"You don't want to go play by the spring?" she asked, raising her eyebrows in exaggerated surprise. "And you don't want to catch grasshoppers to put down Naomi's tunic? And you don't want to go find a really great stick to draw in the dirt with?"

Her brother giggled.

"Go on!" she said, trying to show great enthusiasm. "Go play!"

David ran out of the room, clattering away with the noise that only little boys seemed capable of making.

Alone in the returning silence, Mary covered her face in her hands. She could feel the cool plaster of the wall against her back, and she looked around the room. Their pallets were on the floor, and there was a divider put up to separate off her parent's sleeping place. The blankets were all rolled neatly and the room was swept. It was quiet and clean, all as it should be. Mary tried to pull her knees up to her chest, and realized belatedly that the position was no longer possible. Instead she stretched out her legs and sighed, staring up at the ceiling. She could hear the gentle first rains splattering outside, and she knew it wouldn't slow the boys down at all.

"O, God," she prayed. "O, God, I didn't know that it would be like this! I should have known. But I didn't."

Even her little brothers now hated her. Only David was too young to understand. And if he were older, he would be angry with her too. She felt utterly alone.

"This baby is Yours," she continued softly. "I have not sinned.

Only You seem to know it. But I am only a girl. I'm afraid. And I'm lonely. Everyone hates me!"

Tears welled up in her eyes.

"You said that You would be with me. Oh, don't leave me alone! Don't let them stone me! Don't let them throw me out! And please, please . . ."

But she didn't know what to ask. She didn't even know what would fix all of this! It was too big even to see all the implications. Nothing could ever make it right again in public opinion. The weight of being alone, of being unloved, threatened to crush her. It was unbearable.

"I love Joseph," she whispered. "If You give me only one person, let it be Joseph. Let him love me, too! Let him believe that I am innocent! Let him want me still! I can't do it by myself. I can't be mother to Your child all alone. Please, please, give me Joseph! If you grant me only one thing . . ."

Tears trickled down her cheeks and she lay down on the floor, cradling her head in her arm and covering her eyes as she cried. She felt as if her heart would break.

"And if You would give me two things, let my mother hug me again!"

Suddenly a peace enveloped her, and she felt warm and loved, the way she used to as a small girl in her mother's lap. She sensed God near her, and shutting her eyes, she relaxed for the first time in a long time.

And when she opened her eyes, she felt strong again. She could face this—she could do it . . . for God, and for this little baby growing inside of her. After all, she was now a mother. And a mother needed to be stronger than even a warrior in battle.

CHAPTER 9

I see him, but not now; I behold him, but not near. A star will come out of Jacob; a scepter will rise out of Israel.

—Numbers 24:17

Sheep could be fickle when it came to bonding with their young. If anything disturbed them too much when they lambed, the ewes might lose all interest and forget to let the lambs nurse. From all appearances sheep were stupid animals, but Amichai knew better than that. He'd seen sheep recognize each other after two years' separation. The animals knew the call and distinct whistles of their shepherds. A new shepherd to the flock took a long time to gain their confidence to the point of them listening to his commands. So although the sheep had a certain level of intelligence, they still could very easily become disinterested in their young if something happened to draw away their attention too close to the birth. It was a phenomenon Amichai did not understand.

People could be the same way, of course. He'd heard of women abandoning babies because they were girls, or even sacrificing them to strange gods on stone altars. But those were pagans who did such vile things. For the most part, he shared the opinion that Jews took altogether too much interest in their young. If his own father had taken slightly less interest in him as a boy, Amichai might not resent the old man so much.

But here Amichai was, trying to reintroduce a lamb to its mother, and planning a way to talk to Raold about his behavior. Raold wasn't even his son, only a young kinsman, yet Amichai felt a strange responsibility for the boy. And Raold would likely resent it.

"Stand still, woman," Amichai said gruffly, gripping the ewe's neck so that it couldn't get away. He pulled the lamb closer, encouraging it to nurse. The ewe jerked, its muscles suddenly flexing with a burst of strength, and Amichai lost both his balance and his hold on the ewe. It bolted a little ways away and began to graze unconcerned.

Muttering under his breath, Amichai looked down at the lamb with its long legs and big eyes and ears. The animal was brown and white with a brown patch over one eye, and it raised its gaze to meet Amichai's in an expression of confusion.

"She doesn't want you," Amichai said, picking the lamb up and turning back toward the makeshift camp. The lamb kicked its long legs a few times in an attempt to get more comfortable, then settled into Amichai's arms.

"You'll get milk yet, not to worry. I'll milk her myself."

Amichai was not ancient, although sometimes he felt it. It seemed that life had cast him in the role of someone much older. Did he resent it? He wasn't sure. Life was what it was. God had given him a certain number of days in a certain station. But he sometimes felt like the lamb in his arms, skittish and wanting to run out and try something new.

The temporary camp for the shepherds was a league away from the main camp of the rest of the clan. Raold sat next to a low leather tent, whittling a piece of wood while he watched the food on the fire. It would be mealtime again soon. Only about 17, Raold wore his hair longer than was the fashion, but his curls were as glossy and dark as a girl's. Slender, he had the anxious eyes of a youth trying to act older than he was and unsure if he were playing the part accurately. He looked up as Amichai approached and gave a brief nod.

"'Morning," Amichai said, settling down onto his haunches close to a animal skin of milk. "Pass me a bowl, would you?"

Silently Raold passed the bowl and watched furtively from the corner of his eye as Amichai poured some milk. Since pouring required both hands, the lamb teetered away so that Amichai muttered an oath before putting down the bowl and retrieving the animal. After the first slurp of milk from Amichai's fingers, the lamb began butting his head against the man's arm for more.

"Ah, figured that out, eh?" Amichai said with a laugh. He glanced at Raold, who quickly looked away.

"The ewe wouldn't take," Amichai said by way of explanation. "Pity. This one could be meat, or I could feed it. What do you think?"

Raold appeared surprised at being asked for his opinion.

"I don't know. Feed it, I guess."

"That's what I thought." The young man looked gratified at the affirmation.

"I guess everyone's pretty angry," Raold said after a moment.

"Yeah, well . . ." Amichai said noncommittally.

"I don't want to be a shepherd. I want to live in town. I want to be a merchant or a winemaker."

"Merchants and winemakers are born to the life. They inherit the land or the business. Best to stay where you were born. The family tree offers more shade."

"Everyone is angry at me here, anyway."

Amichai gave him an amused look. "Because you ran off and didn't take care of your responsibilities! A man takes care of his own before he goes off."

"And when would anyone let me leave?"

The older shepherd shrugged. He hated to admit that Raold had a point. "You're young. What do you do out there, anyway?"

"What does it matter to you?" Defiance filled Raold's eyes.

"Some girl, eh?" Amichai said with a laugh. He shook his head. "I know what it's like to be your age. And I'm telling you, the trouble you could cause is not worth the excitement."

"I didn't say there was a girl," Raold snapped defensively.

"Didn't have to." Amichai dipped his fingers back into the bowl of milk and held them out to the lamb.

"So what if I go out and have some fun? What does it matter? If she's willing enough, it's not my problem. My dad always said it's her own fault if her reputation's gone."

Amichai winced. "And if you're the one who ruined it?"

"If it weren't me, it would have been some other guy."

His amusement having evaporated, Amichai turned a direct gaze on Raold that made him squirm. "Let me tell you something as your kinsman," he said, his voice low and angry. "I happen to care what happens to you, and right now I'm not even sure why. You're an irresponsible little rat at the moment, and you'll be getting yourself killed as likely as not. That girl has a family, and that family will require vengeance for ruining her. If you had a scruple at all in that pretty little head of yours, you'd cut the dalliance now and give her a chance at an honorable marriage. Because if I know you at all, you've given her unending streams of promises about your undying love and faithful regard for her well-being. Does she think you're a merchant? Did you convince her that you're rich and will take her away?"

"She knows who I am!"

"Then all the worse for her! Because you were born a shepherd, and you'll die one! And if she can't see that you're beneath her, then her father's whip will open her eyes to that fact! If you want a woman, let your family know it, and they'll choose you a good wife from our clan—not that you deserve it."

Raold gave him a withering glare and pushed himself to his feet. Amichai stood up with the menacing stance of a man who is willing to use his bulk for a purpose. He put a heavy hand on the youth's shoulder and looked down at him, pinning him to the spot.

"Like I said, Raold," Amichai continued in a controlled voice, "I happen to care what happens to you, which is less than I can say for the rest of the men today! Take some advice before you do something irreparable."

"Let go of me." Raold jerked his shoulder away. "You're not my father, you know! You're just jealous that no woman wants an old oaf like you!"

Then he bolted away, leaving Amichai staring after him with a veiled expression. He sighed and shook his head. That hadn't exactly gone according to plan. Squatting back down next to the lamb, he again dipped his fingers into the milk.

No, Amichai wasn't his father. He wasn't even a husband. Maybe he had no right to interfere.

"Your old dad is dead," Amichai muttered to himself. "And he'd be none too proud to see how you turned out."

Simak sat on the edge of his bed and rubbed his hands over his face. It was late at night. What watch, he was not sure—but late enough for the moon to be spilling its light through the windows.

"Third watch!" a voice from outside called out. "All is well!"

Ah, so that was the time—morning would be coming soon enough. He should be using this time to sleep, but his mind would not return to slumber. It was the same dream again . . . the dream about the star and the baby being born.

The Magi often used the stars to foretell the future. Kings had their own court magi to predict the future for them. History recorded countless stories in which the stars announced the death of a king, and in an attempt to thwart death, the monarch had appointed a stand-in to go to all his royal assignments for him. When his representative was assassinated or died by accident, the king resumed his throne. Fate's thirst for blood had been slaked.

But Simak was a ruler and magi himself. He did not have to hire others to foretell the future for him, or to read the stars. Well educated in astronomy, he knew the stars' paths and had his own scrolls of astronomical charts. Magi had plotted and measured every star in its course, whether by month, season, or year. As they charted the yearly cycle, they realized that it ended in a fraction, causing a discrepancy between the new year (the earth's annual cycle), and the new day (the stars' cycle). Was that not always the way? There was never a perfect match between the earth and the heavens. Except for one day . . . a day that had happened 487 years ago, and was due to recur this year—the day that the new year and the new day occurred simultaneously. Was there special power in this day? Not by happenstance alone. There was only special power if Ahura willed it be so. Perhaps Ahura had willed this from the beginning when he formed the earth with his hands . . .

Simak went to the window of his sleeping chamber. It was in a tower high above the city, and he stared out over the slumbering buildings awash in moonlight. The stars were not as bright because of the moon's brilliance, but he could still easily make out the different constellations: King Ribil, the water girl, the hare being chased by the lion, the waterpot . . . King Ribil had always interested him. The stars outlined the form of a man in his regal robes with a crown on his head. Three stars made up his belt, and the center star of that arrangement flickered more intensely than the rest. As a result, King Ribil was the strongest zodiac sign. Who could ignore him?

Down below in the courtyard he could see the guards making their rounds. A servant girl went out to the cistern to draw water . . . a strange time of day, but perhaps someone had been sick. A cloud slid silently over the moon, suddenly blocking the light like a snuffed-out lamp, and Simak stood in the darkness, listening to his heart pound. The cloud moved on, and the light poured out over the courtyard again. He shivered, and as he did, he felt a robe being slipped around his shoulders. Glancing around in surprise, he saw Nadr.

"Nadr! Do you not sleep?"

The servant's response was a slight smile, but Simak had been serious in the question. It was in the middle of the night and he had not called for anyone to assist him. A Magian might be knowledgeable in the stars and religious observance, but the workings of servants was still a dark mystery to him.

"Were you not sleeping?" Simak persisted.

"I was, Your Majesty, but I awoke when some of the servants who had eaten some bad meat were ill. I decided to make sure the mistake did not affect your meals as well. I heard you moving about and—forgive me—I came to check that you were not ill."

"Ah." Simak nodded. "That explains the girl fetching water at this hour. Well, Nadr, since we are both up, come sit with me. I would like to discuss some things with you."

The servant's calm expression did not change, and he edged toward some couches arranged on the balcony. The potted trees that would offer shade in the heat of the day now only served to block the light at night. The men selected two low couches facing each other.

"Is it the dream, Your Majesty?"

"Yes. It returns and returns."

"Any changes to it?"

"None."

Nadr nodded.

"Could it be associated with the approach of the new year and the new day?" Simak inquired quietly. "It is an auspicious time."

"I know less about the stars than you do, Your Majesty," the other said quietly. "But I do know from your father that the ways of the earth and the ways of the heavens do not coincide as often as money-hungry magi would have us believe."

"Indeed. It is why we expose the bodies of the dead on the towers. When the birds of prey and simple time have done their work and bleached the bones, the breath of the man can go back to Ahura. Man is of earth, but when he dies, his spirit is then of the heavens. The dead bodies hang between the two elements so as not to contaminate the earth. Thus it is always the same principle, is it not? Even death is not in step with earthly business. It is never convenient, comfortable, or serves any good unless it is the death of an enemy."

"My death would be a blessing to my enemy, just as his is to me," Nadr agreed.

"Good point. We are the center of the known world, are we not? This palace is situated on the dateline, so that when it is noon here, to the furthest reaches of the western kingdom is yet dawn, and the furthest reaches of the eastern kingdom it is becoming dusk. Yet even this is calculated by humanity. There are other kingdoms that are not in the day when we are."

"But are they blessed by Ahura?"

"There is a baby king to be born in Judah, a king of the Jews, and I dream of it here in Persia, far to the east. How is that explained? If that king is not of worth to us, why am I being told of his impending birth?"

"Why does Ahura care of his birth at all?" Nadr asked. "And why are you dressed as a servant in the dream?"

"It would be heresy to suggest that there are more important things than our religion can answer," Simak sighed.

"It would not be heresy to suggest that Ahura knows more than he can safely impart to man," the servant suggested quietly.

"Much more," Simak again sighed. "Knowledge is both a prison and a key. Enough keeps us locked on earth. Too much sets us free on the towers where our bones are bleached."

"We have always looked to the stars, Your Majesty," Nadr said, looking helplessly upward.

"We have," Simak agreed, his own eyes turning toward the familiar constellations in the night sky. "And the answer will be there. A star will rise, Nadr. It will rise."

CHAPTER 10

O daughters of Jerusalem, I charge you—if you find my lover, what will you tell him? Tell him that I am faint with love.

—*Song of Solomon 5:8*

Naomi pulled her veil up over her hair, carefully tucking any stray curl under the fabric. It was no time to toy with the village's opinion. Rumors were flying like blowing sand from house to house, and women and men alike were gobbling up the details like children with fresh grapes. The delight in scandal could turn into public outrage as quickly as the direction of the wind could change. Naomi was young, but she was not stupid.

As she shut the door behind her, she felt the weight of the family guilt pressing down on her shoulders. She was not pregnant! But her sister was, and in the eyes of the village, the family had been dishonored. They all shouldered the guilt. The worst part was that Mary refused to show proper shame! To keep on insisting that she was innocent was ridiculous. What had been done was bad enough, but to refuse to acknowledge that it had happened when there was such rock solid proof of it was even worse.

Jerking angrily at her veil, Naomi pulled it across her face so that only her eyes remained visible. She squinted against the moist wind that had begun to pick up and made her way in the direction of the market square in town. The hint of rain was in the air. It was the season for first rains and the harvesting of dates and figs. But a little rain would not stop Naomi today. Still, if her mother should watch her from the house, she would see where she was going.

Or supposed to be going . . .

Just then Naomi noticed a group of women walking in her direction. Their voices dropped when they saw her, and two of them looked pointedly away. The third gave Naomi a direct stare, and Naomi averted her eyes, hurrying on. So it had started.

Veering off the main road, she hurried up a rutted track. How many times had she walked this way? How many times had Thaddaeus come out to meet her so they could talk for a few precious minutes?

She could hear the sound of hammering before she could even smell the scent of heated metal and billowing furnace. As she rounded the last corner, she stopped to watch him work.

He was strong from the pounding and lifting. His muscles glistened with sweat and the dust and soot clung to his body, streaming in black rivulets down his back. The anvil was a piece of flattened iron set up on a wooden block. Along the wall of the workshop hung tongs, iron pinchers, and picks. A large oven with holes in the side allowed for air to be pumped in by goatskin bellows. In one hand Thaddaeus held a pair of long tongs that gripped the curved head of a plow and with the other he expertly wielded the hammer, the force of the blows coming down in a perfectly aimed rhythm. Pausing, he turned the plowhead over, nodded to himself, and plunged it, hissing, into the water bucket beside him.

Naomi kicked at a rock, sending it skittering off the path and into some bushes. A blacksmith's hearing was never very good, and a woman didn't hint to a blacksmith with shuffling or sighing. Thaddaeus turned as the rock thudded against something, and his dark eyes caught hers.

She looked around the forge.

"My father has left me to finish while he goes to see my uncle," Thaddaeus explained, anticipating her question.

"Are you busy?" she asked tentatively.

"Yes," he said, but he didn't pick up his tools again. Instead, he stood watching her with a veiled look in his eyes.

"I haven't seen you in a long time. You used to come by my house during the hot part of the day."

"I work hard, Naomi," he replied with a frown. "I get tired. I deserve rest!"

Naomi was silent for a moment.

"I know," she said finally. "But I missed you."

Thaddaeus pulled the plowhead out of the water and laid it aside. He stood with his back to her for a few moments, then turned around, his eyes flashing.

"I heard the happy news, you know!" he said.

"What news?"

"Your betrothal, what else?" he demanded.

"You knew my family was arranging for me to marry Ashi," she said quietly. "We both did."

"Well, I hear that he's very close to coming for you now," he shot back. "You'll be a dutiful wife in no time!"

"I hate it!" Tears welled up in her eyes. "I've been begging my mother for more time! I've begged them to find me someone else! I've done everything that I could!"

"And how do you like your husband-to-be?" Thaddaeus asked, his voice sarcastic and hurt.

"I've never met him."

"He's pathetic." Thaddaeus sneered. "Barely above the size of a boy. His father's got money, though. Not that it matters so much if the boy doesn't know how to make more! I could give you a life of luxury, you know! I could go to Jerusalem and make 10 times what my father does in this little hole of a town!"

"Then ask for me!" Naomi said, approaching, her eyes locked on his. "Ask your father for me! Tell him I'm the one you want!"

"It's not our choice. It's between our fathers."

"But you said you loved me! Didn't you say that?"

"My father says that love fades and what is left is a family."

"And my father says that he knows best. What do we get to say?"

"What can we say?" he barked with a laugh. "Naomi, you know as well as I do that marriage is something arranged between families. And if our families do not arrange it, we have no choice."

"You could ask your father for me," she repeated. "Just ask him . . . you're his oldest son. Maybe he will give you what you want!"

"I did."

Naomi stared at him, the reality registering.

"What if Ashi's family no longer wants me?" she pressed. "What if Ashi's family withdraws?"

"I already asked my father for you," he said, shaking his head. "I asked him last night. My father said no."

Tears trickled down her cheeks. She knew why his father had said no, even if Thaddaeus didn't. Her family was tainted now.

"And what of us?" she whispered.

"We try to forget each other," he answered gruffly. "You'll be married soon enough."

Thaddaeus returned to his work, his back toward her. Forget him? How could she? Even if he forgot her! The thought made her stomach feel sick. Still ignoring her, he thrust a piece of iron into the furnace and bent to work the bellows, the air whistling as it was forced into the furnace. She could hear the rush as the fire flamed up. Finally Naomi walked slowly back down the path, the sound of the hammer ringing out through the air in an angry staccato. Once she stopped to look back at him, the muscles on his bare back rippling and his arms flexed in work. She did not want to belong to another—she wanted Thaddaeus.

Perhaps he had given up, but she had not! She was not married to Ashi yet. If her bethrothed's family did not want the alliance, perhaps there could still be a way . . .

Lydia watched as her cousin walked slowly away from the blacksmith's shop, her head down and her eyes brimming with tears. When Lydia glanced toward Thaddaeus, the son of the blacksmith, she couldn't help noticing his tense stance and angry hammering. She smiled to herself. So Naomi had fallen for that beefy boy, had she? Not bad taste, really, if a girl went for looks. Thaddaeus's reputation wasn't as spotless as Naomi's father would want, however. Even Lydia knew that! She nearly laughed out loud. To think she'd been jealous of her cousin's good marriage arrangement. And here Naomi was pursuing someone else!

"Naomi!" Lydia called. "Wait! Naomi!"

For a moment Naomi froze before turning to face her cousin. Lydia gave a broad, friendly grin.

"I hear your wedding will be soon!" Lydia gushed. "How wonderful! How many new robes have you and your mother made?"

Her face turning stony, Naomi remained silent. She glanced toward Lydia, then looked away, her pace picking up.

"I only wanted to offer my congratulations. You must be so excited!"

"Thank you," Naomi said simply. "But I have to hurry. I can't talk."

"Oh, I can walk with you!" her cousin insisted. "I don't mind! I want to hear all the details!"

"No!" Two blotches of red splashed across Naomi's cheeks. "Leave me alone, Lydia. I don't want you here!"

"Well!" Lydia added more huffiness to her voice than she really felt. "Fine, then! I was only trying to be nice. But if you don't want me to talk to you, then I'll just go back and see if Thaddaeus wants to talk to me."

Naomi's eyes flashed fire, but she seemed to summon all of her self-control and continued on her way. When she did glance back once, her face looking anxious and heartbroken, Lydia felt a pang of guilt. She didn't really care about Thaddaeus or want him. The one she desired was a carpenter, and one already well established. Who wanted the up-start son of a blacksmith anyway? Except, perhaps, Naomi.

The elation of Lydia's brief victory did not last long. It was good to have the information, though. She would stow it away for later use—gossip was always a useful tool! How else could a village keep tabs on each other? And what other weapon did a woman have? The things women did behind their veils could be even more savage than what men did in battle.

Lydia couldn't exactly explain why she hated her cousins so much. After all, they hadn't done anything to her. Tending to avoid arguments, they didn't flaunt themselves unduly. But still they were known as the prettiest girls of the village. Perhaps the thing that bothered her was just the general disinterest toward her on their part. Lydia wasn't pretty enough or interesting enough to merit notice. And while Naomi and Thaddaeus sought each other like spring sheep, Naomi's father was arranging a marriage for her with the son of a wealthy and respected man. It wasn't fair! Lydia was older than Naomi was. Why weren't the men putting their united efforts into a marriage for her?

As Lydia headed slowly down the road, she swung an empty sack in one hand. It was an unconscious movement, one that, when she noticed, she would stop with a jerk. It was not a beautiful thing to do, and a woman who wanted to be perceived as beautiful must act it. But she had not yet noticed, and she swung the empty sack at her side. She was returning from her aunt's house where her mother had sent her to drop off some fresh figs as well as to glean as much information as possible about the upcoming weddings.

As Lydia approached her home, she saw Shali tumbling down the road toward her. The girl jiggled with excitement, and it made Lydia laugh out loud to see her. Somehow Shali had a way of improving just about any day!

"Lydia!" she gasped, trying to catch her breath. She put her head down and waved her arms.

"Some news, I take it? You'll nearly kill yourself rushing about like that!"

"I can't believe you didn't tell me," Shali said, her cheeks red and her voice sounding offended.

"Didn't tell you what? Well, whatever it is, you can spill it out indoors, where it is cooler. You look hot enough to melt."

Shali followed her slimmer friend inside the house where the change from bright sunlight made the indoors seem black as night. Lydia settled her friend on a stool while she poured water from a clay jug into a cup. She passed it to her and refilled it twice before Shali looked calmer.

"I'll tell you everything I heard, but you hold this back!" Shali burst out at last. "I think it's rather mean of you, and if I didn't value you as much as I do, I'd snub you till Passover!"

"I found out only today!" Lydia said, shaking her head. "How you knew so soon, I'll never know!"

"Well, something in your own family would have come to your ears sooner, I'd think. So is it because it is your family you don't tell me? When I told you all about my cousin who married into the poor family?" Shali pursed her lips and fixed Lydia with an accusing look.

"I see my cousins so seldom," Lydia defended herself. "How was I to know that she loved that dumb boy?"

"So you know the father?" Shali exclaimed, leaning forward. "You know it! Tell me now!"

"What father? Everyone knows Thaddaeus's father. What are you talking about?"

"Thaddaeus, the blacksmith's son, is the father of Mary's child?" Shali demanded, her eyes wide in shock. "I don't believe it!"

"What? What about Mary? I'm talking about Naomi being in love with Thaddaeus!"

"Oh, that," Shali dismissed with a wave of her hand. "I would have told you ages ago if I'd thought you didn't know it!"

Lydia felt her face grow hot with annoyance. It was her turn to pierce Shali with an exasperated expression.

"Mary is pregnant!" Shali announced, her voice hushed with awe.

"No!" Lydia slapped a hand over her mouth. "How do you know?"

"The women have been talking about it. It's obvious if you look carefully. And how long has she been locked up in their house now, not coming out into public? And Joseph seems as oblivious as anything . . . or did until yesterday. Now he just walks around looking ready to spit nails!"

"Pregnant!" Lydia shook her head. "I'd never have imagined her . . ."

"It's always the last one you'd least imagine. No point being too shocked over it. The question is, what will they do?"

Lydia turned away from her friend, her mind rushing off in its own direction. Pregnant. It was shocking and sad. No wonder her aunt had seemed so preoccupied.

"I need a new robe," Lydia suddenly announced.

"Whatever for? Besides always wanting something new!"

"I need to look my best, Shali." She ran her fingers through her long, straight hair.

"For a stoning?" Shali asked with a smirk.

"Oh, don't be crude," Lydia said with a frown. "If Joseph's betrothed is pregnant, he might be changing his mind."

CHAPTER 11

Is not this the kind of fasting I have chosen: to loose the chains of injustice . . . and not to turn away from your own flesh and blood?

—Isaiah 58:6, 7

A broad, self-satisfied smile broke over Elias' face, and he interlaced his fingers behind his head, stilting his chair backward on its rear legs. The room smelled of the herbs his wife was cooking with downstairs, and out the window he could hear the sounds of the servant girls' chatter as they cleaned out the rooms that travelers from the night before had vacated. The inn had three big rooms that several families could share. Elias provided clean straw for beds and care for the animals. They could pay extra for food if they so desired. It was surprising the amount of filth human beings and their animals left behind after just one night of sleeping.

Elias' inn consisted of a main two-story house in which he and his family lived, a large kitchen area where his wife and daughter did the cooking for the family and the paying guests, a large enclosed courtyard with a well, and the three long, narrow rooms that surrounded the larger courtyard. It was a good-sized establishment, but like any businessman, Elias was never quite satisfied.

"No one likes an inn with bad wine!" he said with a wink.

"If I know you at all, Elias, you are up to something!" his friend replied, shaking his head. "What is it this time?"

"You have no faith in humanity, Aaron!"

"I have less faith in you," the man said with a laugh. A big man, Aaron had a full, gray beard that puffed out like a sheep ready to be sheered. He had sparkling eyes and a face that made people want to tell him things. For all his jolly looks, however, Elias knew him to be much more self-serving than he appeared to be. He was simply smart enough to cultivate the image he preferred. But who wasn't self-serving? Elias wanted to know. Everyone was at some level. The man who was not looking out for himself was a fool!

"There is an inn in this town . . ." Elias began.

"Yours, I take it?"

"Not mine," Elias said with an irritated shake of his head. "A rival inn. It does well. Not as well as mine, but well enough to lessen my profits. I would like to buy it. If I owned both inns, I would have a monopoly in Bethlehem!"

"And the owner? Is he willing to sell?"

"Not yet. But he will."

"So you will ruin him, I take it?"

"Always jumping ahead of me!" Elias dropped his chair back down on all four legs and leaned toward his friend. "But yes, that would be the end result. I will tamper with his wine. I know who supplies his establishment with it, and I will bribe him to provide only wine that is too young or too old. Juice or vinegar—nothing in between!"

"And if he changes wine providers?"

"By that time he will have lost enough money that my offer will be more than appealing. It's so simple!" Elias let out a laugh that rang through the room.

"And how do you know that his financial situation is so precarious?" An expression of disbelief crossed Aaron's face.

"Because he confides in me," Elias replied with a slow smile. "He trusts me."

"Fool!" Aaron laughed.

"Family!"

At this, Aaron's eyes narrowed, and he pursed his lips in a frown, all humor seeping out of his expression like wine from a broken cup. Elias regarded him nervously.

"What, scruples now?" Elias asked, forcing good humor into his voice.

Aaron's expression did not improve. He shook his head. "Being competitive with another man is one thing, but taking advantage of family? You go too far! If a man cannot trust kin, who can he trust?"

"Himself, of course," Elias replied tersely. "I've always lived by that code."

"Family is sacred, friend. Do not go so far that you lose your good name! A man who will ruin his own kinsman is not going to be trusted by anyone."

"Bah!" Elias waved his hand. "You worry too much!"

"There is right and there is wrong," Aaron protested, his voice beginning to rise. "Sometimes the boundaries can be stretched a little to suit a need, I admit, but family should be sacrosanct!"

"Do you know which member of my family I speak of?" Elias demanded. "I speak of my cousin, Abner, who insulted me at his own wedding!"

"You were drunk!"

"I am still family!" Although Elias recognized the contradiction in his own argument, he chose to ignore it in hopes that Aaron would not notice.

Aaron threw his hands in the air as if pleading with the rafters for strength. He leaned forward. "I warn you, friend, this cannot come to any good! I have always enjoyed your adventurous spirit, but you are going too far. If I were less of a friend, I would not tell you, and I would simply watch you come to your own ruin."

"A friend you call yourself? What kind of friend are you? No support! Not looking at my side and my honor, are you? No, you stand up for that rude little twit, Abner!"

"He confides in you!" Aaron said, his voice growing thunderous.

"Keep it down." Elias winced. "Why must people shout?"

His jaw clenched, Aaron regarded him with disgust. His breath whistled out of his nostrils in gusts that made his mustache quiver.

"I repeat, what kind of friend are you?" Elias demanded, glaring at Aaron's indignation with contempt. "If you are going to warn me or share information with me, make it something that matters! Make it about money!"

"I will tell you something about family, instead." Aaron rose to his feet. "You want information that matters? How about your daughter?"

"What about her?" Nervousness pierced past his anger to make his stomach suddenly clench.

"When I came in, I saw her out by the stables with some man." Aaron's lips twisted in something halfway between a sneer and a smile.

"Impossible! She was in the kitchen with her mother!"

Wasn't she? he wondered. She had better have been! Nona wouldn't have let Orli stray far . . . No, Nona knew her role. Besides, that lump of a girl couldn't attract a man's attention if her cloak were on fire! Aaron had to be lying. He was just angry because Elias wouldn't take his advice. Orli had been in the kitchen with her mother. It was inconceivable that she should be anywhere else.

"Was she?" Aaron smirked. "Perhaps you should ask the shepherd she was with!"

As Orli carefully uncurled her fingers she winced at the pain. She had instinctively raised her hands in self-defense when her father beat her, and the welts were now stinging with new strength. Her back ached from the lashes, and she could feel where the rope had struck her neck and chest. Orli didn't know how bad she looked, and she didn't want to know. As she crouched in her small sleeping chamber, the tears flowing down her cheeks and tasting salty on her lips made her want to vomit.

Orli was not the first daughter to receive a beating, and she would not be the last. Also she was not the first daughter to hate her father with every morsel of her being.

Ugly! Stupid! A drain on my money! What man would want you as a virgin, let alone tarnished? You are a lump of dirt! Disgusting and filthy! How dare you dishonor me? The morals of a common dog! I'll teach you . . . you . . .

And he had beaten her till foam had dripped from the corners of his mouth and his arm grew tired. He beat her until she lay on the floor, her arms curled around her head, her sobs silent. He beat her until the welts broke open and bled, until her mother screamed for him to stop. Then he kicked her solidly, and it was over.

Now Orli crouched in the dim room, trying to pull her blood-encrusted tunic away from her torn skin and crying softly to herself. She was crying from pain, but mostly her tears were hot with anger. She hated him! She despised him! If there were a way to ruin her father without destroying herself, she would take it and never feel a moment's regret.

And so what did it matter if she had met the shepherd by the stables? Her father told all of his friends that he doubted he could find a husband for her. So what did it matter? He was disgusted with her anyway, whether she behaved as she should or not! At least the shepherd had said she was beautiful and hadn't looked repulsed by her. The young man had told her that if she'd only let him, he would come back and see her again. He was her secret . . . her wonderful secret . . .

Or he had been. He wasn't anymore. Somehow her father had found her out and ruined this, too. But if her father thought that a beating would stop her from going to meet the shepherd, he was mistaken. Orli might not be delicate and beautiful, but she was smarter than she looked. She would simply be more careful not to be seen.

Maybe the shepherd would marry her and take her away! Maybe she would travel with his clan and trade wool for lovely fabrics that she would get from wandering traders. Then she would be happy, and the shepherd clan would think she was well above them, coming from such a good family. They would be proud of her, and she would have servants and jewels. Orli didn't have to help her mother very much now. Her mother preferred to do the work herself rather than to redo what her daughter had fumbled. But once Orli was married and the shepherd's clan saw what a highborn young woman she was compared to them, she would never lift a finger again! Then she would command her servants and sleep in till the sun was high in the sky . . .

"Orli?"

The girl glanced up as her mother quietly entered the room. Looking away, Orli tried to ease one arm out of her tunic. She felt her mother's cool fingers as she helped to remove the clothing.

"You shouldn't have done it," her mother said reprovingly. "I've taught you better than that! You shouldn't have done such a wicked thing."

Orli was silent. What did it matter how wicked she was?

"You not only shame yourself, but your father as well. How can you expect to get married compromising yourself this way? Even though I know you didn't let that vile man touch you, it looked horrible for you nonetheless."

"I hate my father," her daughter whispered.

"Don't say such a thing! God will punish you for saying such a thing!"

God would punish her for doing a great many things, Orli was sure, but hating her father would not be one of them. If she could only get away from this house, she would find a wealthy man to marry her, and she would never be beaten again.

"I know that you didn't let that man touch you," her mother repeated. "I know it."

Staring at her mother through reddened eyes, she refused to confirm what her mother so desperately wanted to believe. She had let him touch her. And she was not sorry. Even if she never saw him again, she was not sorry for what she had done.

"Father has always hated me. It is because I'm not beautiful."

"Your father . . ." Her mother faltered and frowned. "He is a man. Men are . . . well, they are men. They are loud and rude and mean, but they bring food for the table, and they keep you fed and clothed. They are necessary for survival. You'd better learn to deal with them now, because husbands are ten times more complicated than fathers!"

Her mother brought a pot of water and a soft cloth and began to dribble cool water over Orli's back. The daughter gritted her teeth against the sting and moaned to herself.

"You're lucky I convinced your father that you are still pure! This was only a lesson in proper behavior, not what it could have been if he believed your virginity was gone . . ."

But her virginity was gone, and Orli wondered if the old wives' stories were true—that a priest could detect the secret. Suddenly she felt a wave of terror that curdled her blood and rocked her stomach. What if people could see a difference? A difference in her movements or her complexion. What if the priest could smell her sin? What would happen to her then?

Lasting only a few moments, at the time it hadn't seemed like a life-changing event in the least, but it was done. There was no undoing it. She was a woman now, even though she and the shepherd were the only ones the wiser. It had just been an awkward, fumbling moment in the stables . . . an uncomfortable, strange, guilty moment, over as quickly as it started.

"You'll be working a lot harder from now on, girl," her mother went on, her voice hardening. "You'll be learning to cook and clean properly, and heaven help you if you waste a pinch of flour! You'll be sweating from morning till night!"

"You hate the way I do things in the kitchen," Orli said.

"Well, you'd better be putting both your brain and your back into it this time. You'll be doing it my way, or you'll be redoing it. You need to learn how to work properly so that you know how to take care of your own home. You have been sadly spoiled all these years, and I intend to make up for it in a few short weeks."

Orli sighed.

"You'll thank me one day," her mother went on. "You'd better sleep now, because tomorrow you'll be up before the birds and learning how to do the work of five women so that your husband will have no reason to beat you."

As Orli silently lay her head on her arms she felt the tears filling up her chest. It seemed as if she was swimming in her sadness. Her mother turned and walked toward the door, but before her sandaled feet slip-slapped away, Orli heard her mutter,

". . . if we ever get you married . . ."

CHAPTER 12

Honor your father and your mother, so that you may live long in the land the Lord your God is giving you.

—Exodus 20:12

Amichai lifted his father's arm and gently wiped the old, sagging skin with a wet cloth. It stank of stale sweat and other noxious odors. His father had been sick again, and being too frail to get himself out of bed, the entire bed now had to be changed and the old man cleaned.

"It was that foul cooking," the father complained. "It was too spicy. And not soft enough. That woman should know better!"

"Shandy's wife gave you only what she gave the rest of her tent," Amichai said patiently. "She wouldn't give you something unfit for her own children, Father."

"She's stupid and slow," the old man said bitterly. "I chose poorly for Shandy."

Amichai was silent. Dropping the cloth into the bowl of water, he sloshed it around, then squeezed it out. He raised his father's other arm and gently wiped a surface as thin as garlic skin.

"Let me be!" his father said petulantly. "Can't you see you're bothering me?"

"You have to be cleaned, Father. You've been sick. You can't stay in the mess."

"I'll clean myself," he exploded, batting away Amichai's hands. Jonah took the cloth in one shaking hand and slid it over his skin, missing most of the filth. "There, see? Clean and fine. Now leave me."

"You aren't clean, Father," his son sighed. "Let me finish, and then I will leave you alone."

His father muttered some curses under his breath and scowled at Amichai as he worked.

"I tell you, boy, stop this, or I'll lay one on you that you'll never forget!" He clenched one frail fist and lifted it, then let it drop.

Again Amichai sighed. The old man always threatened violence, but thank God he was frail as a baby bird now and could do no physical harm. Years ago it had been different. That threat held power and had caused fear so deep that Amichai still remembered it with a shudder.

"You're just like a woman," Jonah went on. "Doing the work of a woman. Disgusting."

"The women won't clean you, Father," Amichai replied, bitterness creeping into his words. "They refuse to come near you, and will only bring you food because my brothers order them to. If you don't want to lay on your bed and die, I have to do the work myself."

"Women used to obey in my day." The old man's voice sounded more like a whine. "They used to bow and cower. They used to do what they were told and respected their elders!"

His son said nothing. Amichai's mother hadn't done much cowering that he could remember. She had been feisty and energetic with a ready laugh and sure hands. But she had died shortly after his youngest brother's birth. Somehow she'd managed to avoid his father's fists most of the time. Most likely, Amichai imagined, it was more her family's intimidation that kept her sour husband under control and his aim faulty. Her brothers would feel no guilt avenging a bruise on their sister's face with a broken nose and split lip.

The boys, however, had a more difficult time avoiding their father's rages. Their mother did her best to come between them, but she could not always be around. And while they were little they had her skirts to hide in, once they were considered men at 13, they couldn't stay in the camp with her any longer. Amichai had never hit his father back. Shandy did once when he was 18, and would have been brutally punished by the clan, had his mother's family not stood up and claimed to have seen Amichai's father trip and fall when he was drunk. The bruises, they said, came from his own clumsiness, and it was wicked of him to blame his own son for something he couldn't even remember. Amichai had always wondered how they had lived with themselves and with God after having sworn an oath to a lie. But deep down he was grateful to them. Shandy hadn't been right to strike their father, but Amichai could not help but understand his younger brother's rage. It was that rage that made Shandy indifferent to the old man's frailty now.

Amichai wasn't sure if he had rage or not. He had a simmering ball in the pit of his stomach when he dealt with his father, but he didn't feel the need to hurt the old man. Sometimes he pitied him. Occasionally he wished that Jonah weren't so fragile—that he could actually do what he threatened once in a while. It was a strange wish, he knew, but the pity he felt for the old man was more disconcerting than anger would be. Anger had its place. Pity was embarrassing and uncomfortable.

"Are you hungry?" Amichai asked.

"I wouldn't eat that slop she brought if it were the last food during a famine!"

"But are you hungry?"

"No."

Finding a fresh tunic, Amichai pulled it over his father's head, stopping to unhook the fabric from his ears and brush the limp whitish yellow hair away from his face.

"Drink something, Father," he commanded, bringing a flask of water to the old man's side.

"I don't want it."

"You've been sick. If you don't drink, you'll get sick again, and I won't be here this time to help you. I'll be out with the sheep again, and you'll have to wait for Shandy's wife to find you."

The threat seemed to work. His father opened his mouth and drank some of the water, then leaned back on the freshly made bed with a sigh.

"It's time you married, Amichai," Jonah said in a faint voice. "I need a woman around here to take care of things."

Amichai shook his head and rubbed his hands over his face. Of course, that would be why his father wanted him to wed. Although too old to have another wife, his father still wanted a woman around to care for him and cook for him. But what about Amichai? What about his happiness?

"I'm not in a position to marry, Father."

"Bah!" the old man grunted, opening his eyes. "There's bound to be some high-ranking servant or ugly girl about who will have you."

After hanging the wet cloth over a rope, Amichai poured more water into a cup. "There are not many eligible girls in the clan. Those that are available are either too young or already betrothed."

"Never too young," his father said with a dry laugh, and Amichai winced. There certainly was such a thing as too young, and Amichai had no intention of betrothing himself to a girl barely out of childhood.

"I would obey you, Father, if it were possible. You are my father, and you still head this family."

His father gave a satisfied nod. "I do head this family, boy," he said with a cough. "And I command you to marry."

The simmering lump in Amichai's stomach began to grow, and he forced it back down with all the mental effort that he could muster.

"I don't have the means to offer a dowry, Father." Amichai tried to keep the edge from his tone. No use in reminding the old man that his drinking and "friendly wagers" had cost the family most of their inheritance and that the dowries for his brothers had soaked up the rest. There was nothing left. Like a family with too many children, the one who lagged behind and didn't snatch his or her share of the stew went hungry.

"I'm tired now—leave me." Jonah shut his eyes. "You are too weak anyway. Too womanish."

Taking a deep breath, Amichai consciously unclenched his fists. He put the cup of water down near his father's bed, then after a moment of thought, moved it further away, just out of the old man's reach. Hurrying out, he stood beside the tent, looking out at the rest of the camp. The smoke from cooking fires rose in lazy swirls upward, and somewhere to the left he could hear the chatter of children. Amichai could smell supper still cooking at several tents and the tang of the sheep's manure used for the fire. His lips compressed in a firm line and his eyes as dark as well openings, he stood motionless. After several minutes of thought, he went back inside the tent where his father was snoring softly, and put the water close enough for the old man to reach.

"Forgive me, God," he murmured.

James, Yafit, and Nasim did not all get together often. It was strange how marriage changed things in a family. Siblings who had been close and virtually inseparable in their father's house suddenly found it difficult to find time for all of them to be in the same room together. Two brothers had been too busy to accept James' invitation. So it was only the three of them at the moment. Not that all of them were no longer close. All of Joseph's children still spoke regularly and cared for each other deeply. It was said that a husband was for children and a brother was for life. Yet marriage was an adjustment for the entire family, and each marriage that occurred, caused more upheaval than anyone had imagined that it would. And while the siblings knew this, they still had a small amount of resentment toward each other that things had altered at all. Now, there was even more change in the air, and none of them were pleased about it.

For the first time in the better part of a year, these particular three were together again in their father's house without their spouses.

"Father should be back soon," James said. "And I think we need to talk with him together."

"I don't know if we dare mention it!" Yafit replied. She was the tallest of the three, with a willowy frame and a long face that looked perpetually mournful. Her voice, however, had the same sympathetic and musical lilt as their mother's had had.

"If we don't tell him, who will?" Nasim asked. "Isn't it worse for him to marry her and find out afterward? It would be more painful."

"He is our father!" Yafit protested. "It is not our place to point out anything to him."

"And she is young enough to be his daughter!" James grumbled, picking up the old theme. "This isn't right. If he wants to remarry, shouldn't it be to a woman his age? Perhaps one who was widowed and needs support. A young woman can easily find a young husband."

"You sound jealous," Yafit said with a wink, and James rolled his eyes in exasperation.

"The point is not her age," Nasim said coolly. "The point is her virginity."

"True," Yafit said, becoming serious. "Our father's honor rests on her purity, which we all know is no more."

"And it is better to hear from us than from a gaggle of toothless women in the market," James said bitterly. "Even though he will resent hearing it from us, as well. But at least if he knows, he can save face and retain his honor."

They were silent, now, sitting together in the old meeting area of their father's house. When they had been children, they had gathered together to share the family gossip and discuss the upcoming weddings. They even talked in this room about their own approaching weddings. Now they wanted to stop a wedding, and they were terrified to do so.

"He'll hate us for this," Nasim stated in a low voice.

"He won't hate us," James countered, his tone less convincing than his words.

"He loves her."

The other two looked at Yafit, aghast.

"It's true," she said defensively. "He loves her!"

"He loved Mother," Nasim said flatly.

"Don't be childish," Yafit sighed. "Mother, as much as we all loved her, is gone. And his life will go on."

"What is love, anyway?" James demanded. "It is duty and respect. It is both parties doing what they should. Mary has not done what she should. How could you call that love?"

"If you've ever seen his face when he looks at her," Yafit said softly, "you would know what I speak of."

"Infatuation!" Nasim's voice rang out harshly. She winced at the sound of it.

"Call it what you will," Yafit continued, shaking her head, "it will still hurt him deeply to hear this. His honor is at stake, yes, but also his heart."

"It is disgusting to speak of our father's heart!" Nasim protested with a shudder. "I might speak of my sister's heart, but not my father's!"

"Father's honor is the only subject we can rightfully address," James said. "His heart is his own business. But his honor affects us. When our father is shamed, so are we."

Hannah, James's wife, quietly entered the room with a platter of figs and dates. She placed it in the center of the group and glanced at them uncomfortably.

"Sit with us, Hannah," Yafit told her, gesturing to a rug close by. "We have passed the uncomfortable part of our discussion, and we are back to a place of comfort again. Now we speak of honor."

Hannah looked uncertainly at her husband, her pretty eyes flickering from his face back to the floor. When James patted the ground next to him, she settled a little behind him as if unconsciously hiding from the others.

Just as Hannah sat, the scrape of the door opening caused them to suddenly hush and look at each other with the stricken expression of guilty children. They could hear Joseph's footsteps, and as he entered the room, his face haggard and his eyes veiled, he stopped short.

"Ah, some of my children are here!" he announced, a smile coming to his lips. But he looked older in that moment. His eyes seemed strained, and lines had appeared on his face. They all looked up at him mutely.

"Father," James at last broke the silence. "We . . . we would like to respectfully tell you something painful that we heard."

"Father, we didn't want you to hear it elsewhere first," Yafit added quietly.

"H'mm." Joseph remained standing, crossing his arms over his chest, studying his seated children.

"It is about your honor," Nasim said feebly, and as her voice trailed away, they glanced at each other again uncomfortably.

"Let me guess," Joseph began. "You have heard rumors in the marketplace, or from friends—"

"More than rumors, sir," James interjected.

"About . . . her . . ." Joseph's voice tightened.

They were silent.

"And you fear for my honor."

Again, they were silent.

"You are my children, and your honor is bound in mine," he went on sadly. "You have a right to protect the name of the family."

They all seemed to relax at those words.

"Is it true, then?" James asked slowly. "That Mary is with child?"

When Joseph visibly winced, tears rose up in Nasim's eyes.

"It appears to be true," Joseph said, swallowing hard.

"What will you do, Father?" Yafit asked suddenly.

Joseph looked down at them. They were all adults, but sitting in the room they had grown up in . . . sitting together as they used to when they were young . . . sitting with their expressions so confused and pained . . . they looked like children again. Each appeared so small and in need of comfort and protection—as if they needed their mother.

"I am not willing to discuss this," Joseph said gruffly. "I have made a decision, and that is all you need to know."

With that, he walked from the room.

Silently they sat staring at each other.

"It's breaking his heart," Yafit said finally, deep sadness in her voice.

"Oh, shut up!" James and Nasim said together.

Yafit gave them a slightly amused look. "Look at us, returning to the way we acted as children," she said with a low chuckle. "I don't know about you, but I have a husband and children waiting for me. There is a house where I am a mother and wife—where I am fully grown! And I am returning to it."

CHAPTER 13

The rabbis taught, "It happened once that a man wedded a woman with a mutilated hand, and did not discover it until she died." Said Rabh: "Behold how chaste this woman must have been, for even her husband did not discover it." R. Hyya retorted: "This is nothing! It is natural with women to hide their defects, but note the modesty of the man, who did not discover it in his wife."

—*From the Talmud*

That evening, when he could hear the gentle sounds of his daughter-in-law cleaning up after the family meal and the low tones of his son speaking with her, Joseph escaped the warm confines of his home to be alone. The night was balmy and calm, and a slight breeze cooled his face as he walked, his eyes cast down, watching the rocks and moist ground with a strange fascination. It was the rainy season—the season everyone counted on, and the smell of fresh rain would have been invigorating if his heart had not been so heavy.

Everything had changed in a moment. From being excited and nervous and scared . . . looking forward to his wedding . . . he was now depressed, lonely, isolated. He felt all over again the way that he had after his wife's death. His son's domestic bliss with his young wife only served to remind Joseph of all that he was missing.

Things had been so uncomplicated with Hadas. He had not expected a choice in his wife and had not gotten one. Nor had he expected her to adore him, and she had not. She had respected him, though, and been proper in everything she did. Because he had not expected to feel passion or longing, he hadn't experienced it. But he had been happy with her nonetheless. Things had been uncomplicated because they were being done as they had always been. His marriage to Hadas joined two families. Their fathers reminded them at every chance meeting on the street that their union was the will of the collective family, and that when they behaved as they should, they received the support and goodwill of the family. What more could a young man want?

But the years had passed, and Hadas had died. His children were grown. And life stretched before him like a lonely, rocky path. He did not want to face old age alone. Once he had thought that his children would be a comfort, but he was beginning to realize that their lives would increasingly go on without him. They would love him, yes, and care for him. But life would never be the way it was when they were small and he was the sun and the moon for them. They were adults now, and he would be just an old man.

Mary would have loved him, even in his old age. That was a comfort. She made him feel young again. And somehow he had thought that she would make him happy . . . that he would make her happy . . . that life could be exciting and luminous again.

All that had been dashed. She was pregnant, and he most certainly was not the father. The thought still tore at him like a dull knife blade. Whom had she been with? What beast had dared to touch her? What kind of man had seduced her? What was it about him that she had found so irresistible?

Mary . . . his own sweet Mary. But yet not his own. No, she physically belonged to another man now. Despite how much he wanted her to be his, she could never be. He must stop thinking of her like that.

But he wanted to see her . . . he desperately wanted to see her.

Yet what good would it do? No, he shouldn't see her. It would only make things worse. He needed to think—to decide what he had to do.

His honor was at stake. That was what was important! Mary had deceived and betrayed him! What kind of woman did that? He had believed that she was a good woman—virtuous and pure. Had believed that she had returned his unexplainable, deep feelings of longing. Strange as it was to feel that way . . . unexplainable as it was . . . insane as it was to make decisions based on such a feeling . . . he had believed that it had united them somehow.

"Why, God?" he prayed miserably. "Why did this happen? How could she do this? How could she give up our entire life of happiness for . . . for . . ." For another man? For a moment of pleasure? For what?

Joseph stood on the narrow road, looking numbly out across the countless miles toward the horizon. In a single day everything had changed. And somehow he must get used to it.

"It's a long way, that road," a gravelly voice said beside him. Startled out of his reverie, Joseph glanced down at a knobby, grizzled little figure beside him.

"Good evening, Borah." Joseph dipped his head in deference to the old man.

"Is it?" Borah stared down the road thoughtfully. "Not all evenings are as good as others, son."

"No, sir, they are not."

"But that road won't take you any further away from it all," the aged man went on. "It would only make you tired and muddy as well as sad."

"Am I so transparent?"

"As water, my friend." Borah chuckled. "But isn't that what women always say about us? That we show our feelings too readily?"

"I must think of how to live my life," Joseph said quietly. "The hopes I had for the future must be . . . altered . . ."

"Marriage is as much for the clan and the town as it is for the man."

So he knew. Everyone knew! Why was Joseph surprised?

"I was married three times," Borah went on. "Childbirth is a difficulty for women, and oftentimes it leads to their death. Each marriage was chosen by my family. Each marriage was happy."

"Perhaps I should defer to someone with more perspective than I. I am a father of three married children, and still unable to choose wisely for myself."

"We have done things this way for generation upon generation. Our grandfathers had wisdom, son. Why question their ways now?"

Why, indeed. Because he loved Mary, that was why. Because someone else would have chosen a suitable widow in need of support. Because the one elder in his family was a crazy old man who might marry him off to a goat!

"Once in every lifetime, and sometimes twice, if you are a man with luck, you will feel that kind of overwhelming longing," Borah said. "I felt it myself. But my family married me to another woman, and I was still happy. Perhaps that longing, had I satisfied it, would have eaten me up like a snake does a rat."

"Who was she?"

"A pretty little thing who worked in my father's house." A smile crinkled the old man's face. "So sweet and gentle. We would talk for hours, she and I. I adored her. I would have walked over burning coals for her. I begged my father for her. I swore I would do anything for him. But the only thing he wanted was for me to marry the girl the family had chosen. So I did as I was bidden."

Joseph did not say anything.

"Her name was Kisha," Borah said softly. "I still wonder what became of her."

Would this be Joseph in 30 years . . . old and weathered and still remembering the woman who had made his heart leap and his stomach refuse food? Would this be him, old in body and still young in heart?

"I had three wives after her!" Borah said. "Life goes on, son. Don't forget it!"

The younger man nodded. Borah looked up at him through squinted eyes, then nodded back and turned away, ambling crookedly back toward the town.

Joseph couldn't marry her. No, he could not marry a woman who would betray him in such a way. It was unthinkable! But could he stop loving her?

He'd break the betrothal carefully, so as not to draw attention to it. Her father couldn't protest now. No, her father would send her somewhere else. But he would do it quietly. No matter what she had done to him, Joseph still couldn't bring himself to hurt her.

While his mind had reached a decision, his heart refused to understand.

Reuben pushed open the door of his house and listened to the familiar sounds of his wife's off-key humming while she cooked. He knew exactly what she would be doing and how she would look without having to glimpse her. Her gray hair would be uncovered since she was indoors, but worn back in a twist to keep it out of her face. Although her figure had thickened about the waist and hips, she still had delicate and pretty shoulders. With her sleeves pulled back and tied behind her to keep her arms free to move, she would be covered in flour up to her elbows. She always seemed to be covered in flour up to her elbows, no matter what she was doing. To this day he could still remember when he first met her—his cousin on his mother's side—and even then, she had had flour up to her elbows.

His sons were working late in the vineyards, but Reuben did not have to. It was the joy of having sons. Still young and learning the business, they took pride in their seniority over the workers. But Reuben was their father. He was old now. It was his right to come home early and rest. Soon his eldest son, Seth, would marry and take over the running of the vineyards completely—in function, if not in name until after his father's death.

"That boy has a head on his shoulders!" Reuben called out as he entered. He could hear his wife's sandals slapping toward him, and she appeared around the corner with an anxious, pent-up expression on her face. Reuben ignored it. Women were known to get worked up over trivialities. Let them deal with it in the kitchen and let him have peace.

"He discovered a customer cheating us and saved us a week's work to make it up!" her husband went on. "Seth is a good boy—he'll make me proud."

"I've always told you that he would make a good manager," Ruth said, compressing her lips in a prim line. "A mother knows these things."

"Ah, of course, of course," he agreed with a wave of his hand. "I will have no worries leaving the decisions to that boy. He needs me still, but given another year, he'll be fine to run it himself!"

"H'mm."

Reuben gave his wife a sideways look. What was with her? Normally, she was thrilled to discuss the merits of her eldest son, but today she seemed to be simply doing her duty toward him, letting him talk after he returned home, without much interest in the subject herself.

"Well, what is it?" he demanded.

"What is what?"

He rolled his eyes. "What is it that has you all twisted up like a new rope?"

"Just gossip, that's all," she answered with a slight lift of her still slender shoulders. She cast him a flirtatious glance and turned back to her work. "Nothing for a man to worry about, I'm sure."

Something in her voice told him otherwise, and Reuben sighed. It was always like this. Usually he refused to listen to her prattle about women's gossip, but at times women could glean rather important information. In such instances dragging the information out of her was difficult, as if her pride depended on her being obstinate.

"What is it, woman? Obviously this is more than your regular jabbering."

"Well, who's to say if it is?" she asked innocently, turning her attention to wiping the flour from her arms. "I wouldn't want to bother my husband with women's talk. It is beneath him and not worth his valuable time. He should be resting and enjoying some of the food I have worked so hard to prepare for him . . ."

She always referred to him in the third person when she had something particularly interesting to say. Annoyed, he shook his head.

"Fine, then! Keep it to yourself! I'm going to rest!"

Muttering a few phrases about the obstinacy of women beneath his breath, he turned to leave the room.

"Well, if you are so certain that you want to know," she said, pouring some water from a dipper into an earthen cup and holding it out to him submissively. "I will be happy to share my small bit of information."

With a grunt, Reuben took the cup and drank, then handed it back to her for more.

"Our daughter heard this from a rather reliable source," she began. "And it has been confirmed by quite a few women as well."

"I don't care about the pedigree of the source," he growled. Hot and tired, he was getting hungry, and this was getting on his nerves.

"Our family has a blot on it," she announced, looking up at him triumphantly.

He glared at her.

"What are you talking about, a blot? What has that daughter of ours done this time?"

"Oh, our daughter has done nothing! It is wicked of you to assume she has done anything, husband."

"Then who?"

"Your niece, Mary. Ebenezer's girl."

"I know who she is. What did she do?"

"She's pregnant."

Reuben let his eyes rest on his wife's, and they shared a look of disgust before rage began to slowly simmer up inside of him.

"Pregnant?" he demanded. "By who?"

"She claims by God," Ruth said with a sneer, "adding blasphemy to lies. That girl is a disgrace!"

"Pregnant!" he muttered. This was impossible! He had always resented his younger brother for having girls that the village seemed to value more than his own, but he had never imagined that his nieces would be a shameful blot on the family!

"Most likely that man she's betrothed to," Reuben said, his eyes narrowing. "He'll be made to take her immediately, that's no doubt!"

"Rumor has it that he claims he isn't the father," Ruth said simply. "And it's hard not to believe it when you see that haggard look about him."

"So Mary has been . . . Lately I've been wondering why no one has been asking for our daughter! We have money! Any family would be lucky to be tied to me in family! But if my niece has been wandering around like a common prostitute, it would explain a wariness to associate with us."

"She makes us all look bad." Ruth scowled. "My daughter is a virgin! She is good and hardworking! She is beautiful as well. And Mary has ruined my daughter's prospects of a good marriage!"

"Marriages—is that all you can think about?" he roared.

Ruth gave him a petulant look and tossed her head.

"Family honor is what this is about!" he said. "My honor! I am the head of this family! I am the oldest son of our father! I am the one who bears responsibility for our good name. The shame lies on all of us, but I shoulder the greatest burden, woman."

"Something must be done, husband," she said quietly. "You will be shamed further if no one desires to take your daughter."

He didn't need to be reminded of it. Why must women be such animals? A good woman kept her mouth shut and her head covered. A good woman was unsure of what a man even looked like before her wedding!

Reuben had worked hard, demanding the best of his family, and invariably had gotten it. His sons were admirable. His daughter was beautiful. His wife was dutiful, albeit irritating. And his brother? What had his brother done? The man had let his girls run wild and ruined their name! He should have been more involved in that household!

"Ebenezer is an old fool," Reuben spat out. "Even as a boy he was bright-eyed and idiotic! Idealistic and trusting as a baby . . . Idiot!"

"Something must be done," she repeated feebly, expectantly looking at him. Was he God? She was staring at him with that dutiful look of hers, waiting for him to fix the problems of the entire clan. While sometimes he enjoyed her complete and total trust, at times such as this he resented it. What was he supposed to do?

"The shame," he muttered. There was only one way to be free of it . . . to restore the family to its proper position in public opinion. He must show them that he did not stand for such sin in his own clan. He must let punishment fall—and in fact, encourage it—or the village would always wonder where the original sin had sprung from in the clan. They would talk behind their hands and refuse to be united with his family in a marriage.

"That stupid man!" Reuben raged. "Stupid! Cannot even control women!"

His wife stared at him mutely, her eyes wide.

"She'll have to be stoned," he said quietly, and as the words came out of his mouth, he knew that it was the only way out. His niece would have to be offered up to village justice, and he would have to lead in the punishment to prove that he did not support such wickedness. It was his duty to his family—his duty as a man!

And when he looked at his wife, her expression had turned from dutiful expectancy to a malicious smile. She was enjoying this. And something inside of him felt fear.

CHAPTER 14

And thus he was caught between hatred and love; he was frequently disposed to punish her for her insolence, but being deeply in love with her in his soul, he was not able to get rid of this woman. In short, although he would gladly have punished her, he was afraid that by putting her to death he would thereby, through this loss, bring a heavier punishment upon himself than upon her.

—Josephus, on Mariamne, Herod's wife

Herod was having one of his more lucid days, and he could sense it. He could recognize that things seemed more logical to him as his mind absorbed information, sights, sounds, and smells with more clarity than he had been aware of for a long time. Also he felt the urgency of making as much use of this time as possible. Able to see things for what they were, he could judge for himself what was happening around him. As he remembered the past 20-some years in chronological order he knew that Mariamne was dead.

It had started that morning when he woke up. For the first time in years he came awake unconfused. He knew where he was. People who were supposed to be there hadn't vanished into thin air. No one had aged unexplainably. In addition, he also noticed how people watched him warily. They eyed him with a tinge of fear.

"I am not crazy," he now said softly to himself, and in saying the words he felt as if he were. Wasn't it the insane who talked to themselves?

But today must be used to its greatest capacity. It must not be wasted! As king of Judea he was powerful and must not let anything thwart him. In his sudden clarity he understood that he was vulnerable when his mind got muddled and confused. People could too easily manipulate him. Today he must make decisions to protect himself when he was again in one of his confused states.

As Herod looked at himself in the mirror he saw an older man with chubby cheeks and a carefully sculpted beard looking back at him from the polished bronze. He noticed the gray streaking his hair, the lines around the eyes, and the tired expression. Ruling a nation was exhausting. And he was not getting any younger. His belly protruded in a paunch that betrayed his love of delicacies. Even worse, his knees had started aching when he crouched and when he knelt. And he found himself letting out small grunts when he rose to his feet from a sitting position. No, he was not a young man—he would not live forever.

That thought saddened him, and he felt grief moving up into his throat like a lump, threatening to cut off his breath. He would not live forever. After he died, who would remember him? Who would love him after his death?

"Oh, Mariamne," he sighed. He loved her, even after her death. And he loved their children despite their deaths.

They were good boys . . . why had he not seen it? Alexander and Aristobulus, the latter named after Mariamne's brother. She had loved her brother. It was unfortunate that Mariamne's brother had been a traitor and villainous. But you could not blame a woman for a treacherous family. After all, she had not chosen to be born to them. No, God had done that. And he, King Herod the Great, had chosen her. They had had five children together. Three boys—one of whom had died of a fever when he was attending school in Rome—and two girls. Girls. Useless for a king. Who needed daughters? No, what he needed were sons! He needed heirs! The girls were nothing like their mother. Had they been more like her, he might have felt more favorably disposed toward them. As it was, he married them off quickly to form political alliances as soon as they reached puberty. And what would their lives be like in the homes of their husbands? He did not know and did not care.

And the boys . . . they were good boys . . . He remembered how Mariamne used to go to the nursery and hold them. Little Alexander and Aristobulus would sit on her lap, and she would quietly talk to them and tell them stories. They'd look up at her with such adoration in their big, dark eyes, their tousled curls tumbling across their foreheads. He would watch from the door, and when Mariamne noticed his presence, she would turn away from him, protectively putting her body between his gaze and the children.

Mariamne was a fiercely devoted mother, he thought with a smile. And how could she have been so fiercely devoted to her young if she truly hated the father of those children? No, it was impossible. She loved him, but for some reason had wanted to maintain her personal power. Some women were like that. He had always loved Mariamne's spirit.

But the boys hadn't been careful about appearances, he reminded himself bitterly. They hadn't known enough to guard what other people thought. And when their older brother, Antipater, had told him that they were plotting with rebels to overthrow him, he had been furious! He had remembered how Mariamne had used to shield them from him, and he resented her for it. Perhaps she had been filling their heads with treason all along!

Herod let his face fall into his hands.

"My boys . . ." he sighed. "Oh, my little boys . . ."

They hadn't died badly. Their deaths had been quick. And of course they had no longer been children, but young men. Old enough to know where their allegiance lay—and to be a threat.

Someone tapped on his door.

"Come!" Herod barked.

The door opened soundlessly, and he felt, rather than heard, his son's entrance. The king slowly turned, letting his eyes rest on the mature man before him. He was taller than Herod, with the same black curls, but the rest of his features were nothing like his father. Still, he was strong and solidly built—a man with an aura of power about him.

"Father," Antipater said, bowing his head respectfully. "Your Majesty."

It was curious that Antipater should choose to call him "Father" before addressing him as king. Herod noted it with acid irony, a dangerous smile flickering at the corners of his mouth.

"Come inside. Sit there." Herod pointed to a seat, then watched the uncertainty cross Antipater's face as he glanced quickly over the chair and behind it. So the man did not trust his own father? Perhaps a man with something to hide suspected traps in every seat offered to him.

"You look like your mother," Herod said thoughtfully, studying his son's soft features and weak chin. He certainly didn't take after his father! Doris had been a daughter of an influential family—well, influential for the moment. They did not amount to much after Herod was king.

"How is my mother?" Antipater asked quietly.

"How should I know?" Herod asked tersely. "I sent her away—what was it? Five years ago? More?"

That had been the most recent incident. He had dismissed and re-called her several times during his reign. Not that he would make that stupid mistake again.

Antipater looked at a point just over his father's shoulder. So this man resented the fact that he had exiled his mother. Yes, that made sense. He would. Just as he had also resented the children of Mariamne. He had known that Herod loved Mariamne and had not loved his mother.

"Your Majesty," Antipater said quietly, "what may I do to serve you?"

"A good question. What have you done in the past? You made up stories about your brothers."

"Sir?" Antipater looked up with quick, wary eyes. "I did not lie to you! You are my father. I wanted to protect you!"

"Protect me?" Herod laughed. "You? You have the intelligence of a foot soldier—good for orders and not much more! And you would protect *me?*"

Herod saw the slight confusion pass over his son's expression, and then, when he noticed as the younger man's eyes sharpen, he watched him warily. Looking for signs of mental confusion, no doubt.

"Your Majesty, that was years ago!" Antipater continued.

"They were still my children!" the king snapped. "The children of the woman I loved!"

Antipater closed his mouth and stared at his father. Antipater was not a young man anymore. He had reached his maturity, peaked, and begun the downhill slide that all men must face. Now close to 35, he had lived a hard life of late nights and parties. And he was smarter than Herod had ever given him credit for, as well.

"I did not lie, Your Majesty," Antipater stated calmly. "I reported to you what I had overheard in the palace. I did my duty as your son."

"Your allegiance has always been to your mother," Herod replied, his lips twisting with disgust. "And I have no doubt it was her you were thinking of when you lied to me about my sons. They did not wish me dead. It was you all along! You wished me gone!"

"Father!" Antipater shook his head and started to rise. As Herod turned away he felt quite shaken. He had not expected to feel so emotional in this interview. But it was all so clear now. It was all coming together for him . . . all those confusing moments that seemed to occur in the midst of a fog, now shining forth as clearly as a bright new day!

"I don't really expect you to admit it." Herod turned back to face his son. His voice had turned gentle, and he looked down on his son affectionately. "You would be stupid to admit to anything but deep filial love and duty, young man. I do not expect you to confess to me that you have always wished me dead. You are my firstborn. You want to rule. Who doesn't? I am like God! I stand between life and death for even you, son. Do you not covet this power?"

Antipater did not answer.

"Well? Do you not covet it?"

"No, Your Majesty," Antipater said quietly. "I am satisfied to be the son of a great man. I am honored to be in your shadow."

Herod chuckled at this. Honored, was he? Who was ever honored to be in a shadow? His son lied well—he had to give him that.

"I loved Mariamne," Herod said truthfully. "I did not love your mother."

"I realize that," his son said calmly. "But women are for children, are they not? My mother served you well."

"You fantasize about your mother, no doubt. I don't know what she told you after you were grown, but when you were born, she did not touch you. Did you know that? She passed you off to a wet nurse who fed you, and she looked down at you once or twice, but she never did touch you. Did you know that about your mother?"

Antipater was again silent.

"I think you cling to thoughts about her that are not true," Herod went on quietly. "I think that I never saw you as a threat because even your mother did not love you."

Antipater's complexion had turned ashen, and his lips were clamped together, his eyes flashing. *So this was what got a rise out of the man!* Herod thought to himself.

"Why are you telling me this?" Antipater barely kept his voice under control.

"Because today I am thinking more clearly than I have in a very long time," Herod explained with complete truthfulness. "And I would like my son to know the truth of things."

"Are you planning on killing me, Father?" he asked in almost a whisper.

"Killing you?" Herod laughed. "Oh, my boy, no! I could not kill the first sign of my virility, could I? You are my son! You have only ever tried to protect me. I was testing you, that is all. I see your true nature. Did I worry you?"

Antipater let out a hoarse laugh.

"No, no, Father, I was joking!" He stood to his feet, wavering a little as he did so. "It was a poor joke, I'm sure, but a joke nonetheless."

"Good." Herod put his hand on the man's strong shoulder. Too strong, that shoulder was. Able to pin him to the ground if he wanted to. Able to kill, with that kind of strength . . .

"Now, leave me, son," Herod said, smiling warmly at him. "I need some rest. I will drink with you later. There are things we must discuss about the future of our land!"

For a long time Herod stood motionless after his son had left.

Chapter 15

Such action is permitted only when a man is not in an actual fury, but wishes to appear as if enraged in order to command obedience (from his family), as R. A'ha bar Jacob used to do; viz.: "When he wanted to show displeasure at the deeds of his family, he would take up a broken vessel and shatter it, making his family believe that he was furious and was breaking whole vessels."

—*From the Talmud*

Ebenezer glanced at his wife as she bent to offer his brother some new wine and cheese. The sharp tang of goat cheese and the warm scent of fresh flatbread wafted through the hot room. Esther moved gracefully for her size, and she kept her eyes respectfully averted. He could always count on his wife to be proper and polite when it most mattered. And if it had ever mattered it did so now! Just knowing that her silent support was there enabled him to relax. Something in her stance, though, hinted of her tension. Her eyes, though tactfully averted, showed strain, and her lips were compressed into a prim little bow. While she would never give Reuben a reason to speak ill of her, she was tensed like a lioness ready to defend, if anyone cared to learn her signals. As she knelt near him Ebenezer put a hand on her ankle, and she stayed in that position, waiting just a moment longer than she needed to for him to select his choice of cheese and dried dates. Like him, she was drawing strength from the hidden physical contact.

It was strange how even a marriage arranged by parents could lead to this kind of need for each other. Somehow he could not fathom facing life without this woman by his side. And now, as he must deal with his older brother, his wife's presence in the house meant more to him than he realized that it would. He glanced in her direction as she retreated to the kitchen, her robes swinging from her ample hips.

"God be with you, brother," Ebenezer said, leaning back and regarding his brother's stony expression. Reuben was older, but only by two years. He had the same full, gray beard and shoulders that slightly hunched forward. And he had the same eyes, lined and direct.

"This is a solemn visit," Reuben said slowly. "I hope we can join together as a family and put this problem to rest."

"And what problem is that?"

"You know the problem better than I do, brother," Reuben said acidly. "Your daughter." The last two words dripped with venom.

Ebenezer nodded. No use denying it. Everyone knew by now, and hiding it would be impossible in a couple more weeks. Or was he fooling himself? Perhaps hiding it was impossible now!

"She was such a good girl," Ebenezer said sadly. "You remember her as a child, don't you? So sweet and obliging! So understanding of people's feelings. She had promise to be a good, godly wife."

"Then you fooled yourself. She is pregnant, and the good and godly do not find themselves in that situation before the marriage is finalized."

Ebenezer met his brother's eyes, biting back the retort that sprung to his lips. No, insulting the man's own daughter would not help. It did not matter how empty-headed and selfish his niece Lydia was—she was not pregnant. The proof of her virtue stood before them.

"I love her," Ebenezer instead said simply. "She's my eldest child. You must understand that kind of love we hold for our children."

"I understand love, brother. I also understand properly rearing a family so that our honor remains intact."

"You think I failed." With a nod, he added, "Obviously, I have. Do you think I have not blamed myself every hour since I discovered my daughter's condition?"

"Then you can take it upon yourself to remove this blot from the family," Reuben said, his voice low.

Ebenezer was silent, his stomach curdling at the words. "You do not really mean that," he said finally, his voice hoarse.

"How could I not? You know what this will do to us! And this is not my doing! It is yours! You didn't supervise her. You didn't teach her to be a moral young woman! The fault lies in your home, brother!"

"So you would let the village stone her?" Ebenezer asked, tears welling up in his eyes.

"Justice is not always pleasant. But it is necessary."

"It is not!" Ebenezer said, his voice beginning to rise. "She is my child! Stoning her is not necessary!"

"You have another daughter. She will bring you joy and wait on you in your old age. Forget the one who is undeserving."

"Forget your daughter!" Ebenzer snapped. "Try not to think of her every moment? Try not to worry about her? Try to act as if her pain does not cut you deeper than your own?"

"My daughter is not pregnant."

"She does not need to die," Ebenezer said, his voice quivering. "She can be sent away. You would never see her again. The village would forget."

"A village never forgets." Reuben laughed. "Never!"

"The memory would dim, brother," Ebenezer insisted. "They would see that you had done your duty as the head of this family by sending her away. They would see how honorable you were by casting her away from this village!"

"A village forgets only when it exacts its own vengeance."

Ebenezer stared at his brother's lips, twisted in disgust. Why was he doing this? Why was he coming to him, discussing it as if Ebenezer would allow anyone to lay a finger on his daughter, no matter how wicked she was? Was the man completely heartless?

"How could you expect me to agree with you?" he demanded at last, tears of frustration and helplessness beginning to blind him. "How could you expect me to allow this?"

"Because the family honor has as much to do with you as it does with me," his brother said, his voice low and even. "You have another daughter who must marry. You have sons who must marry. You have children who depend on your decisions to allow them a future without shame."

"I have a daughter relying on me to protect her life!"

"Then we cannot come to a family consensus," Reuben declared, jerking himself to his feet with a wheeze. He stretched his limbs out carefully and then turned his cold eyes onto his brother. "You disappoint me. I had hoped to pull together in a difficult time like this for the good of all of our clan. Instead, you go against your own flesh and blood."

"Mary is my flesh and blood too!" Ebenezer bit out in disbelief.

His brother just shook his head in a slow sway, like a cow brushing away flies.

"The village will require justice," Reuben said simply. "And whether you allow the shame that stays on your head and the heads of your children to be washed away or not, is your concern. I will look to the honor of my own children. The village must see that at least I do not condone such sin."

Ebenezer stared as his brother stoically headed toward the door. He walked out with slow, purposeful steps, leaving the door open behind him. For several moments Ebenezer could see him disappearing down the path, shoulders rigid and spine erect, his steps the same slow, purposeful pace.

"That wicked old goat!" Esther's voice shattered his thoughts.

As he turned to face his wife, Ebenezer felt as if his body was moving with exaggerated slowness.

"No," he said quietly. "He is not wicked."

Her mouth moved, but words did not come out. Instead, her eyes flashed fire, and she looked ready to tear her own husband apart in her fear and anger. He could fully understand her rage at his standing up for his kin at a time like this.

"Wife," he said gently, "Reuben did not have to consult with me. He is giving me warning of what he is about to do. While he could have simply come with the village to our door, he did not. He came alone and told me exactly what to expect."

"Her death!" Esther sobbed, her face crumpling into tears.

"Oh, no, wife!" Ebenezer roused himself and let out a booming laugh, then took his wife into his arms in a strong, rib-cracking embrace. "Oh, no, wife! There is time! Reuben walks slowly! Get her things packed—Mary leaves Nazareth now!"

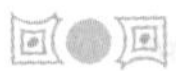

Thaddaeus crept forward, cringing with each snap of a twig or clatter of rocks. He froze for a moment, letting his eyes adjust to the shadows. Where was she? She said that she'd come! The night was dark, the moon, barely a sliver, hidden behind clouds. It was as if the night sky was rebelling against the earth, siding with the youths against the archaic adults with their tradition.

Had his father never been young? Had his father never longed for a girl? It was as if his father had stopped feeling and had forgotten what it was like to be young and alive! Tradition! It was what he always went on about.

"This is how we've always done things," he would say. "This is how my father did things, and his father before him. Are you better than our fathers, son?"

Everything looked different at night. The rocks appeared jagged and fierce in the faint starlight. The road behind him resembled a mouth ready to swallow whatever stepped onto it. And still the moon turned its face away, refusing to look down like a petulant child.

Tradition! Tradition ruled them like law. Tradition was law. They cooked the way they did from tradition. They ate, talked, walked, celebrated, rested . . . they slept, married, died, and breathed the way they did because of tradition! Tradition unwritten—the oral law that was taught from birth. And what if someone wanted to do something differently? What if someone sought to break out of those clutching arms of tradition? Tradition was like a clinging, crying old woman . . . her frail arms stronger than one ever imagined. And if you hurt her, if you broke one of her brittle bones, everyone would look at you in horror and turn their backs on you forever.

The well . . . he was here. He could see the rock and mortar sides rising up, the leather cover stretched over the opening to protect from debris or curious animals falling in. Even in the darkness he could see the worn ground where countless feet had shuffled and stood, and would shuffle and stand in a few hours when morning came . . . waiting their turn at drawing water. The well was a memorable place for a boy. As a small child, he waited here with his mother. Then as an older boy he had watched the women from the bushes, hoping for a veil to slip or a calf to be exposed, and trying to listen to their strange woman talk. Now he stood here in the dead of night, waiting with his heart pounding for a young woman.

"Thaddaeus?"

He turned when he heard her whisper, and saw her, swathed in her robes and veil, looking more like a shadow than a woman of flesh. For one superstitious moment he felt his flesh crawl when he thought of spirits and the dead, but the closer she came, the more detail he could make out. It was Naomi, with those plump lips and those big, almond eyes. Her hair was carefully covered and tucked away, and she had wrapped her robes around her like a swaddled baby.

"Naomi!" he sighed, moving toward her. "Did anyone see you?"

"No, they are sleeping. When I come back, I will tell them I went to the kitchen to be alone. I do that sometimes."

As he nodded she came up beside him, then leaned against the rim of the well.

"I had to talk to you," he said. "I'm sorry about the other day."

"It's all right," she mumbled, looking down. "It's been a hard time for my family, too."

"Yes," he said awkwardly, "your sister, and all . . ."

She winced at the words, and he resented them as soon as they were out.

"Ashi might not want me now . . . because of my sister . . ."

"My father arranged a marriage for me," Thaddaeus blurted.

She turned toward him, distress visible on her features even in the faint light.

"Who?" she asked, her voice sounding more like a wail.

"My cousin."

"Which one?"

"Does it matter?" he asked glumly. "It's one I have never met. She lives in another village. My father told me this morning."

"And what do you want?"

"I want to marry you," he said, his voice low and lifeless. "But the wedding will go forward. My father and my uncle agreed to have it as quickly as possible."

"Why her?" Naomi asked miserably.

"Because that way they can keep us close to my father or hers, and I'll never have a chance to go to Jerusalem and establish my business! I'll be poor, dirty, and insignificant for the rest of my life. It's what they want. And they're getting it."

"She wouldn't go with you to Jerusalem?"

"She's devoted to the faith of our people, my father says. That means she would report me immediately if I tried to make plans to set up a business that catered to the Romans. But why should she care? It would be money. Gold is gold, whether it comes from a Roman purse or a Jewish one."

"I would go with you to Jerusalem!" Naomi exclaimed, tears welling up in her eyes. "I would go with you!"

"And that is why my father doesn't want me to marry you. Because you wouldn't hold me down, keeping me under this festering pile of tradition!"

"Who cares if you made your money off the Romans?" she asked, shaking her head. "You'd still provide well for a wife! She'd live well! She'd have powerful friends! She'd have gowns and veils of silk . . ."

"That's what I keep saying."

"And there is no way out? There has to be a way out! I've got my sister's reputation that will let me out of my betrothal. There has to be something for you . . ."

"I don't know. If there is, I can't see it. Maybe I could take you as my second wife!"

Naomi gave him a flat glare.

"Maybe not."

"I hate her," Naomi said, her lips quivering. "She'll have you to herself, and I'll be stuck with Ashi—some dull, religious man."

"Look." Thaddaeus turned her to face him. "We won't give up yet, all right? We won't give up yet! I'll still try to find a way out."

Just then the moon burst out from behind the clouds, and the small sliver in the night sky illuminated their anxious faces. Thaddaeus felt his heart suddenly throb as he looked down onto her tearful eyes and her parted red lips.

"My business will flourish!" he announced with sudden passion. "And I'll give you gowns and jewels!"

"Oh, Thaddaeus!" She bit her lip and said nothing more. He reached toward her, but she suddenly seemed to realize how exposed she was, and she pulled her veil up across her face, darting panicked eyes around her.

"I don't dare get caught!" she breathed. "I have to go!"

And with that she hurried away, casting one glance of longing back at him. He watched her till she disappeared, and then he turned and kicked at the rocks at his feet, sending them skittering across the dirt.

They'd tie him down with this blasted tradition if they could . . . tie him down with a dutiful wife whose allegiance lay with her father and not with her husband. It was what his father wanted—to keep him nearby and stuck in this hole of a town.

He wanted Naomi! And he wanted out of Nazareth and into the money!

CHAPTER 16

The wise woman builds her house, but with her own hands the foolish one tears hers down.

—*Proverbs 14:1*

The donkey was tired, and so was Mary, but the animal was more obstinate. With every step and hollow clopping of its hooves, it seemed to be threatening to stop entirely. The road stretched before them—a muddy, rocky track through the hills of Judea, meandering from one tiny village to another. Mary walked in front of the plodding beast, the lead rope in one hand, and her other hand on her swelling belly.

"Miss, we should stop and rest," Nathan, the servant, said. A stout individual, he had a bushy white beard that Mary had never seen grow longer than a finger's length. The top of his head was bald, but his body was still strong and muscular. Anyone who mistook him for an old man would be rudely surprised if they chose to face him hand to hand. He was leading his own donkey, and his eyes anxiously watched Mary's progress.

"I'm afraid to stop," she said simply.

"I'm here with you, miss. I'll protect you. I've protected you since you were a tot, remember? Would I stop now? Your father asked me to protect you, and I swore to the God of our ancestors that I would do so."

"They want to stone me, Nathan." She glanced in his direction. "My uncle wants it the most. What if they come after us?"

"Bah, you're safe enough now! But we'll go on if you can keep that donkey moving."

"Will they try to hurt my father? For sending me away?"

"Hurt him? No, not hurt him. They'll be angry with him. He'll be shamed, no doubt. His business will falter. But your uncle will make it evident to the village that he was willing to have you stoned. That will salvage your uncle's honor."

"Honor . . ." she murmured.

"Don't worry about it, miss. In your condition, you should let your mind rest."

"And let my father suffer?" She shook her head.

"You didn't ask for this, miss," Nathan reminded her. "God appointed you. And if this is from God, He will take care of the details. He won't let your father suffer because of it."

Mary's donkey halted in its path, and she did also. It was no use. Mary knew as well as anyone else that donkeys could not be dragged. Nathan untied the water bag made from a sheep's stomach from his donkey's saddle and passed it to her. After taking a long drink, she carefully replaced the stopper.

"Look." Nathan pointed. "There is some shelter. Sit down for a while. You need rest. The rain looks as if it will start again any minute."

The day was cool and damp. A little off the road a grove of fig trees provided a small amount of shelter. The broad, lobed, leathery leaves drooped like tired hands dangling from the gnarled branches, dripping slowly. Mary let Nathan take the rope, and she sank to her heels, her back against the trunk of one of the trees, and leaned her head against the rough bark.

O, God, I'm afraid.

Unshed tears seemed to have filled her chest, making it difficult for her to breathe. She'd never been away from her family before. Having grown up in the same house that she had been born in, she had spent every morning of her life in that courtyard with her mother . . . and now she was traveling to a distant relative she had never met to avoid being stoned before the front door of her father's house.

"Take this," her father had said, tears in his eyes. He pressed a bundle of clothing in her hands. "Don't stop, Mary; just go as fast as you can to your cousin's house. Tell her who your mother is, and she will know you. But you don't have much time. Your uncle just left."

"Can't you come with me?" she'd pleaded.

When her father hadn't answered, her mother had taken over at that point, loading up the donkey with food and a water skin, her strong arms working quickly, but her fingers shaking when it came to tying the knots.

"Rest when you can," her mother had said gently. "If you start feeling pain here" —she put a cool hand on Mary's belly— "then lie down and do your best to stay calm. Sometimes resting can save it."

"Save what?" she'd asked desperately. "I can't do this alone! I don't know what to do!"

"You're early still," her mother continued. "You should be able to walk quite a ways, and ride when you need to. You're a healthy girl. I don't suspect that you'll have trouble."

"But what if I do? Don't send me away alone!"

"Nathan has said that he'd go with you," her father had said. "I trust Nathan."

"But what about you?" Mary had asked, looking desperately from her father to her mother. "When will I see you?"

"You'll come back, love," her mother said, her lips trembling. "But you must let the anger die down first! We'll send word when it's safe!"

"And Joseph?"

"There should be enough food for a few days. Don't let yourself get too thin . . ."

"What about Joseph?" Mary pressed. "Can I see him? Where is he?"

"We don't know," her father had said, pushing her toward the donkey. "But there isn't time! Joseph has been very upset by all of this. We will explain to him where you are. But there is no time!"

He'd been upset by all of this? Mary knew what that meant. Joseph didn't believe her. Something deep inside of her knew that he would call off their betrothal. How could he not? How could she blame him? And her parents had wanted to shield her from that terrible truth as long as possible.

Do not fret a pregnant woman, people said. Babies were lost that way. How many lies would be told to her on that pretext? No longer Mary, daughter of Ebenezer, she was now Mary who was pregnant, and the rules of dealing with her had changed. And there was no one here to explain them to her.

The ground was hard and rocky beneath her, and she felt the hot tears overflowing her lids and trickling down her cheeks. Mary squeezed her eyes shut, images of her mother's familiar form and her father's sad, gentle eyes running through her mind. She didn't want to be without her parents. In fact, she had never wanted to live more than a short walk from her parents' home, even after she was married. How many times had she promised her mother to come to visit her every day? And she'd meant it! Then she had seen no reason she shouldn't be able to, but now she was traveling a long distance on her own with promises that they would send for her. But what if they didn't? What if it was another half-truth told to the pregnant girl so that she wouldn't be too upset? What if she never saw them again?

If she had Joseph, perhaps the grief would be bearable. But even he had been mysteriously silent. The family would go on without her . . . close the gap and continue the life of a clan. Joseph would find another girl whom he believed was more worthy and marry her. Good, kind Joseph didn't deserve any of this!

"Oh, miss, don't cry!" Nathan said, looking worried and perplexed. He squatted in front of her and peered at her with the confusion of a man unused to dealing with young women.

"I don't think Joseph will marry me," Mary said, lifting her eyes to meet his. "And he'll marry someone else!"

"Not a chance!" Nathan said, but his voice was unconvincing. His eyes clouded as he chewed on the side of his cheek. Then after a moment of consideration, he said, "And what if he does?"

Mary took a deep breath and wiped her eyes with the corner of her veil. She looked down at the wet cloth and pondered Nathan's question seriously. What if Joseph did call off their marriage and marry someone else? It would be the worst possible thing to happen . . . but what if it did? It terrified her because it was a very real and likely possibility.

O God, give me strength. I'm being weak. Make me brave.

"I would be mother to the Messiah," Mary said quietly after a moment. "And God must provide for me as a husband would."

Nathan gave a satisfied grunt and shoved himself back to his feet.

"I've seen women with a worse lot in life," he said with a sniff. "Husbands aren't all easy to bear, girl."

"Let's keep moving," she decided, standing and vigorously brushing off the grit and dirt that stuck to her robe. She wiped her eyes with her veil once more and took a deep breath.

Nathan gave her a surprised look, and she met his gaze evenly, raising her chin and managing a matter-of-fact smile.

"They say that when a girl gets married she has to grow up quickly," she said, tugging at the ties on her donkey's saddle to check how secure they were. "Well, I'd better get to it. I'm going to have a baby, and I don't know about the future, but right now I'm on my own. They say mothers are as strong as 10 men in battle. I guess that I'd better start finding that strength of womanhood, Nathan."

"All right, then, miss," he said with an admiring glance as he turned his attention to his own donkey, his experienced hands tightening the load with greater dexterity than one would have expected of him.

"Little girls cry," Mary said softly to the donkey as she let him drink the last of the water Nathan had provided. "Grown women face life with a veil. And when their veil slips, their faces should reveal less than the fabric did."

Looking down the long road ahead of her, she started walking, each step taking her farther away from home.

"Lydia," Ruth said to her daughter, "put down that comb and start the bread!"

The girl pulled the bone comb through her hair twice more before heaving a sigh and setting it aside. She examined the ends of her hair, then flipped it behind her shoulder and gave her mother a bored look.

"My robes are all so old and dull," she complained. "I want something new."

"If you have so much time to mourn over your robes, perhaps you should work harder," the older woman said pointedly.

Heaving another sigh, Lydia went to the jar of flour to begin measuring out fistfuls into a clay bowl.

"You could take one of your oldest robes—the one that is torn—and make it into a new veil or two," her mother suggested. "A thrifty woman is a jewel to her husband!"

"A thrifty woman's husband can't afford jewels," Lydia said with a smirk.

"Go saying that kind of thing in the marketplace, and you'll have no husband at all!" Ruth snapped. "Then how clever will you be?"

Once again Lydia sighed. She knew her mother was right. Appearances were everything, especially in such a small town. One questionable phrase, and the entire village would be talking about it and spinning their own tales about what exactly it meant about her character. Men might be kinder when thinking about a pretty face, but women were vicious. And it was the women who formed the village's unofficial council on marriageable virgins.

"Pay attention to your work, girl."

Lydia glanced at her mother, who was unnaturally irritable today. Normally Ruth was quite indulgent with her only daughter, especially when it came to her taking care of her looks, but today the older woman's mood seemed off. Shrugging to herself, Lydia added a dribble of oil to the flour, kneading it in with her fingers.

As she set the small jar of oil down, there was a knock on the door, and Lydia and Ruth looked at each other, silently comparing their hands to see who was cleaner to open the door. Lydia had one clean hand, and so with yet another sigh she pulled her veil up over her head and went to answer the knock.

Probably my aunt, she thought to herself.

As Lydia opened the door, her thoughts had returned to her desire for a new robe. She wanted something in red, or perhaps a pale green. Green would compliment her hazel eyes, and with the right cut, it would make her look taller, she thought. And as she opened the door, she was focused on how unfair it was that her father didn't deem her beauty of more importance to give her what she wanted—so focused that for several moments she didn't fully recognize who was standing before her.

"Oh," she gasped, putting her dirty hand behind her back and ducking her head bashfully. "Good morning, sir."

"God be with you," Joseph said. "I was hoping that your father was in."

"My father?" she managed to say, feeling flustered. "No, I'm sorry, sir, but he has gone out on business. I'm not sure where, because business isn't a woman's concern, you know . . ." She glanced up coyly through her lashes.

"Oh, I see." Suddenly he seemed uncertain of himself. Tall, with that glossy black beard and the strong arms and broad hands, he stood looking somewhere to her left, his expression preoccupied. She could guess what was on his mind, what with the recent gossip! Lydia took a moment to gaze at him.

"But if you would like to come inside, sir, my mother . . . I mean, I have cooked some food that you might enjoy."

His eyes showing worry and strain, Joseph glanced back at her.

"Who is it?" her mother asked, coming to the door. When she saw Joseph, she stopped short and adjusted her expression to one of doting hostess.

"Oh, Joseph, we are so happy to see you!" she gushed. "God be with you, friend! My husband will be happy to see you when he returns. I believe my daughter told you that he will be back soon, did she not? Well, he will be back any minute now! Please, come rest yourself!"

"No, thank you, mistress," Joseph said politely. "Perhaps I will meet him on the road."

"Well, suit yourself," she said, pursing her lips. "I'm sorry to hear about your situation, anyway. I hope you forgive me mentioning it, but the whole village has been abuzz. Of course, I have not said a word to anyone. I am not the gossiping kind of woman, you see. But I heard of it, and I said to myself, that poor, dear man! To think that a hussy like that could have hidden her true nature!"

"I'm . . . I'm sorry, mistress, but I should be off," Joseph announced, casting an uneasy glance at the two women in front of him. Lydia sighed. This was not going well!

"Gossip aside," Lydia said quickly, "our family is very horrified by my cousin's lapse in sanity."

"Horrified!" her mother chimed in.

"Is Mary here with you?" Joseph asked, fixing his intense gaze first on one woman and then the other.

"Here?" Lydia asked.

"Certainly not!" Ruth said, expelling her breath in disgust.

"It was just that her father told me that he'd sent her away to family, and I thought perhaps she was with you for a time . . ."

"We do not condone that kind of sin, sir," Ruth declared primly. "She would never be harbored in my home, I can assure you!"

"Well, thank you," he said, his voice low and sad.

"I know that you must have called off the wedding," Ruth said with a sigh. "We are not exactly on speaking terms with Ebenezer's house after this episode, but word does travel, you know. To give up on a wedding is a strong disappointment!"

Cringing, Lydia cast her mother a pleading look. What was the woman doing? Lydia wanted Joseph to see her as sophisticated and beautiful, not the daughter of a crude gossip! Of course, her mother was not on speaking terms with her aunt right now, but she certainly was with every other busybody in the village!

"I'm not willing to discuss that," Joseph replied curtly.

Apparently unfazed by the retort, Ruth put out a confiding hand on his arm, ignoring the fact that he pulled back.

"I'm sorry to be so bold, sir," she said. "But the wedding can still go forward! I have a daughter who is eligible, beautiful, and virtuous. With a more appropriate bride, your day of celebration will be even happier!"

Burning with embarrassment, Lydia pulled her veil closer around her face and tried her best to melt into the ground.

"Please, Mother!" she begged, then turned her humiliated gaze toward Joseph to see what damage had been done.

"She's healthy," her mother said, pinching Lydia's arm in demonstration. "And she's strong! She's also a most thrifty young woman."

"Thank you for the kind offer," Joseph said coldly. "Perhaps I will think it over at a later time."

With that he turned and walked stiffly away, leaving Lydia with a bruise on her upper arm from her mother's enthusiastic pinch. "Mother!" she hissed. "What have you done?"

"I think it's promising," her mother said, putting her chin up. "He said he would consider it."

"He hates you for it!" Tears began to well up in the daughter's eyes.

"He might resent it now," her mother retorted. "But he'll think of it later when the sting of his recent embarrassment is past. And he'll know he's welcome here! There will be no question of whether he'd be accepted or not by your father."

"If I'm never married, you can't blame me for it!" Bursting into tears, Lydia turned and stomped back into the house, too angry to say another word.

Chapter 17

Whatever wisdom may be, it is far off and most profound—who can discover it?
—Ecclesiastes 7:24

Simak stood at the back of the schoolroom. Only the brightest boys were permitted into this weekly class at the palace, and they ranged in age from 4 years old to 14. Right now they were drawing from memory the constellations in relation to each other on their wax tablets. If one did not know where the stars belonged in the heavens, how could one ever note a difference in them?

The older boys could do this exercise with their eyes shut, repetition having cemented the position of each star into their memory. As a result they could help their younger classmates who looked up to them. With a sense of pride Simak watched the boys working together, the low hum of concentrating voices moving through the large room like a lazy bumblebee. Only the best of them would have a chance at becoming Magi—religious leaders and experts in the stars.

"Today, boys, we will discuss a phenomenon of great importance," Simak announced, raising his voice above the low murmur. The class grew silent, looking up at him expectantly. His gaze shifted to a small boy in the front row sitting alone. The lad had large, luminous dark eyes and a small, thin mouth. He always looked serious, and his child solemnity always brought a smile to Simak's lips.

"And what do you think it is, Anoush?" the Magian asked.

"I do not know, Your Majesty," the lad said quietly.

"Truthful," Simak said with a nod. "But I always wish to know what goes on in a boy's mind. For me, those years are too far away."

The boy glanced up silently, his eyes questioning. A closed child, he did not reveal much about himself, but seemed to absorb information quicker than a fleece soaked up water. He would make a good Magian, Simak knew. If only he could be guided properly . . .

"Today we will talk about the moon," their teacher went on, looking out over the boys. "And in particular, the meaning behind the moon's disappearance."

As the boys' eyes widened at this, Simak smiled to himself.

"But first, I want you to guess—each one of you! What would the meaning be if the moon turned black in the sky before your eyes?"

Most were too young to have witnessed the last total eclipse. And most were too young to have experienced the widespread panic of the people at such an event. The gods or demons were about to smite them, they were sure! Partial eclipses happened about twice a year, but only the most observant noticed them. And most people, sadly enough, would be unaware if their own faces were eclipsed.

An older boy raised his hand, and Simak waved him away. "You have heard this lesson before," he said with a shake of his head. "I want to know what the younger boys think."

"The gods are angry?" one suggested. "They are denying us light at night because we have offended them?"

Simak gave a noncommittal response.

"Something awful is about to happen?" another guessed.

"Someone important has died?"

"A shrine has been desecrated?"

The guesses began to dwindle, and Simak looked inquiringly at young Anoush. "And you?"

The boy was thoughtful. "Has it happened before?"

"A good question," Simak said with a smile. "Yes, it has."

"What did it mean then?" Anoush continued.

"Aha! The beginning of wisdom and knowledge is to know what you do not know, and what questions to ask!"

Anoush was a bright boy, and Simak knew beyond a doubt that he would one day be a powerful Magian. But that was not his only interest in the boy. The lad was special, doubtless, but he was also the son of someone special.

Salma had been the most beautiful girl that Simak had ever seen. He had been young then, and had not seen many women, but he was convinced that she would outshine even the sun given a chance. Not only was she delightful and delicate, but one day he had discovered that she was also intelligent. They had been walking together, respectfully at a proper physical distance, and not looking directly at each other. That was the custom to show that they intended no immorality. He had been trying to show off his vast knowledge of the stars, and in his monologue about eclipses she had interjected, "But Simak, that happens quite often. I've counted as many as three in one year. And each time I find it difficult to find anything in common with each, besides timing. There may be a mathematical formula to predict them."

And he had been stunned. For a woman, she was marvelously intelligent. And even for anyone, she was marvelously observant. The fact terrified him.

He had been young, and young men are not always as wise as they imagine themselves to be. Unfortunately, he had decided that a wife must be beautiful as the stars, but never brighter than he was. So he stopped walking with her and simply watched her from afar, intimidated and in love.

Anoush, it seemed, had inherited his mother's intelligence. She was not only bright, but gentle and kind and sympathetic to the pain of others. She was as beautiful on the inside as on the outside. And since Simak had seemingly lost interest in her, her father arranged a marriage for her with another man, and she was lost to Simak forever.

Oh, not forever, his friends had laughed. A man of Simak's wealth and influence could easily attract her as a mistress, could he not? But no, Simak knew that her strength of character would not allow her to dishonor her husband so. And Simak would not want her to. It would topple her from the stars and make her tawdry and ordinary. So she was indeed lost forever. And the very knowledge of his inability to have her made him love her even more.

"The moon has eclipsed in one way or another at least twice a year for as long as our lunar catalog record," Simak explained, and the younger boys all gasped in awe. "This happens when the moon turns partially or completely dark. Sometimes it is totally blackened. Other times it turns a bright orange or a dusty brown. When one charts the eclipses, a complicated pattern emerges, but a pattern nonetheless. If there is a pattern to these events, does that mean that the gods are trying to tell us something particular?"

Silence.

"An older boy, perhaps?" Simak asked.

Still silence.

"These are the questions that a Magian must contemplate," Simak said quietly. "These are the questions that brings him to sacrifice and ask the gods for guidance."

"Perhaps," Anoush began, then his voice trailed away.

"Yes, Anoush? Out with it."

"Pehaps, if it is a pattern, it tells us something about the gods and universe that is unchanging."

"And what unchanging attribute might that be?"

Anoush looked down at his crossed ankles, silent.

"There is no set answer to these mysteries," Simak continued. "Each time in the past that an eclipse has occurred, there seems to be no consistent parallel on the earth. There seem to be no consistent deaths or births. There seems to be nothing we can relate to here . . . But perhaps there are things that happen above that are so vast and immeasurable that our small plot of dirt does not share in their significance."

The first eclipse that he had noticed after his break with Salma, Simak had felt an incredible sadness. She was noticing it too, he knew, but she was now married to another. And now, each time he saw the darkening of the full moon, he felt that strange emptiness inside of him. Some things, it seemed, were so much bigger than he was that he was not a part of them, except simply to observe.

"We are finished for the day," Simak concluded. "Think about these things. And we shall meet again next week."

A rustle filled the chamber as the boys rose to their feet, then the growing sound of their voices as they conversed together. The school room echoed with their ringing tones, the cool stone tiles reverberated with their sandaled feet.

Salma. Perhaps she was happier without him. The man she married was a good, kind individual. Hardworking, he was respectful to her and never unfaithful. Yes, he was a good person. Salma had a good life with her husband, and she never seemed to glance at Simak with any sort of interest beyond that of a citizen to royalty. No longer a man to her, he was just a role—a Magian. And perhaps it was better that way.

Dedicated to his studies and intent on gaining knowledge as well as proud of his own achievements and his own wealth—could he have made her happy? Would she have been anything more than an ornament?

Yes, some things were so much bigger than he was, that all he could do was to observe. But a passage from an ancient Jewish scroll he had read said that their God would bless the eunuch with something more lasting than children. And while Simak was not a eunuch, he was just as alone, and just as cut off from the woman that he had foolishly cast off. Could it be that there was something even bigger to fill that emptiness inside of him? And was it heresy to hope?

Naomi measured more salt into her palm and dropped it into the pot of lentils simmering over the fire in the courtyard. Cumin and garlic were already mingling with the other scents. Cooking outside spared the inside of the house from getting even hotter, but it didn't keep Naomi any cooler. Sweat trickled down her spine and stood out in beads on her nose and forehead. When she flapped her robe, it let a small finger of air work its way through the fabric. She stirred the pot with a long spoon. The lentils were almost done, and she eyed the glowing coals beneath the pot. No point in adding more wood. Covering the pot, Naomi turned and left the food to finish cooking with the last of the coals' heat.

"I wonder how Mary is," she sighed as she entered the house. Her mother looked up at her, her eyes heavy with dark circles and her square jaw set in an expression of determination.

"I pray she is safe," Esther answered in a low voice. "That is all I can do."

The boys stuck closer to their mother lately, and they sat nearby amusing themselves. Children could sense when something had gone horribly wrong, and while they doubtlessly understood what had happened, the repercussions on the family still confused them.

"Why don't you go play, boys?" Noami said, peeking her head around the corner.

"Why?" Japheth demanded.

"Because you are children, and you don't need to worry like this. You need to go play by the well or find your friends."

"They won't play with us," Adam announced. "They said our family is wicked."

"Our family is not wicked," Naomi said, her stomach sinking. "Then go play together. Sitting in the courtyard won't do you much good! Off with you! Go play!"

The boys got up unwillingly and shuffled off farther from the kitchen area, but Naomi couldn't help noticing that they didn't leave. With a sigh she returned to her work. Her mother glanced up.

"Even the children . . ." Esther muttered. Naomi wasn't sure which children she was speaking of—her own, or the other children of the village. But did it matter?

"Mary is gone now," Naomi said, hearing the sharpness in her own tone. "Soon they'll forget."

"Will they?"

Naomi grimaced. A cloud had hung over their house ever since the unfortunate discovery of Mary's pregnancy. It was her sister's fault, yet they all had to pay for it! Even the boys, who had nothing to do with her guilt.

"Mother, I need to talk to you." Her daughter edged closer and lowered her voice.

"Yes, dear?" Esther continued kneading some dough.

"It's important," Naomi suddenly said, and her mother frowned and looked at her inquiringly.

"It's about my marriage. Don't get angry at me . . . I just don't want it! I hate it! I don't want to marry that man!"

"You can't remain unmarried, silly girl," her mother said with an indulgent smile.

"I don't want to," Naomi said seriously. "I want to marry Thaddaeus."

Esther did not speak.

"He loves me," Naomi added feebly. "He said so!"

"Well," her mother said, methodically scraping the dough from her fingers. "Well . . ."

"Don't you understand what we're feeling?" her daughter blurted out. "Didn't you ever love anyone? I love him! I want to marry Thaddaeus, not some stranger. He loves me! He wants to marry me, but our parents stand between us!"

"Your parents stand there for your own good," Esther replied evenly.

"He's . . . he's everything to me. How can I explain it? He's so good and strong! He wants to make money and clothe me in silk! He wants to make his father's business prosperous!"

"His father' business is already prosperous."

"He wants to improve it. Why can't you see what a good man he is? Why don't parents ever look at what their children want?"

Her mother's expression softened, and she patted the ground next to her. Naomi shifted closer to her mother, smelling the scent of sweat, yeast, and dust mingled together in that comforting way that she remembered since she was a small girl.

"I do understand what you are feeling." Her mother wiped the last of the dough from her hands on a cloth. She put one broad hand on her daughter's leg and gave it an affectionate pat. "I was your age once. I know what the young feel. And I know how strongly you feel. But I can assure you that your father has chosen a good man."

"And if I never can stand him? What then?"

"You will," Esther said quietly. "You will grow accustomed to him. He will be kind to you, and you will learn to feel fondly toward him. And in time you will forget about Thaddaeus."

"I won't!" Tears caught in her voice. "I never will!"

"In the future you will understand. That I can promise you. You will see the life that Thaddaeus's wife has, and the one that you have. Then you will know why your father chose the man he did. You must stop questioning your father's wisdom, girl. He loves you more than Thaddaeus ever could."

"How can you even talk about Thaddaeus's wife?" her daughter wailed. "How could you?"

"Then let us talk about your husband. He is very kind, you know. And he's gentle. He works hard, and his father has complete trust in him. He's handsome, too, I've been told!"

Naomi sat sullenly, her mind tuning her mother's voice out. It was always the same. They wanted her to marry Ashi and would not change their minds. What parents ever did? Like battering her fists against a mountain, whatever she said did no good.

Unless she took things into her own hands, and Ashi refused to marry her . . . But what if Thaddaeus's marriage went forward, and she had neither man?

The thought was sobering to a girl like Naomi, who did not intend to sacrifice the rest of her life for anyone—even Thaddaeus.

CHAPTER 18

When you get scalded from hot food, you blow when you're served even cold.
—Ancient Jewish saying

Amichai!" the old man shouted. "Amichai!"

His eyes still scanning the hillside, Amichai sighed. He wished he were out with the sheep, watching them graze . . . planning for the next cropping. He wished he were bullying that stubborn ewe that kept forgetting about her young. Or he wished he were sitting around the fire during long wet nights with the other men, exchanging stories and watching the flames crackling and sizzling upward into the damp darkness. But he was not there. Instead he was here, in the camp, for at least a few more days.

"Amichai!"

"I'm coming, Father." With a sigh Amichai pushed open the flap of the tent and ducked as he entered. His father lay on his bed scowling and petulant, propped up with pillows and sheepskins. The old man's bushy eyebrows were drawn low over his watery eyes.

"What's wrong?" the son asked, trying to suppress the impatience he felt.

"This bed is lumpy. And I'm too hot."

After helping his father to loosen his tunic, Amichai pulled the blankets away from the man's thin, pale legs. Amichai knew what the problem really was. His father was lonely. But the old man would never admit to it. He'd spent his life being a bully and a brute, refusing ever to admit to any weakness.

"Everyone will be happy when I die," he muttered. "I'm not a respected patriarch, I'm a weight on my children . . ."

"Of course we respect you, Father."

"No, you don't," Jonah said, pulling his legs up, obviously now chilled.

"Are you cold now?"

"I said I was hot, didn't I? Stop treating me like a newborn baby!"

Amichai groaned.

"I'm cold," his father announced after a moment.

As Amichai pulled the cover up over his father's legs he thought how strange it was that the human body, once aged, felt chilled in the middle of a hot day. While it was hard to anticipate his father's comfort, it was even more difficult to anticipate the man's moods. No, that was wrong. It was quite easy to anticipate them, since most were foul.

"I don't know what's wrong with your generation," his father went on. "When I was young, our fathers were honored and cared for! We were grateful for all that they did for us. We cared about their opinions and did as we were told."

"You're tired." Amichai began to rise.

"I am not tired! You make excuses. You say we have no money . . ."

"Father, we are taxed more than we can bear. I do not blame you. I blame the Romans. How can we afford to live when they take every penny? They'd snatch the food out of our very mouths, if they could get it before our teeth clamped down!"

"Teeth clamped down," the old man said with a hoarse laugh. "Yes, teeth . . . Funny. You've got some spirit, boy."

When he laughed again, Amichai felt somehow mollified. Although he knew that his father would never approve of him, somehow giving the old goat something to chuckle about made him feel as he'd succeeded in a way. At something.

"When the Messiah comes, it will be different, boy." His father shook his head. "He will come with power and swords, mark my words! He will rally us all together, and we'll stand up as one to fight off these heathen invaders!"

"Yes," Amichai agreed with a smile. "Things will be different."

"And what we grow, we will eat! What we make, we will set aside for our children. We'll have money enough to have families the size of villages! The Romans will be outnumbered five to one, and they'll be our slaves . . ."

It was a familiar conversation, this wishing and hoping for their deliverer. Such discussions had taken place in many a tent, in many a house, between many a Judean. And it always began with outrage at their unfair treatment at the hands of pagans, and then it moved on to a dream of what it would be like . . .

"I'll have a Roman to cook my food," his father laughed. "The filthy swine!"

Amichai smiled at the irony.

"Do you want them to work for you, Father? Or do you want them to be expelled from our country?"

"I'd work them like donkeys!" His father's eyes crinkled with humor. "I'd make them watch the flocks. I'd make them carry our loads. I'd forbid them to marry!"

"And when they got old with no children to care for them?"

The old man's humor evaporated, and he gave his son a sour look. "It's people like you that let them!" he spat out. "Spineless and weak! If men were still men like they used to be, the Romans wouldn't be ruling us!"

The Romans had ruled when his father was young, too, Amichai thought with a grimace. And things were more complicated than a new political leader could fix. Would a new king take away this core of anger in the pit of his stomach whenever he thought of his father? Would a new king stop the beatings that young boys received at the whim of the man who sired him? Would a new king bring back his dead mother—the only one who had loved him? No, things were much more complicated than the rheumatic old man cared to admit. And fixing things was not so simple as ridding themselves of the Romans.

When God sent the Messiah, it was supposed to bring peace and harmony. But was that even possible in a family like theirs? Would a Messiah make any difference to a man like Amichai? Why hope for a Messiah when it wouldn't alter anything that mattered? Why do anything but pay the idea lip service if the political change wouldn't touch your own personal hell?

Unless there was something more to the coming Messiah than a political ruler . . . unless the Messiah was something that none of them expected . . .

Jonah watched as his son ducked his head, his spine still straight and angry, and left the tent. It was always the same. Amichai came to help, and he would leave again offended and aloof. If he were stronger, Jonah would take out his rage on something nearby. But instead he was a feeble, pathetic thing that smelled. He knew he smelled—of age and rot and weakness. He hated the smell of himself worse than anything else.

Amichai was so predictable and easy to goad. As a boy he'd always been weak. And now that he was a grown man, his body had matured and acquired a beard, but the weakness was the same. Jonah could see it deep down, all soft and wet like underbaked bread. He wouldn't take it if he were a real man. Nor would he let anyone speak to him the way that Jonah did—the way his own father always had. But Amichai would never raise a hand to him. Amichai would never shut his mouth for him. No, Amichai would just continue to take it, because he knew that his father, weak and feeble as he was, was still more of a man.

Jonah hissed angrily to himself, kicking at the cover that felt so heavy against his legs. This wasn't what old age was supposed to be. Old age was supposed to be his chance to rest and be cared for. Daughters-in-law should hold his hand and feed him broth and cater to his whims. His sons were supposed to be respectful and seek his advice for their family decisions. And his word should be law! He should be . . . he should be . . . loved . . .

But old age had stolen up on him and leaped on his back like a thief. Old age had thrown him down and held him in the dust. He hadn't seen it coming. If he had, he could have been prepared somehow. Perhaps made peace with his children. If that were possible. They hated him, and he knew it. Even Amichai, the weak one, couldn't hide his dislike.

Ungrateful little pigs! Hadn't he sired them? Given them life and a name? What more did they want from him? To act soft and pathetic like a woman? No! He had fathered and raised them! And he was hard on them for their own good, just as his father had been on him. To let them see that the world was hard so that they would never be disappointed, he had never spared the rod. And his children were never spoiled! So what was their problem now? Why the anger and bruised feelings? They were acting as if he had coddled them!

It was difficult to dislike one's own children. Wasn't a man supposed to be proud of his brood? Wasn't he expected to love them and feel tender toward them? But he didn't like them. They were nothing like what he had hoped they would grow into. A disappointment and pathetic, they would fail at life, he knew, and he had little choice but to watch it happen.

Jonah leaned back against his pillows, wishing that Amichai hadn't left. He was lonely. And pathetic as Amichai was, at least he was another warm body in the tent. Someone to talk to, even though the conversation was always irritating at best.

"Amichai!" he called out feebly. "Amichai!"

A few moments later his son's tired, irritated face appeared through the tent flaps.

"I'm thirsty," Jonah said.

Elias stopped short, the muscles in his face twitching in an effort to control his rage. Orli was walking toward the house, her small eyes bright and her lips moving in a conversation with herself. Her soundless words stopped, and she smiled, the corners of her lips upturning like a pink bow. She did not see her father at first, and when her gaze passed over his shadow, she flinched visibly before her eyes rose to the level of his chest and stayed there, refusing to look him in the face.

"Where are you coming from?" Elias demanded.

His daughter hung her head and glanced at him sideways in a look of barely controlled fear. But beneath that terror there was something steely—something he couldn't beat out of her. Conflicting emotions pinched her broad, plain face as she stood there flat-footed, her shoulders hunched as if awaiting the blows.

"Well? Where are you coming from?"

"I was checking on the goats," Orli said in low voice. "I thought the she-goat had given less milk this morning, and I wanted to see if she was sick."

"The goat is fine," he snapped. "Who was in the stables?"

Orli was silent, watching him through veiled eyes. When he made a move toward her, she took an involuntary step backwards. He stopped, too hot and tired to chase after her and beat her. It wouldn't be worth the energy. How many times had he punished her? And still the same stupid excuses to go out to the stables, where he kept missing the opportunity to catch her at her sin.

Or perhaps the goat was sick. How could he know? Maybe she just went out there to be alone and get away from work. It was possible. He wasn't a complete brute.

"Get back to work!" he barked. "I don't want to see you away from the kitchen, or I'll make you regret it!"

She paused just a moment too long before turning back toward the house. Insolent! That was what she was! Why he didn't have her stoned, he did not know. A shame to his name, she was hulking and ugly and not worth a two-pigeon dowry! And now this?

Plodding like a tired donkey, Orli drifted away. There had been a time that while she was not pretty, at least she had been deceived into believing she was. That was better than this. It was as if she'd suddenly realized exactly what she was and had started to act like it.

But she wasn't so ugly, really, Elias thought to himself. She had nice qualities. Her large frame promised to mature into a nice full-figured woman. She would have strong arms. And when she was happy, which seemed ages ago now, her plain face had a way of lighting up into an almost likable smile. The shape of her face reminded him of his sister. Her nose resembled his mother's a little, and her hair was too much like his own. The girl took after his side of the family instead of her mother's, and the combination had not been to her advantage.

Why was he feeling this strange pity at a time like this? After resenting her for so many years, he finally had reason to be rid of her! At least send her away . . . But, now the thought made tears prick at his eyes. It was disgusting weakness! He was pitying her disastrous looks when she was toying with his honor!

Stalking toward the stables, he squinted into the dim interior. The goats had fled from the heat and were chewing some hay audibly in the back corner. The smell was overpowering as usual, and he kicked at some loose hay, eyeing the floor for some sign of a man's recent presence.

Nothing. But he didn't know what he was looking for anyway . . . a carefully made bed and cooking fire?

When he turned back into the sunlight he caught his daughter staring in his direction. It was difficult to read her expression from this distance, but she turned quickly away and disappeared into the darkened confines of the house.

"How is the goat?" Nona called from the door.

"You ask me, woman?" Elias retorted, glancing around to see if any of his friends had seen her speak so casually to him.

His wife cast him a look of cool superiority and disappeared back inside after her daughter. So there was a problem with the goat after all. He should have known. The stupid beast had been a gift from Nona's uncle, the cheap old man. Elias should have guessed that the animal wouldn't be strong.

But Orli . . . he'd had such big dreams for her once he had gotten over the disappointment of her gender. And somehow she'd always been too . . . too . . .

What was she? He didn't even know. She was tough and strong. She was sullen. She was carefully defiant. She was silent and stubborn. He didn't understand girls. Had she been a son, he would know how to deal with the lad. But a girl—they were confusing. Complicated, they didn't answer to logic! As a little girl, she had made more sense, laughing and giggling and trusting him. But now she was a young woman and beyond his understanding. He couldn't fix this for her . . . couldn't make the world kinder to a girl like her . . .

And she was his daughter—as much a part of him as his own foot. She even looked like him, the poor girl. Although irritating and disappointing, she was still his. And he would be dashed to pieces before he let some dirty shepherd put his hands on her again!

What Elias did not realize was that his confused heap of feelings that he had toward his daughter could be defined as love.

CHAPTER 19

The wife of R. Joseph was accustomed to light her (Sabbath) lamp late. Said he unto her: There is a Boraitha: It is written: "The pillar of cloud did not depart by day nor the pillar of fire by night"[Ex. 13:22]. From this we infer that the two pillars always closely followed each other. She then wanted to light up too early. Said a certain old man to her: "There is another Boraitha, however, that (whatever is to be done) should be done neither too early nor too late."

—*From the Mishnah*

The old man in the road said this is the place," Nathan explained, reaching out a hand to grasp the reins of Mary's donkey when the creature appeared to be quite willing to walk on past. "Second road on the right is what he said."

Nathan squinted down the narrow road. Dust rose in small clouds with every breath of breeze as they started along it. A sprinkling of gnarled trees shaded it, and Mary found herself feeling breathless and excited. She had almost reached her destination! A woman on her own . . . visiting family that she had never met . . . While she should have felt fear, she instead had a sense of elation. God had protected her, and she had survived! There was something exhilarating in simply being conscious and drawing breath.

A woman stood outside the house, her back to them. Mary could tell that she was elderly by her posture. As they drew closer, she turned toward them. Her face was lined, and a wisp of hair that had escaped her veil was white as salt. She must be ill, Mary thought, because if it weren't for her age, the girl would guess that the woman was pregnant! What kind of strange disease could cause a belly to grow like that?

Nathan held out a hand and helped Mary off the swayed back of her donkey. Her balance was changing with her growing stomach, and it seemed that even simple movements could cause her to stumble. It was a strangely vulnerable feeling.

And then, at that moment, Mary felt something for the first time—the baby inside of her suddenly leaped, as if it were stretching out all its limbs at once! A strange sensation—one that only a mother can know—it was the feeling of life inside of her. Not the idea of life . . .

not the knowledge that all the signs pointed to life . . . not a small fluttering inside of her . . . but the feeling of a baby—a strong healthy baby!

"Oh!" she gasped, her eyes widening. And she was suddenly filled with such joy and relief that she laughed out loud, one hand on her belly and the other against the flank of the donkey.

"Miss?" Nathan said, looking worried.

"Are you Elizabeth?" Mary asked.

The old woman suddenly glanced down at her own belly, her eyes widening. She rubbed her belly in a circular motion and shook her head in wonder.

"Who am I that the mother of the Messiah visits me?" she asked, her face creasing into a broad smile. "You are blessed, girl! You have been blessed with the role that all women have been coveting since Adam fell! Don't ask me how I know it . . . but this baby of mine leaped up inside of me when I heard your voice, and I knew it!"

She knew? Mary was completely bewildered. How could she know before Mary had even spoken?

"My soul praises God, and the very breath in my body rejoices in God who has saved me!" Mary said, the words suddenly coming together inside of her and flowing out in a tumble. As she spoke, her voice got stronger, and she could feel her cheeks growing warm.

"God has seen the state of one humble girl . . . and because of that, every generation after me will call me blessed! God has done great and miraculous things for me—no one is as magnificent as our God! He is merciful to those who believe in Him, and He humbles the proud and arrogant with one glance. He topples rulers off their thrones of gold, but He takes a humble, poor girl like me and raises her up! He gives delicacies to the hungry and sends the pompous rich away with nothing. He has remembered Israel . . . He has not forgotten us! He hasn't forgotten those age-old promises He made to our fathers."

Tears coming to her eyes, Mary laughed again. This child inside of her was the Messiah! This child, that she could feel, was a real baby sent from God!

"What is your name, girl?" the old woman asked.

Looking up in surprise, Mary saw the old woman standing next to her, her hand in the small of her back and her other gnarled hand rubbing her great belly.

"Mary. My mother is Esther. My father is Ebenezer."

"Mary!" the old woman said, her face lighting up with a smile. "Esther's girl! I haven't seen her since we were about your age!"

The old woman took Mary's hand in her dry, firm grip and began her waddle toward the small house.

"I am Elizabeth—your mother's cousin. Your mother and I were inseparable! But then we both got married, of course, and life changes, as I'm sure you know . . ."

Mary faltered and Elizabeth looked back at her, her shrewd eyes examining the girl's face in a quick glance.

"Not married then?"

"This baby is not from a man!" Mary said. "God told me that I would conceive, and that this child would be His . . ."

Elizabeth did not say anything, instead biting her lip, her eyes narrowing in thought.

"Well, I'd believe it," she said finally. "God works in strange, strange ways, I have learned lately. Look at me! Barren every day of my life until I was old, stooped, and rheumatic! Then suddenly an angel comes to my husband and says we'll have a child! Can you blame poor Zechariah for being a little incredulous? Look at me! I'm ridiculous! Have you ever seen a woman my age in this condition? Now I can understand why Sarah laughed out loud when she heard that she would conceive! Well, that is all in the past now. Zechariah hasn't been able to say a word since the angel spoke to him, and that was six months ago!"

The younger woman felt her eyes misting with tears.

"Oh, no use for crying!" Elizabeth said, giving Mary's arm a vigorous pat. "Come inside then . . ."

"I'm not alone!" Mary burst out. "I'm not by myself anymore!"

"Oh, who ever is?" Elizabeth asked with a chuckle. "But sometimes the company isn't so good, that's all . . ."

Mary smiled. She liked this strange old cousin of her mother's. But she wasn't alone. Mary knew what she had meant. She wasn't alone in being pregnant—alone in experiencing this strange miracle. Here was a woman who believed her and didn't judge her. Elizabeth would answer questions for her, and show her some affection. A hug, perhaps. Some kind words.

"Nathan?" Mary said, glancing over her shoulder.

"Oh, don't worry about him," Elizabeth said. "Zechariah and your servant will get things organized the way men do."

As Mary looked back, she saw Nathan casting her an agonized expression of exasperation as Elizabeth's husband gestured broadly in an entirely incoherent manner.

"I don't understand," Nathan was saying to him. "The donkeys . . . water? What about the ground? I don't understand!"

Mary stifled a chuckle. Well, Nathan was an intelligent and patient man. Eventually the two would come to some sort of understanding—even if that was to stop trying to communicate altogether!

"Two miraculous pregnancies under one roof," Elizabeth kept repeating to herself with a low laugh. "Generations from now, girl, stories about us will be told! God is doing something that is bigger than anything we could ever understand."

"How is it that you believe me?"

"Timing, my girl. Tell me that you were a pregnant virgin a few months ago, and I would have tossed you off my property. But now . . . it's all in the timing, my girl. All in the timing."

The moon rose late that night, a shining crescent in the vast dark heavens, bathing the small villages, groves, and vineyards with its light. In the small house of an aged priest with his bizarrely pregnant and elderly wife a young woman, a visitor to that house, sat staring up at that crescent, rubbing her belly as she gazed at it, her lips moving in a silent prayer.

And across the rocky landscape . . . across the vineyards, and across the Roman roads that plowed across the landscape like ruthless arrows . . . across the meandering tracks left by shepherds and traveling caravans . . . that same milky crescent shone its light down on the city of Nazareth.

There Joseph lay in his bed, motionless, one arm flung above his head, his breathing deep and rumbling. It was the first deep sleep he had experienced since he had heard the heart wrenching news about Mary's pregnancy. Every other night he had lain awake, knowing that the next day he would be even more exhausted and more irritable. But he could not sleep. Even the cool night could not give him rest from his broken heart. And the more sleep he lost, the more hopeless his life seemed and the more lonely he felt.

Until tonight. The thought had suddenly come to him with the force of a hammer. Life was not happy. He was very much alone.

So this night Joseph had prayed. But it was not the same prayer he had been praying for the past few weeks. It was not the angry, confused prayer or even an indignant prayer of lost honor. No, it was a different prayer. It was a prayer of desperation—that of a man who had given up and did not know what that meant. The prayer of a man who saw the shattered pieces of his life strewn around him and did not know how to pick them up again, was not even sure if he actually wanted to try.

And this night, the night that he fully realized what his life was without Mary . . . without that ray of light to give him a reason to crawl from his sleeping mat every morning since the death of his wife . . .

This night, Joseph finally slept.

In his dreams he saw Mary as he had when he first realized that he had to marry her. He saw her laughter and her bright eyes as she bent over the water pot, dipping and pouring, dipping and pouring as she filled it at the well. And when he saw her walking away, he felt his heart break all over again.

There was the color blue . . . that he would always remember. The blue of the sky that seemed to melt into the blue of that beautiful fabric he had seen at the marketplace . . . the fabric that had cost so much, but would have been so lovely on Mary. And the color blue seemed to fill him up until he wanted to cry like a baby just to release it. But he could not cry.

Then the swirling images were suddenly blown apart by the most dazzling light he had ever seen or imagined. It obliterated everything—every thought and memory.

"Joseph," a voice said.

In his dream he tried to look around, but everywhere he turned was the same dazzling light.

"Joseph of Nazareth!" The voice was commanding.

"Yes, Lord!" Joseph called out. "Where are You?"

"He is with you," the voice answered. "He is with your betrothed. He is with the child inside of her . . . His own Son."

"God's son?" Joseph said, bewildered.

"The child that Mary carries is not a child of sin," the voice continued, softening now. "The child inside of her is the child of the Lord God. Mary has not sinned. She has been chosen to be the mother of the Messiah."

Joseph was speechless.

"You have also been chosen, Joseph," the voice went on. "Chosen to be the earthly father of the Messiah."

"Me . . ." was all that the man could say.

"You will name him Jesus. He will save the people from their sin."

There was silence—a rich, beautiful, restful silence that Joseph did not want to break. The first rest that he had felt in weeks, it seemed to seep into his very bones, revitalizing him from the inside out. It was as if for a moment Joseph could see the immensity of the sky—the stars that went into eternity, the swirls of lights and cloud amidst the blackness of nothing. For a moment Joseph felt the stretch of time and the enormity of what he had just experienced in that progression, and he was filled with a gratefulness so deep that it had no words.

"My son," the voice said finally as it faded away, "do not be afraid to take Mary home as your wife. Do not be afraid to love her."

Then the light vanished into a soft, thick blackness. And Joseph woke with a start.

James rubbed a finger under his nose and sniffed.

"My father is a man of honor," he said with a shake of his head. "Obviously the marriage has been called off. It is a shame that the girl couldn't have been more virtuous."

This realization made him feel aged. The near miss of shame, as if he'd felt the breeze of it as it swung past them . . . the proximity of another man's pain . . . it made him feel much older than his years. James suddenly felt experienced—wise.

"Are you sure?" his wife asked him gently. "I don't know why, but this seems more complicated somehow."

"Oh, Hannah," he said indulgently, "you don't understand these things. A man must do what he must do. Duty is sometimes painful, but how can a man face himself if he does not perform it? His duty is to his family, Hannah. Just as my duty is to you!"

She smiled and blushed prettily.

"And, of course, to my father," he added with a wave of his hand. "My father has been through enough, and I am tired of people talking about him. They jabber on as if there is nothing else of interest in this entire town! Well, I will stand for him."

"How?" Her eyes pinned on his face with an expression of impressed awe.

"That little fox," James said, standing taller and letting his disgust creep into his eyes. "Her family insisted that she was dutiful and virtuous! They swore to her character and piety! And they acted well, I'll give them that . . . Perhaps she had them duped too. Could it be that she was wicked to the very core of her being, and no one was the wiser? But I doubt that. I think someone knew her true character and chose not to speak. Someone decided to let my father make the biggest mistake of his life!"

James let out his breath in a huff and turned around in time to see his father standing in the doorway, the muscular bulk of him filling up the space. The older man stood motionless, his eyes fixed on his son with an expression of barely concealed anger. It was the look that used to stop the son in his tracks as a boy, and it still held the same power.

"James," his father said a low, controlled voice.

"Yes, Father?" The son's sense of self-importance suddenly rushed out of him in a flood. "I was just . . ." His voice trailed away.

"Never," Joseph said in that same low, controlled voice. "Never, son, speak of my betrothed in that way again. Not in my hearing. Not out of my hearing. Not beneath your breath in a locked room. Never speak of Mary like that again."

James stared after his father in shock as Joseph turned and walked away. Then he glanced back at his young wife who looked up at him in wide-eyed innocence.

"I think, husband," she said softly, "that it is very, very complicated."

CHAPTER 20

Now the Pharisees simplify their way of life and give in to no sort of softness; and they follow the guidance of what their doctrine has handed down and prescribes as good; and they earnestly strive to observe the commandments it dictates to them. They also show respect to the elders, nor are they so bold as to contradict them in any thing they have introduced . . . . Because of these doctrines they hold great influence among the populace, and all divine worship, prayers, and sacrifices are performed according to their direction.

—*Josephus*

Ebenezer crossed his arms over his chest and frowned thoughtfully as he watched his daughter bending over a bed of coals outside the house, baking flatbread. Naomi made a wonderful flatbread. It was always crispy on the outside, but fluffy and moist on the inside. And as she knelt before the coals, her veil modestly covering every stray hair as she worked, he felt a wave of sadness. She would have made a good wife to Ashi and would have eventually been happy with him. Oh, of course, she had not wanted to marry the young man . . . thinking she knew better . . . but once she realized what a good man her father had chosen, she would have been grateful. A rabbi for a husband was nothing to sniff at.

But there was no chance of that now. And he couldn't bring himself to tell her. He couldn't face her surprised delight at the failure of the betrothal. Ashi's father had visited Ebenezer early that morning and made his family's views known. They would not join themselves to a family through marriage that had a pregnant daughter before the marriage had been finalized. The union was now entirely undesirable—in fact, their family was now entirely undesirable.

Children were not as levelheaded in this generation. Unable to see the benefits of the ways of their fathers, they thought the old religion was tedious and merely followed the rules without seeing the heart behind them. Why couldn't they just open their eyes and recognize the wisdom of the old ways? Why always fight things? Why must every generation learn the hard way?

Not that it mattered now. It was not because of Naomi that the family had canceled the betrothal—it was because of Mary.

And at that thought Ebenezer felt very tired. He just wanted to sit and ignore the world, perhaps sleeping hour after hour, and forget about the burdens that he must shoulder for his family.

Naomi looked up at him with her sweet smile that reminded him of her as a little girl. He smiled back sadly.

She handed him some fresh flatbread, but when he dutifully took a bite and made the appropriate noises of enjoyment, it tasted like sand in his mouth. Swallowing with difficulty, he turned back into the house.

Ashi had dreamed of being a rabbi since he was old enough to attend school at the synagogue. Most communities had a synagogue. A true Jew must worship, whether the Jerusalem Temple was within walking distance or not. So a true Jew worshipped God where he was, and kept his mind in the Torah while his body must remain in earthly chores. Thus synagogues began to be a part of the Jewish tradition, and people continued to establish them in their communities. They sent their sons to the synagogues to study from the rabbis there. The rabbis chose only a select few boys to continue in their education. Those young people would one day be rabbis as well.

Always a bright boy, Ashi had learned the Torah quickly, and he had lapped up the legal opinions of respected rabbis much as a dog does water. Midrash had been no problem, either. Finding a rabbi willing to take him on as a student had not been difficult, and it was assumed that Ashi would become a rabbi. Everyone expected it. His parents, his family, his friends, his community. And when everyone expected something, you did not go against it.

Other boys had dreamed of becoming rabbis too. They had studied hard, burning precious oil late at night as they copied out passages from the Torah in the dust and memorizing, memorizing, memorizing . . . But it wasn't only memorization that guaranteed a boy success in the school. He also had to have a flexible, quick mind, able to grapple with the scriptures and discuss the Midrash intelligently. Such a person had to back up his ideas with solid proof from Scripture and argue his points persuasively. It was a long and arduous education. Without notice, boys sometimes got sent home, never to return. They had not lived up to the standard. The rabbi teaching them was not suitably impressed by their advancement. But Ashi had remained, continuing under the tutelage of his rabbi. And soon, he expected, he would be advised that he was now ready to be called Rabbi in full title.

It had been his dream since a boy. When he was small, he dreamed of the ornate prayer shawl that he would wear. He dreamed of the people following him . . . the respect his family would show him, listening to his opinions in grave silence and bragging about him to anyone who would listen. But now, as a grown man, his dream had altered. Now he dreamed of growing knowledge, of understanding prophecy, and of better grasping God. The Torah was His Word. The Mishna and Midrash were the collective studies of His students. And beyond it all was the Almighty God.

"Your mind does not seem to be in the Torah today, son," Samuel, his rabbi said. "What is bothering you?"

"I'm sorry, Rabbi," the younger man replied, shaking his head. "It is nothing of importance . . ."

"But it is of importance if it draws your attention away from your studies. It might help to have a spiritual perspective."

"My family would have me marry," Ashi said with a tight smile. "It is the same for all young men. I am not special in this."

"And you do not wish it?"

"I don't know. I have not met her. I know that my father will find a girl from a good family with a good reputation. He knows the importance of the right kind of wife for me."

"And what kind is that?"

"What kind?" Ashi looked surprised. "A proper wife for a rabbi! A godly woman. A modest woman."

"H'mm," came the low, rumbling reply.

"But I don't feel that the timing is right, Rabbi," Ashi continued shaking his head. "I am still a student. When I have been elevated to full rabbi, then it would be appropriate to marry."

"So that she will always know you as a rabbi, and never as a student?"

Ashi blushed. Was he so transparent? He was terrified to marry! The right girl would bring happiness and peace. The wrong girl would be an irritation for life. But if she knew him only as rabbi, perhaps a proper respect for him would curb her somewhat . . . if she were the wrong kind of girl . . .

"In the beginning God created the heavens and the earth," Samuel commented quietly. "And Adam was not happy until he saw Eve."

"Yes, I know. A woman completed him. And I will one day be completed as well. But perhaps it is too soon . . ."

The rabbi let out a short laugh.

"All young men feel this, son." The man put a reassuring hand on Ashi's shoulder. "But life does not slow for us just because we wish it. You must respect your father and do as he bids you. Honor your father and your mother."

His student nodded. The betrothal was being called off even as he sat in the synagogue with his rabbi. He knew this. The girl his father had chosen had come from a family that had recently lost honor. A rabbi could not have a sister-in-law who was a harlot! But this would not deter his father for long. Eventually he would find another girl, and as much as Ashi hated to admit it, he was afraid.

"We are but each a grain of sand on the seashore," Samuel continued. "God promised Abraham that his descendants would be like the sand of the sea. So much vaster tides and currents flow through the tiny lives that we live, that we cannot fully comprehend what it is that God is doing. But He is working, nevertheless, and specks of sand that we are, we are swirled around and gently laid down exactly where we are supposed to be."

"And one of those currents," Ashi said thoughtfully, "is the promised Messiah."

"The king to come!" his teacher replied, warmth filling his voice.

"But are we sure? We assume that the Messiah will be a king, a ruler."

"The prophets tell us, son. He will hold a scepter. Is that not clear enough?"

"But if the king comes in disguise . . . like the flames of a burning bush? What other things must we recognize if the Messiah does appear the way that we imagine? God is bigger than we can fathom. What if we are not understanding the prophecies properly?"

"Would God be unclear to us, knowing our limitations and fallibility?" Samuel questioned.

"What if we have simply looked at the prophecies in the same way for so long that we cannot see them any differently? What if tradition is blinding us?"

"The same old theme you refuse to give up." Samuel gave an irritated shake of his head. "You want to be a rabbi, but you don't talk like you want it."

"I do want it, Rabbi! I've always wanted it! But I also want to understand. I do not say that the Midrash is not correct. I only seek to look at all sides to be sure of our position. I want to understand all that I can!"

"Tradition, my son, is also powerful. Do you suggest that greater men than you are all wrong in their interpretations of Scripture? Are you somehow better than they are?"

"No." Ashi glanced down to hide the irritation in his eyes. "I am not better, Rabbi. I am young and foolish compared to those great men. But . . ."

"The position of rabbi is a great social responsibility. You must lead, son. And leaders do not concoct their own position. They rely on the solid bed of tradition and heritage to give them support. A leader is nothing without people to look up to him. And a leader is nothing if he does not bolster up our Jewish nation and pride."

"Is there not pride in truth?"

"The truth was given to us long ago," Samuel replied coolly. "There is pride in remembering it."

Ashi did not know why his stubborn streak kept getting the better of him. But he knew why he had not yet been elevated to rabbi. It was because he had these ideas that consumed him . . . ideas that he could not let go of . . . ideas that irritated the man who would suggest that he was ready to be a rabbi in his own right. Why could he not simply follow the well trod path before him? Why could he not allow the traditions and social structures to engulf him like that tide, let them buoy him up, whirl him about, and deposit him in a position of grandeur and respect? Was this not what he had always sought?

"You are intelligent, Ashi," Samuel continued quietly. "You are quick and brighter than any young man I have ever taught. You are promising and exceptional. But you lack discipline."

And as long as he "lacked discipline," Ashi knew that he would never be a rabbi. At most he would be an upstart . . . a radical . . . nothing permanent. Nothing memorable. Nothing to be proud of.

Yet, why could he not curb his stubborn curiosity?

As Ashi left the synagogue on his way back to his father's house, he dropped a few coins into the lap of a beggar. He did not notice that the coins were not mere pennies, but silver. The beggar scooped them up with excited, fumbling fingers, calling, "God bless you, sir!" in a high, nasally whine. Ashi looked at the pennies remaining in his purse, and realized his error. But he did not go back. No, the old man with the crutch deserved the money more than he did.

But then he heard a scuffle, and when he turned around, the old man who had received Ashi's accidentally large gift was being kicked and cursed by some beggars nearby. It broke Ashi's heart to see it. The man had curled his misshapen legs underneath him, and wrapped his tattered arms over his head, and his voice rang out in a piercing cry.

"Get off of him!" Ashi shouted, racing back to the scuffle. Grabbing the thin shoulder of a wiry beggar, he tossed him to the side. The attackers scurried back into the alleys.

"They took it!" the old man cried, tears brimming up in weak eyes. "They took it all!"

"Come on, then," Ashi said, pulling his arm, trying to bring the old man to his feet. "Come on. Today you will eat with my father."

"No!" the beggar gasped. "No! It is not my place, good sir. I am who I am. I belong where I belong. Do not do such a wicked thing!"

So Ashi left him, feeling embarrassed and frustrated.

"Another penny, good sir?" the beggar cried after him. "They took it all! Another penny?"

Frustrated and irritable, Ashi went home to his father's house, to hear the news that his betrothal was officially canceled. And he went home to the pride of his mother and the expectant gaze of his sisters and brothers. Because he would be a rabbi. They knew it—expected it. If he did not become a rabbi, what were they but a common family? Ashi brought them honor.

And what if he did not become a rabbi? What if he simply worked in his father's pottery shop?

Suddenly he laughed out loud, the sound ringing out through the streets and bouncing off the stone walls of houses. When people looked up at him, he laughed harder, tears streaming from his eyes. Ashi laughed because he was what he was, and he belonged where he belonged. He did not know his father's trade—only the Torah. He understood persuasive argument and rabbinical teaching.

And somehow, with the laughter, his spirits lifted, and he felt like that piece of sand, whirling dizzyingly through the currents of the sea . . . in the hands of God. What a ride! And where would he drop? Only God knew.

Behind him, in the street, a homeless beggar split the proceeds with those who had attacked him. It was not a successful ruse. If it had been, the sympathetic young scholar would have given him more to make up for what had been stolen. But he had not. The beggar had miscalculated.

Next time the ruse would work better, because they would hone it. They would become better at their act.

"God send the Messiah," someone muttered, avoiding the stinking beggars as he lifted his robes as if wading through filth.

But the beggars did not wish for the Messiah. They wished only for another penny. Because they could spend a coin, and the Messiah would never even glance at the likes of them.

"God send me a gold talent!" the beggar belted out, and the others laughed along with him.

CHAPTER 21

He who guards his mouth and his tongue keeps himself from calamity.
—Proverbs 21:23

Word had spread, as it does in all villages, at the speed of a runaway goat. Dashing from corner to corner, skittering in the pebbles and making off again . . . word spread from house to house, from woman to woman, from group to group in the market square. While news of a wedding was something to pass along, its cancellation was more exciting still! And the betrothal between Ebenezer's daughter Naomi and Ashi, the soon-to-be rabbi from the neighboring town, was off.

Lydia, being well informed at the best of times, was even more knowledgeable in the worst of times. She heard the news within exactly two hours of the actual visit between Ashi's father and her uncle Ebenezer. A woman passing on her way to the market had overheard one of Ebenezer's servants telling another. That woman told her friend whom she encountered on the road, and those two women stopped and told the next neighbor within sight. They told the news the way all godly women gossip . . .

"It is horrible news! I don't know how the poor family will endure this! What can we do to help them, I want to know? A good Jew always helps their neighbor."

"But should we help?" another asked thoughtfully. "There is sin in that family. The pregnant one, you know. Maybe it is best to distance ourselves."

"Let the family deal with the sin alone, you mean?"

"Well, yes, and protect ourselves. You know how people talk."

"Yes, it's disgraceful. Gossips are horrible creatures with nothing better to occupy themselves!"

"I couldn't agree more! Now, don't breathe a word of this, of course. I wasn't telling you to gossip, just to share the news of a neighbor's misfortune in case we might be able to help, which, of course, it is *obvious* that we cannot."

And so the word spread. Not surprisingly, it was Shali who told Lydia. Shali was Lydia's main source of village gossip, and say what you like about her, Shali's information was usually frighteningly accurate. She used little variation in the godly woman's gossip formula.

"Oh, Lydia! How horrible for your family! Naomi's wedding called off now, too! All because of your wicked cousin . . . Don't you worry, Lydia! No one will think you are like *them.* You are nothing like them, and even a blind old woman could see that!"

Lydia nervously pondered Shali's words as she walked through the village center. She had always imagined herself to be beautiful, and she had enjoyed the glances she received from both men and women alike. Most people resented beauty, she had realized quite early. Women especially. So when she received unfriendly looks, she simply walked with a little more determination. An older man might also resent her beauty, but there would be young sons who would beg their fathers for her!

Today, however, as she walked, she felt uncomfortable when people glanced in her direction. What were they thinking? Certainly, today, it was not about her appearance. She pulled her veil closer over her head and ducked beneath its comforting folds. For the first time, she wondered if she had always assumed incorrectly. Perhaps she had been naïve in believing her mother's declarations of her startling beauty . . . Could it be? The thought was too contrary to her entire upbringing to take seriously.

As Lydia passed a group of men, she recognized the rumble of her father's voice, and she slowed her steps. It was not often that a girl was able to overhear the business of men, and curiosity got the better of her. In truth, she always hoped that she would overhear the discussions surrounding her own betrothal.

"Disgraceful!" one man was exclaiming. "It's good of you to stand up for what is right, Reuben."

"We can always count on you for that," another said.

"I can see Ebenezer's position, of course," a third man added. "She is his daughter, after all. He loves her. It would break any father's heart . . ."

"One heart broken, but the sin expelled," she heard her father declare. "You may pity Ebenezer, as do I. He is my own brother, after all! But let's be objective, shall we? Who did not instill her with morals? Who did not supervise her properly to keep this from happening?

Whose home was not strong enough in our ways? We may pity him, but the man brought this on his own household. Can we let a woman go about like that and escape punishment? What will our daughters think? What will our own wives think?"

"True enough!" someone else stated. "I don't want the same thing happening to my girls because they see sinful women brazenly going about. It's disgusting, I say! My own girls wouldn't know the first thing about their wedding night, and they'll remain that way! Why? Because I watch them like a hawk, that's why!"

"Something must be done!" Reuben insisted. "And soon!"

"Agreed!" another man put in, old and grizzled. "I've got a young wife. What will happen if she thinks that these things are tolerated in Nazareth? What then? Are any of us safe?"

"We can't turn a blind eye!" Reuben pressed. "Don't consider only the consequences to our own families. Think about the religious ramifications! It is a heinous sin—punishable by death!"

"It is our obligation as righteous men," someone declared.

"It is!" Reuben said, his voice rising. "It is our duty! Now, who is with me?"

A hum of approval spread through the crowd.

"She's been sent away," Reuben said. "But when she comes back, the punishment should be no different! Time does not forgive sins—only God!"

And Lydia recognized that something much bigger than she was at work. She realized that her own wishes for marriage and matchmaking were not the focus of the village life. Forces much stronger than her own demands were whipping the village into a fury, and she saw the world in a different light than she had ever seen it before.

Lydia had always regarded her family and her future as the center of her world—her own discomfort or pleasure as paramount to anything else. But suddenly she perceived things in the stark light of reality. As her father riled up a group of men, she witnessed the anger simmering beneath the surface at the very thought of an impure woman. The culmination of those currents rose up like a wall of sand whipped up in a desert storm. She saw it as clear as day in her mind—death. It would mean the death of her cousin. The ultimate, cruel, unstoppable death of a girl her own age . . .

"Oh, God!" she gasped. And in that one short prayer was concentrated all of her fear, horror, and shock.

"Oh, God!"

But she was not blaspheming, no matter what a village woman might say who overheard her. No, Lydia was not blaspheming, because they say that God hears the meaning behind the words. He hears what we don't know how to articulate—even the words stuck in the throat of a spoiled, self-centered girl standing in the middle of her village and realizing that the world is ever so much bigger than she could possibly imagine.

Amichai stopped to shake a rock out of his sandal, but did not take his eyes off of the young man hurrying toward town ahead of him. Raold moved with the alacrity of a mountain sheep, his feet finding sure footing with each step as he bounded forward. Already feeling short of breath, Amichai shook his head at the energy of the young. Why did youth take energy and strength for granted? But then youth took life itself for granted. Every young man thought he was invincible. It was age that taught the lesson of mortality.

Not that Amichai was aged. No, he had learned life's lesson's quickly and efficiently. And yet even now, nearing the age of 30, he could feel his body changing again. His energy was waning. He had begun to gain some weight around his middle—something that he'd never done before.

This morning, while young Raold slept too late as usual, the others had taken it upon themselves to discuss the young man's future.

"Warnings do nothing!" one man said, spitting on the ground with a sour expression on his face. "Out of his head faster than water runs off a plate!"

"Punishment is a little more memorable!" another observed with a vicious wink.

"Punish him for the wrong thing, and he'll never turn around," Amichai said thoughtfully. "You can't just beat him for something he might have done. That works on children, not on grown men."

"He's acting like it!" another protested.

"No, let one of us follow him," Amichai suggested. "Find out what he's up to, and if he deserves punishment, at least he will be punished for the right offense!"

"Too much work," one shepherd muttered. "As if I have time to follow after some young buck with no brain in his head?"

"I have children of my own to raise!" another added. "And the sheep to watch . . . my wife's brother's children add to my responsibilities."

"If he were closer kin, I might not mind," someone commented.

"Let Amichai do it! He's the one with the great idea! I say, either Amichai follows him, or we all beat him! I vote for beating him!"

So Amichai had agreed. And now that he was chasing after the young man across the hill country like an outlaw, he couldn't remember why it had seemed such a good idea! Except that he couldn't abide injustice. It might make the men feel better to vent their frustration, but it would do nothing for Raold. He would not see the clan's perspective—as a hotheaded young man, he would see only his own.

As Raold approached the edge of Bethlehem, he angled off toward the main road leading into the town. Amichai paused, watching the young man as he sauntered into the traffic of clattering carts piled high with goods for market, and covered with tarps. Men moved in both directions, the travelers more noticeable because of the packs they carried on their backs and the walking sticks of knotted wood that they carried. Amichai allowed a little more distance between himself and his young kinsman, keeping his robe always within sight.

"Careful, shepherd!" someone barked, and Amichai stepped back to let a cart clatter past him. Raold rounded a corner, and Amichai picked up his pace. When he reached another corner, Amichai found himself breaking into a jog in order to keep up. One quick turn, and Raold would be all but lost in the confusion of the village.

As Amichai swung around the next corner, he took a precautionary step backward. Raold was slipping toward a stable for livestock, looking furtively first one way, then another. Amichai felt like cursing the stupidity of the young. Was he stealing goats now? If Raoul came out of that stable with anything living in tow, Amichai would beat him black and blue himself!

Then, a few minutes later, he saw the girl, and it all made sense. She was a pretty thing, Amichai would give him that much! Sturdy with pleasant features. Her eyes were alight with excitement. For a second her gaze shifted past Amichai without noticing him, then flicked back toward him. She pulled her veil closer over her head, turned back to call something into the house, and then made her way toward the stables.

The stables had been constructed inside a cave in the rocky hillside. The cave was high and rather shallow, like a scoop had been made out of the rock ages ago, leaving the stone surface pockmarked and dusty. Wooden poles and fences served to corral the animals, and a tarp had been hung to act as a makeshift barrier between the animals and the driving sand, or rain, depending on the season.

The young woman, for now that Amichai could see her better, he realized she was not quite the girl he thought she was, went into the stables and grabbed the rope halter of a nanny goat, obviously getting ready to milk her. Something deeper in the stables attracted her attention, and she let out a laugh, then looked anxiously behind her. Amichai saw a hand reach out and grab her arm, and she allowed herself to be tugged inside. The nanny goat wandered away, chewing lazily on its cud.

So that was what Raold was up to . . . Yes, the easiest answer was normally the right one. But to do the young man a last shred of justice, Amichai slowly approached the stables and stopped to listen by the tarp.

". . . I don't know . . ." Her voice.

"It can't be!" His voice. "You've got to be wrong!"

"I'm almost positive!" She was sounding less happy to see him now, and more distraught.

"Then you'll have to get married!"

"To who, Jeb?"

Jeb? Had Raold given the girl a false name as well? Amichai rolled his eyes in exasperation.

"Isn't your father arranging anything? I don't see what you want me to do!"

"Take me away with you!" There were tears in her voice now. "Take me somewhere else . . . To your family! You said that they are kind and wealthy . . . You said that they would think I was beautiful!"

Well, Raold had been right about the young woman being beautiful, but the claims to wealth were a stretch. What shepherd clan had any wealth to speak of? The only assets they had was in the form of livestock, and even the flocks were slim lately . . .

"They are kind." Raold answered. "But my father is a very picky man. He had recently decided upon my marriage to my close cousin. The flocks must be kept together. You know how these things are. I have no more choice than you do."

"But I'm pregnant!" she gasped. "I cannot change it! I cannot stop it!"

"You might be able to stop it. I heard there are herbs . . ."

"A crime against God!" she wailed, then seemed to become aware that her voice was traveling, and she lowered it to a shaky whisper. "What will I do?"

"My clan is moving on. Pasture has been exhausted here," Raold told her. "I'm sorry, but there is nothing I can do, my pet. Nothing! I will always think of you, though . . ."

Amichai darted out of sight as he heard some rustling, and the young woman made some more entreaties. Raold came out of the stables, his face ashen. And as he stepped back into the sunlight, Amichai caught him on the back of the head with a solid cuff that rattled the younger man's teeth.

"What the . . .!" Raold barked, turning to face Amichai with a look of rage that quickly evaporated into fear.

"Wealthy, are we?" Amichai demanded. "We might be if you did an ounce of work! All we do is pick up after you like you're an infant, and you run off to the city to dally about with the girls!"

The young woman's eyes were round with terror, and she looked caught between running away and flying at Amichai in defense of her lover. Amichai noticed her father coming in their direction, and he felt his heart sink with pity. The last thing he wanted to see today was a stoning!

"Good thing you called for my help, miss!" Amichai said loudly. "You never know why these stupid brutes like to sleep off their drunk in good people's stables! But you did well to ask for assistance!"

The young woman looked confused for a moment, then seemed to catch on.

"Thank you, sir!" she said, her voice quivering with obvious terror. "I didn't know what to do! But there is my father!"

"I'm sorry, sir," Amichai said to the innkeeper, who was now red-faced with fury. "My young kinsman can get into the drink. A stupid little goat he is, and trust me, we'll be taking care of him in the family way . . ."Amichai gave the portly man a meaningful nod and grabbed Raold by the back of his neck and steered him back toward the street.

"Someone check the livestock!" the portly innkeeper was shouting. "Wait! Don't let that rat get away! Wait!"

"Run!" Amichai hissed in Raold's ear, and he didn't need to repeat it. Raold was off like an arrow from a bow, and the two men raced toward the street and dodged between carts and villagers as they dashed out of the town. They were both breathing hard by the time they were convinced they had lost their pursuers.

"What were you thinking?" Amichai demanded. "The girl is pregnant now! And you were going to feed her some milksop of a story and never see her again? Nice way to uphold your father's name, boy!"

"Don't speak of my father!" Raold snapped.

"He might be dead," Amichai said in disgust, "but he would beat you within an inch of your life if he were still with us! Your father was 10 times the man you're turning into! I knew him! He was a good man. You . . . you're . . ."

Amichai bit back the words.

"So I learned my lesson," Raold said glumly. "I'll never go off to visit a girl again. You have my word."

"So does she, apparently," Amichai muttered.

"It's over now!" Raold shouted. "You heard me end it!"

"Over?" Amichai barked out a laugh. "She'll be stoned, O wise one! Pregnancy doesn't just go away because you don't want it! Her life will be over! And if she manages to lose the child before anyone finds out, she might die as a result anyhow!"

Raold gave Amichai a sideways look. The boy was worried, that was for sure. Amichai hoped he felt more than worry.

"Can we just forget it?" Raold asked quietly. "Just let it go? I'll make my father's kin proud. I swear it! I've learned!"

"It isn't my place to let anything go," the older shepherd replied coldly. "We'll let the clan decide what needs to be done."

"Who hasn't done it before?" Raold complained. "You did, I'll bet! Every man did it, and if the girl was willing, how can we be blamed?"

"I have never done it!" Amichai replied, and he saw a look cross the lad's face . . . one of amusement and mocking.

"You have a head like a rock!" Amichai snapped. "Idiot! You are an embarrassment to our entire clan! I'll be surprised if you can stand upright when your kinsmen are through with you! You think you are a man? You are like a little girl, all pathetic and sniveling!"

And as he said the words, Amichai heard his father's voice echoing in his head, using the same ones on him when he was a boy. And he physically flinched. Was he becoming his father now? Was he becoming everything that he had tried his entire life to avoid? Of course, he could say that Raold completely deserved every word that Amichai had spoken. Raold certainly wasn't blameless! But the nasty bark in his own voice had mirrored his father's voice a little too closely, and it sent chills down his spine.

"Look . . ."Amichai brought his voice under control. But the expression on the younger shepherd's face dripped with loathing, and the words caught in Amichai's throat.

As the sun was lowering on the horizon, he walked with his young kinsman back to the camp . . . back to the family . . . back to the sheep. He accompanied Raold back to everything he had been running from.

CHAPTER 22

Mariamne herself went to her death with a calm demeanor
and without a change in the color of her face,
and so, even in the last moments of her life,
made clear to those looking on the nobility of her lineage.

—*Josephus*

The story of Mariamne was widely known around the palace. It had been 25 years since her death, and a few servants still remembered her. Those not old enough to have seen her alive knew the stories better than they did their own family histories. Mariamne was more than a dead queen. People said that she managed to reach past the grave and torment her husband in revenge.

To those who knew her before her marriage she had been a beautiful young woman with a contagious laugh. She had eyes that sparkled and a sharp sense of humor. Many cousins had hoped for her hand in marriage. Countless friends of the family would have been delighted to take her into their home. But Herod was an up-and-coming politician, and his mother was not a Jew. And everyone knew that the Jewish identity passed down through the mother.

The marriage was entirely political. Herod's father was a political follower of Mariamne's grand-father, Hyrcanus. Hyrcanus wanted the throne of Judea for himself, and he hadn't seen Herod as a real threat. But Herod had seen marrying Hyrcanus' grand-daughter as an ingenious political move. Not only was she Jewish, which would perhaps divert the Jewish population's attention away from his technically Gentile status, but children with her would perpetuate Hyrcanus' line—a necessary political move after defeating Hyrcanus' nephew, who had made a claim to the throne.

Politics drove both Rome and Judea. The Roman authorities sought to install a Jewish king who would pander to their wishes. Mariamne, however, did not share either Herod's or her family's motivations. Strongly Jewish in the sense of nationality and allegiance, she hated the Romans and longed for the day that Jerusalem would be free of Gentile influence.

Mariamne loathed Herod and hated everything that he stood for—the Roman occupation, his ruthless pursuit of power, and his insincere adherence to the Jewish faith. Every time he touched her she felt his Gentile blood like a personal assault. And soon those eyes that used to sparkle with humor began to glint with rage and hatred. The voice that used to laugh so infectiously began to crackle with sarcasm.

As a very young bride Mariamne recoiled from her husband. She did not want his attention or affection. But whatever she did, it seemed, it only drew him more and more to her. He gazed at her across rooms. He stole moments alone with her, running his finger down her clenched and rigid arm. He attempted to recite poetry to her, idealizing her beauty. The more she hated him, the more he desired her.

"I hate you!" she would hiss when he came to her at night. "I hate you! Don't touch me, you snake! Get away from me!"

At one point she struck him with a small statue and knocked him senseless on her bedroom floor. But she knew what would happen to her if he were to be found dead. She would be quickly killed too. So she did not finish what she had started, but waited next to him until he moaned and regained consciousness. And all that long hour she had cried into her hands, sobbing out her frustration and misery.

Royal heirs were always necessary. Mariamne would reluctantly bear him five children, and each one she guarded as carefully as a lioness with her young. She did not trust or respect her husband. Nightly she prayed for his death at the hand of God.

Married at an early age, Mariamne rapidly had to learn the ways of the world. Her husband was demanding, cruel, and paranoid. Quickly she realized that he was not normal in any sense of the word. Power had corrupted him, and its pursuit had broken him. And still he longed for his wife like a young lad did for a village girl. She did not understand it. How could a man love a woman who hated him so completely?

Soëmus was a steward in the palace. A kind and gentle man, he worshipped sincerely, and hoped that somehow even in the palace of the king he might be able to do God's bidding. In Mariamne he encountered a woman in misery and a fellow believer close to the end of her endurance. Seeing in her someone with nowhere to turn, he did something he should not have—he allowed her to turn to him.

Herod had sent him to Mariamne to convince her of his undying love for her. But the king had also admitted to Soëmus that if he were to die, he wanted Mariamne to be killed as well so that he would not be separated from her even in death. It was not Soëmus's fault that the queen fell in love with him. But it shouldn't have surprised him. A desperate woman will cling to the one who offers her any kind of solace. Soon adoring Soëmus, she made excuses to call him to her and would exchange glances with him across the room.

Salome, Herod's sister, was not blind. She hated Mariamne. Mariamne was more beautiful than she was and drew men's hearts to her. Jealous and filled with hatred, one day she pointed out to her brother the attraction between Mariamne and Soëmus. Then she went further and suggested that Mariamne had been unfaithful to her husband. That was all it took.

In a fit of jealous rage Herod ordered the immediate public execution of Soëmus. Mariamne managed to convince her husband of her fidelity. He loved her so passionately that he wanted to believe her. However, plots were at work in the palace, and through stories about love potions that had never been mixed or even conceived, Herod's sister convinced her brother that Mariamne was trying to murder him so that she could rule Judea by herself and become queen of the Jews.

In a fury Herod had Mariamne and her mother set under guard while he went on a political journey. Upon his return, Mariamne stood trial for treason. The charges were serious and the evidence strong. Herod ordered her death.

Mariamne stood in the center of an arena. She knew that she would die. She glanced at the furious face of her husband, with his ashen complexion and quivering lips. Then she looked up to heaven and wondered if somehow she had gone terribly, terribly wrong.

God forgive me!

Her last conscious thought was not of the Jewish nation, her hope for its future, or of the man that she had fallen in love with and who had been killed for the same perceived crime. And it was definitely not of the husband she had loathed so intensely during her marriage.

Rather, her last thought was of her Maker, and her silent prayer that He would accept her.

CHAPTER 23

He who seeks good finds goodwill, but evil comes to him who searches for it.
—Proverbs 11:27

Lydia stopped in front of the solid door and licked her lips nervously. She wasn't supposed to be here. Slipping away during the hottest time of the day (when the household lay down to rest), she had tiptoed out of her home and hurried down the street, praying silently that she would attract no attention. And now she stood in front of Joseph's door, her stomach sinking in dread and her mouth dry as dust.

"The family is resting," the servant girl informed her.

"It is important that I speak with Joseph immediately!"

Hearing the spark of aloofness in her own voice inspired a bit of courage in Lydia. She sounded like her mother, and no one dared to cross her mother! The servant girl compressed her lips and gave the visitor an evaluating stare.

"If you do not fetch him for me," Lydia said in a low, even voice, "I will tell him the next time that I see him that his business is being affected by an overzealous servant. He will not be pleased, I assure you. Now do as I command."

The girl appeared to believe the threat, much to Lydia's relief, and a few moments later Joseph appeared at the door. His eyes were puffy from sleep, and he bit back a yawn as he looked at her. It took him a moment to realize who she was, and when he did, his eyes narrowed in annoyance.

"May I help you?" he asked, his voice carefully modulated to be polite, but possessing no warmth.

"Please, sir," Lydia burst out. "Please, I just need to speak with you! Forgive my mother. She means well! If she offended you, please . . ."

"Do not worry about that," Joseph said, his voice softening. "Your mother does the best she can for her children. You can go home and rest your mind on that account."

"That is not why I came." She looked down and to the side, giving him a full view of her long lashes. As long as she was here, he might as well see her at her best!

"Miss, it is not proper for you to be here." A hint of warning tinged his tone.

"I know." Abandoning her attempts at charm, she continued, "My father will beat me if he discovers it. I must ask you to promise to keep this a secret!"

"I cannot promise anything. You are standing in the middle of the street."

Lydia glanced nervously over her shoulder.

"Sir," she said quietly. "I don't come for myself, whatever you may think! I come for Mary."

Suddenly snapping to attention, he stepped back.

"Thank God! Come inside. Tita, call your mistress!" he said over his shoulder.

Yes, a woman would need to be present to keep propriety. But Hannah, Joseph's daughter-in-law, was a good woman, and Lydia had never known her to be a gossip. However, she did not put much confidence in the discretion of anyone. People talked, and anyone who assumed otherwise was a fool.

"Did Mary send a message?" Joseph asked once they were all settled in the courtyard. "Where is she?"

"Her father sent her away. No one but he knows were she is. And he will not say."

"But she contacted you? Does she need me?"

"No, she has not contacted me," Lydia replied, her stomach writhing in nervousness.

"You said this had to do with my betrothed. What is it?"

"I overheard something I should not have." She swallowed quickly. His expression turned tired.

"No, it is not idle gossip, sir! I promise. I overheard my father, our kinsmen, and some men of the village talking."

"You should not be listening to the talk of men."

"No, I should not," she admitted readily. "I know it. But I did overhear, and they said that they are planning to stone Mary upon her return."

His eyes glittering now with a frightening intensity, Joseph said nothing for a moment.

"Would you lie to me?"

Lydia felt her face grow hot with indignation. What did he think of her? That she would lie to him in order to ingratiate herself to him? All she would gain would be a beating from her father and to press her cousin into his arms! Here she was, risking her own safety to tell him what she knew, and he distrusted her intentions.

"No, sir," she said primly, rising to her feet. "I would not lie to you."

As Lydia went to the door, eager to get out . . . eager to get away from the man that she wished she could marry, but who adored her cousin . . . eager to put all of this behind her, she heard Joseph's gentle voice.

"Lydia?"

She turned, allowing her eyes to rest on his dark ones for just a moment before she dropped her gaze to the floor.

"Thank you."

To be thanked meant that the relationship was over. There would be no favors in return for her aid of his betrothed. His thanks would be all that she would receive from him, and his thanks were a very obvious goodbye.

She dipped her head in acknowledgment and fled.

Hannah watched as the girl dashed away from the house. If others discovered her visit, they would beat Lydia within an inch of her life. And Lydia's father was not a man to ease up on his punishments. He was a harsh man—harsh enough to stone his own niece. In addition, he was a righteous man who did what he knew he must. And that was a dangerous combination.

While Hannah was newly married, she was not a foolish girl. Quiet and observant, she recognized that Lydia longed for her father-in-law. She also knew that her father-in-law would abide no flirtation from her. Joseph was a kind man, but he never toyed with morality.

"Father?"

Joseph turned, and when he did, she saw the anxiety in his eyes.

"They will stone her over my dead body!" he exclaimed. "No one touches my betrothed, I assure you that much!"

Nodding, Hannah believed him. She'd never seen a man truly love a woman before. Her parents were fond of each other. Her own husband admired and respected her. But she had never seen this—a man ready to lay down his life to defend the woman who had been unfaithful to him. Although strange and frightening, it was yet something to be envied. Whether Mary was deserving of his devotion or not, she certainly had it.

Would James defend Hannah with his life? Would he live in misery if he had to face the rest of his days without her? She wondered, not sure that she wanted to know. Hannah suspected that her husband was like most men who would mourn the passing of his wife and move on to marry another in a short time. If Mary died, would Joseph ever marry again? She doubted it.

The servant girl was whispering avidly to another servant, and she hushed when Hannah approached, looking up with exaggerated innocence.

"What are you talking about?"

"Nothing, Mistress," the girl said submissively.

"If word gets out about what Lydia said here today, I will not beat you myself."

The girl watched her warily.

"Instead I will ensure that you are given as a gift to Lydia's father's household, and I will let her deal with you herself," Hannah finished.

The girl's eyes widened, and she blanched.

"She risked her safety to save her cousin. I will not allow you to endanger her just to provide yourself with gossip!"

Who was to say what Lydia deserved? Or Mary, for that matter? But punishment and mercy belonged to God, and not in the hands of gossiping servants.

Simak let go of the scroll in front of him and let it curl back into a roll on the broad wooden table. The table legs were intricately carved with elephants and flowers, and the surface had been rubbed with fat until it shone. The scroll that Simak held in his soft, slender hands was of the lesser legal quality—barely adequate for scratching out the ciphers—but it held information that was priceless to the two men before him. They stood awkwardly, refusing to look up, but hunched as if trying to sense his reaction through their bodies.

"This deed shows that the well belonged originally to Deepak's great-grandfather," Simak said. "But how do you know that Deepak's great-grandfather, or his grandfather, for that matter, did not strike a verbal agreement with the neighboring family?"

"Your Majesty, he did not," the first man said.

"He did!" the other declared. "In fact, my family tells the story often! We have the right to the use of that well!"

"You trespass!"

"You pig!"

Simak slapped his hand on the table, the sound echoing through the chamber, and the men fell silent, glancing furtively at his face, then dropping their gaze back to the floor.

"What has happened between your houses that you cannot share something as simple as a water source?" Simak sighed and looked back down at the scroll before him. "I must make my judgment in favor of Deepak, because he has shown proof of ownership. However, if Abdul can bring three witnesses that there was a verbal pledge between the two families, I will reconsider my decision. I will look to the stars tonight and seek the truth."

Simak watched as the two men left. Even with a decision given to them from their own ruler, they were still rigid and furious with each other. Somehow he doubted that their antagonism had anything to do with their own generation. The quarrel had most likely started with their fathers or grandfathers. Perhaps the quarrel had always been about the well. Or perhaps it was because of something as simple as declining an invitation to a feast. There was no way to know anymore—but the remnants of that original insult had festered and boiled until it involved two entire families and would not be resolved through the ownership of a well.

His fellow Magi taught that the stars gave answers. The constellations, if properly read, could point to lies and ill omens. Yet Simak had noticed more often than not that he and his fellow Magi did not have the knowledge to truly read the stars. Yes, they could try. And the population at large would believe in their ability to milk the future out of the night sky, but too often Simak relied on superstitions to aid him in his decisions. The men who had come to him believed that he could see a lie in the stars, so if a man were guilty, he would act so and lose all his confidence. He would fumble, and his story would become convoluted. Was that really an answer from the stars? Did the gods always communicate? Or did they simply reveal their wishes when it was their desire to do so?

"Ahura Mazda, great Creator, the Uncreated . . . God of gods, Beginner of all life . . ."

The prayer was a formal one made during the season of sacrifice, but it did not encompass the questions now filling him.

"I am a mere slave," he whispered. "I feel the emptiness inside of me. I have power, wealth, position, and proper birth. I am respected, even revered. I am a ruler. Yet I feel that while I have amassed treasure and cultivated the esteem of my people, I have missed the greatest treasure of all . . . And I do not know what it is . . ."

The silent, cool chamber did not answer him.

"You speak through the stars," he said quietly. "You show Yourself through Your creation. We see the tension between good and chaos. We try to understand, but there is too much to comprehend.

"Only You, O great Ahura Mazda . . . only You give wisdom. Only You show us how to read the unreadable cosmos. Show me . . . show me . . ."

And Simak's eyes fell on the Jewish scroll he had put aside. Isaiah, the writer's name was. A Jew. An outsider. An other.

"Lift up your eyes and look to the heavens:
Who created all these?
He who brings out the starry host one by one, and call them each by name."

Simak began to think some things that his people could consider heretical. But scholarship, he argued, must not begin and end within one's own borders. True wisdom was not anchored to the earth, but found in the stars. And the night sky covered more than the plains of Persia . . .

Chapter 24

Do not withhold discipline from a child; if you punish him with the rod, he will not die. Punish him with the rod and save his soul from death.

—Proverbs 23:13, 14

As Amichai and Raold approached the camp, Amichai's stomach began to rumble at the smell of food. The camp was busy. It was evening, and the women were cooking and chatting together, or else shooing away children who were trying to snatch food before it was time. People did not chastise only their own children. They were all kin and all part of the same community. The children belonged to the camp, and a misbehaving boy wouldn't be able to take another step without someone reaching out to remind him of proper behavior. Some men stood guard over the camp, watching for predators and keeping their slings ready. When they saw Amichai and Raold approaching, they called something behind them, and the entire mood of the camp shifted noticeably. The voices lowered, and as Amichai approached with his young charge, he could feel the tension.

"Tsk!" an old woman muttered as they entered camp. She was Raold's great-aunt, but at the moment she would not have admitted to such a close relationship. Instead, she pulled some boys aside and shooed them in another direction.

"Better to face the clan now than wait till morning," Amichai said.

Raold was silent and looked unconvinced. The men were already migrating toward the center of the camp with its meeting circle. The women moved discreetly away to let the men take care of business. And Raold was getting more skittish by the minute, like a yearling feeling trapped.

The young man had grown up with his kinspeople. He knew what it was like to be punished by an uncle or cousin for poor behavior. But this time he would be facing several adult kinsmen, and this involved more than a slap upside the head for rudeness or sneaking away at night.

"He came of his own accord," Amichai said simply, nudging the young man forward. The men grunted their replies and refused to look directly at Raold. There were five kinsmen in total. The eldest, and therefore the most senior in respect and authority, was Daniel. A big man with a bushy beard streaked with gray, he had a booming voice and strong, knotted hands that cracked when he clenched them into fists. The men avoided looking at the miscreant and instead directed their questions to Amichai.

"And what was he up to?" Daniel questioned.

Amichai looked at Raold, waiting to see if he'd stand and speak for himself, but the lad was digging his toe into the rocky soil and glaring at the ground accusingly.

"Visiting a girl," Amichai said. "A pretty little thing, at that!"

"I don't care if she was the queen of Sheba!" one of the men retorted. "He was sloughing off work that was his responsibility. And defiling himself with a woman!"

"What's her name, boy?" Amichai asked.

Raold was silent.

"I hope she was worth the punishment you'll be getting!" another put in. "You're a man now. And you go off embarrassing your kin?"

"He is a man," Amichai added. "I say he's almost old enough to be married."

"Not to one of my girls!" one elder laughed. "If he wanted a good marriage, he should have been acting that way!"

"The situation is more complicated than we'd anticipated," Amichai explained slowly.

All eyes turned to him, flickered toward Raold with a look of shocked silence, then returned to Amichai.

"Go on," Daniel urged.

"Would you like to tell them?" Amichai asked Raold. It might be better coming from him—if he'd take some responsibility for his actions. Otherwise, the elders would feel the need to instill an understanding of his responsibility into him . . . and that would not be pleasant!

When Raold did not answer, Amichai sighed. "The girl is pregnant."

Raold still stared at the ground, and Amichai noticed his cheek twitching nervously. The young man clenched his fists at his sides, and his eyes had misted over. For the first time Amichai realized how surprised Raold must have been to find out that the girl was carrying his child. Perhaps the reality of it was just beginning to settle in. He would be a father. There would be a little boy or girl who would look like him, walk like him, have his same tastes . . . his.

"How did you know?" Daniel asked, crossing his thick arms over his barrel chest and pursing his lips.

"She was telling Raold when I approached. I overheard."

"Did you believe her?" someone else questioned.

"I did," Amichai told him. "The girl had had too much desperation in her voice for her to be lying. And what would she gain? She had only been asking to be taken away from her home (in which everyone would know), and where she could be stoned." An unforced girl wanted a legitimate marriage, of course. Anything else was unthinkable and would exclude her from society.

"Well," Daniel said, his brows furrowed and his eyes glaring fire. He shook his head slowly and eyed Raold through narrowed eyes.

"I broke it off!" Raold finally said defensively. "I said I'd never see her again!"

"And that will fix this?" the elder roared. "That will cancel her pregnancy? How stupid are you, boy? And what happens to her? Or do you care?"

Confusion filling his face, Raold muttered something incoherent.

"We'll discuss this without the boy," Daniel announced abruptly. He flicked his fingers in Raold's direction. It took the young man a moment or two to realize that they had dismissed him. Looking up furtively, he glanced around with anxious darting eyes before slinking away.

"Now," Daniel said, shaking his head and putting a hand over his eyes, "what do we do with him?"

Raold sat a short distance away from the men, sitting in the shade of a tent and watching them nervously. Part of him wanted to run away, but he was smarter than that. The punishment would only be heavier if they had to search for him. What would they do? Would it be a thrashing? Would he have to work longer hours until he'd proven himself? Would he be given the most menial jobs as penance to the clan? Perhaps a combination of all? Having never known anyone caught at something as wicked as what he had been doing, he didn't know what would happen to him. She wasn't the daughter of a kinsman, so they could not force him to marry her . . . or could they? He wasn't sure.

They'll beat me . . .

The thought of a lashing with a leather whip sent shudders through him. He wouldn't be able to sit or lie down for days! Once he'd seen his cousin whipped for stealing a sheep from his father and selling it in a town. Even now he could still remember the whistle as the leather thong lashed through the air, and his cousin's quick intake of breath when it connected with his back.

He was wicked . . . no good, and no one expected anything better out of him. But now he'd gone too far. For a time he'd thought that it was fun. Orli had seemed willing enough, after he convinced her, of course. After he visited her, he'd feel miserable and guilty, but eventually he forgot the sense of guilt and went to her again, telling her that she was beautiful and that he loved her. Raold had claimed that his family was wealthy and that they traded with caravans for treasures that she could only imagine. At the time it had been fun as he composed new stories in his head as he made his way to the stables where he would meet her. And she'd believed him. That had surprised him. In fact, at first he had expected that she would laugh at him and send him home burning with embarrassment. Instead, she had looked at him with awe in her eyes and believed every word.

And what was he supposed to do then? He couldn't go back and tell her he'd lied. So he told her more stories . . . making up an ancestry filled with intrigue and drama. Thus he had regaled her about maidens from the east who had been sold to his grandfather and had borne him children with strange talents. About a father who was wise and caring and a mother who was more beautiful than any of the other women in the clan. He said that Orli resembled his mother.

And then, when she'd finally done what he'd wanted her to do, he couldn't help wondering why he'd wanted it so much. It had been rushed and awkward. And she no longer seemed quite so alluring or so exciting. Breaking it off would be a relief!

In fact, he had been planning on terminating the relationship as he made his way to see her. But he wanted to do what they had been doing just once more. Then he'd walk away, promising not to return and never intending to. But she'd sprung her news on him—saying that she was pregnant! And he couldn't get away fast enough. She just told him and ruined it all.

Stupid girl. He should have not gone back. That way he never would have known, and she wouldn't have grabbed at his robes in that clinging way she had about her. And he wouldn't have to remember her desperate, gasping voice telling him about it . . .

"Raold."

It was Amichai. Amichai, who was always trying to be nice. Pathetic Amichai was too old to be his friend, but wasn't married, either. Amichai with his silly expression and shy way of looking at people. Amichai, who was always trying to do Raold some sort of favor by standing up for him in front of the men.

His heart hammering in his chest, Raold looked up, then shoved himself to his feet, brushing off his clothes. He gave Amichai a small smile.

"A decision has been made," the older shepherd announced. "Come on, then. You'd better hear it out."

Cautiously Raold glanced around. If there was a whip in sight, he wasn't going! But there didn't seem to be one, and the men had stood in the same circle discussing while he'd watched them, so no one had gone off to get any. Slowly he followed Amichai back to the men, afraid to look at them, but too wise not to lest he miss the signs of a cuff coming to his head. If you were prepared, it didn't have to rattle your teeth.

"Anything to say for yourself?" Daniel demanded, large and menacing.

Swallowing hard, Raold shook his head. No need to plead now. They knew the worst. Let them say how many lashes and have it over with!

"Fine. At least you're wise enough not to defend yourself."

Raold felt hope begin to rise in his heart. Maybe it wouldn't be so bad after all . . . Besides, they'd probably done it when they were young. He wasn't the only one! The other boys talked about it. Some told stories that would curl your toes! Raold hadn't managed to do any of the things the other boys bragged about.

"We've discussed it," Daniel continued. "It's too bad you don't have a father to speak for you. Amichai took your side, though. There will be no beating."

When Raold flashed a glance in Amichai's direction, he saw the man staring uncomfortably at the ground. Good old Amichai! He'd come through after all!

"There is the question of the girl, however," the elder said. "For all you know, she might get stoned. She should be spared if at all possible. And if a marriage cannot be suitably arranged, her family might justifiably desire vengeance against you. You are not too young to marry, and it might just do you some good. There'd be no time for idleness with a family to feed, that's for sure."

An expression of horror filled Raold's face.

"Yes, yes," Daniel said with a bellowing laugh. "So you understand, do you? May I be the first to congratulate you, boy! We are going to arrange your marriage!"

Frantically Raold looked from one man to another. Amichai still studied the ground.

"Well," Daniel corrected himself, "not so much we as Amichai. I would rather have let her father beat you."

Orli stood motionless, staring after the young shepherd who had said that he loved her. He had dashed out into the street, followed by his older kinsman, and they had vanished into the milling crowd of the Bethlehem markets. Her father, at first, was more concerned with getting his hands on the boy, but after it became clear that the shepherds would not be so easily caught, he turned his attention to his daughter.

"What were you doing?" he demanded.

"Going for milk!" she said, hanging her head.

"And what were men doing in the stables?"

"Like the man said," she replied, keeping her voice quiet and respectful. "The boy was sleeping there. I came upon him and screamed. The other man came to my rescue."

"I heard no scream."

"I was too afraid to make much noise," she whispered. "But luckily the boy's kin was nearby."

The girl didn't dare look up. And as she felt her father's gaze boring into her, she felt terror because of the beating that she knew he would gladly give, and also because of her own conscience. She was lying—and pregnant.

"You don't suppose you will see that man again, do you?" he asked slyly. "Because if I should see him, I would kill him for trespassing on my property." He watched her closely, eyes narrowed.

"No, I don't think I'll see him again," she replied without even a quiver in her voice. The shepherd would not come back. Obviously he hadn't even told her his real name, and had promised things that he would never give her. No, he would not return.

Orli had recognized the caged look that came into his eyes when she had implored him to take her away. She knew what it meant—that she was by herself in her trouble. Her father and mother had sheltered and taken care of her for her entire life. Now the very people who had protected and provided for her would turn against her. Never before had she felt more alone.

"Where are you going?" her father shouted, and she turned, realizing that she had been walking away.

"I'm going to milk the goat. It can't be neglected."

Her father let out a grunt and didn't argue. She walked toward the stable—the cave behind their enclosed compound where the nanny always preferred to be. Forced into the enclosure, she would panic and stop producing milk. She was an odd goat, but her milk was sweet. Orli walked into the cave, feeling the cool darkness close around her. Sinking to the ground behind the hung tarp, she covered her face in her hands.

"O God," she breathed. "I'm so wicked . . . so very, very wicked . . ."

She did not know what to do. Should she compound her guilt and try to kill the child inside of her? Should she run away? But what chance did she have by herself in another city? Prostitution would be worse still. But her father might have her stoned! Unless she lied and claimed to have been raped . . . No, that would be another lie. Another sin to pile on top of the mountain of them that she had already accumulated.

"I am wicked," she repeated.

And she did not know what to do.

Chapter 25

There is no heart more whole than a broken heart.

—*Ancient Jewish saying*

Ebenezer sat down in the courtyard of his home, crossing his legs and watching his visitor nervously. Joseph had come with a solemn expression on his face, and Ebenezer feared the worst with this visit. The betrothal would be canceled. A divorce would be given to his daughter, and she would be free to marry. Free to marry? It was a joke, really, because who would want a divorced woman with an illegitimate child? She would never be free again.

Esther had spread out blankets for them to sit on, placing a tray of dates and nuts between the two men. A deep sadness pressed on Ebenezer's heart, and he felt his chest constrict and a strange flutter go through it. Somehow he forced himself to look the younger man in the eyes, and gave what he hoped was an encouraging smile. It was best to get this over with. Why sit around pretending to speak of other things?

The sun was getting lower in the sky, and its golden light spilled onto the sealed jars of wine and vinegar that lined the opposite wall, lengthening the shadow of the wall that the men sat in.

"God be with you," Ebenezer began. "I am glad to have you in my home."

His visitor nodded.

"This is a difficult time, Father," Joseph said slowly, and Ebenezer felt another wave of sadness at that familiar address. "It is a complicated time."

"I cannot pretend that it is not," Ebenezer agreed reluctantly. "I wish I could say something to alter your view, but I cannot in truthfulness . . . No, I cannot."

"Your brother would have her stoned," Joseph said bluntly.

"I know." The older man rubbed his chest, trying to relieve the tightness. "He warned me of it in his own way. It is why I sent her away."

"You must tell me where she is," Joseph declared fervently. "You must tell me!"

"No." Ebenezer shook his head. "Never."

"Please, Father. I want to save her. How can I protect her if I don't know where she is?"

"She is safe. No one but me knows where she is, my son. And it will remain that way as long as it needs to."

"Her pregnancy reflects on the family only if she is unmarried. A betrothed woman who becomes pregnant can be endured as long as she marries her betrothed. When we are married, her pregnancy does not reflect on your brother in the least, but on myself."

Ebenezer's eyes sharpened, and he stared at the younger man across from him in slight confusion. What was Joseph saying? That he still wanted to marry her?

"You are not calling off the betrothal? Is this what you are saying?"

"I do not know how to explain it to you, but your daughter is not the wicked girl you must think she is. I was going to divorce her quietly, but then I had a dream from God."

"A dream?"

"An angel of the Lord told me that the child conceived in Mary is not from man, but from God Himself. The child will be the Messiah. No, Father, I will not put her aside. I will marry her as Yahweh instructed me to do."

It took a moment or two for what Joseph had said to sink into Ebenezer's mind, and when it did, all the tightness and weight lifted from his chest, and he laughed out loud. Looking at Joseph more closely, just to be sure of what he had heard, Ebenezer laughed again.

"My son!" he roared. "My son!"

Joseph laughed, at first uncomfortably, and then he joined in the happiness of the moment. Ebenezer pushed himself with a wheezing grunt to his feet in order to hug Joseph and kiss his cheeks.

"Did you say that the child is of God?" Ebenezer asked, releasing his son-in-law and shaking his head. "The child is really of God?"

"It is. I am convinced of it. Mary is still a virgin, just as she has claimed all along. She hasn't lied."

Again Ebenezer shook his head and felt hot tears welling up in his eyes. "She is pure after all," he murmured. "And I didn't believe her."

"Neither did I," Joseph said, squeezing the old man's arm. "But now we know, Father. And we can do right by her. I'll protect her, sir.

You can be assured of that. I'll love her every day of my life, and I'll be good to her. I swear it."

Ebenezer nodded, a smile breaking over his face once more. Again he put his arms around Joseph in a fierce hug and belted out another laugh.

"Esther!" he roared. "Esther! Come celebrate!"

A son! He had another son. A good son. A strong son. A son who would love his little Mary and protect her . . .

"God of mercy and love," Ebenezer said, seizing Joseph's face between his hands and patting his bearded cheeks in happiness. "You have blessed us today with a son, and the return of a daughter! Praise God!"

More than anything, Ebenezer longed to bring his little girl home.

Naomi could hear the excited chatter of her parents in the courtyard, and she knew what had happened. Somehow Mary's betrothed had not canceled the wedding. Somehow it was all patched up again, like a mud-and-lime roof after a particularly bad storm.

"Where are you going?" Adam asked.

"I'm going to get water."

"No, you aren't. Where is the water jar?"

"Never mind, Adam," she said irritably. "Never mind! Go see Father and Mother in the courtyard. They are celebrating, and you are missing out."

This attention successfully diverted, Adam ran through the house and into the courtyard with Japheth at his heels. Naomi looked back at them for only a moment, then pulled her veil over her head and rushed out the door.

Free! Now she did not have to marry Ashi after all. His family didn't want her, and she would not be taken away one night by a bridegroom that she had never met. She would not be installed in the home of strangers who would be watching her for her homemaking skills and whispering about her behind her back. And perhaps . . . perhaps, if God would grant her one wish, she could have Thaddaeus—the only man she could imagine being wife to. The only one she had ever wanted to be wife to!

Naomi had to stop herself from skipping in happiness down the road. No, now was not a time to draw attention to herself. The villagers glanced up at her with uncertainty as she passed. Her family was not yet shamed, but people were only waiting for the sign that Ebenezer and his house were outsiders. They were only waiting . . .

As she passed some serving girls Naomi looked away. She did not care what the girls thought of her. Not today. Nor did she care what anyone thought of her, as long as she had a chance to marry Thaddaeus!

Some clucked tongues and muttered comments greeted her, but she did not notice. When she turned up the path that led to the blacksmith's shop she felt as if her feet were floating on air. But as she approached, she felt the weight returning to her feet, and the elation ebbing out of her heart. Even before she approached closely enough to hear anything, she knew something was wrong.

Thaddaeus's father stood with his back to Naomi, but his happy voice was carrying. His son stood awkwardly, nodding his acceptance of the father's congratulations.

"She is a good girl, and her parents are well positioned. We arranged it all this morning. You will be very happy! I am so proud! We have agreed that the wedding should be sooner rather than later. We'll arrange it all, son. No need to worry!"

And Naomi realized from the expression on Thaddaeus's face that the man was not speaking about her. The son's eyes were clouded with suppressed emotions, and his gaze locked on hers for one anguished moment.

His father turned then and looked at her questioningly. "What can I do for you, miss?"

"I have come for a new pot, sir," she said, looking down uncomfortably.

"My son can help you with that. I have things to take care of inside. Thaddaeus, see to it!"

Naomi watched Thaddaeus silently as his father disappeared. The son forced a twisted smile to his lips. She didn't recognize him like this. He seemed a stranger.

"You will be married!" she said, her voice almost a wail.

"So will you," he responded woodenly.

"Not anymore. They don't want me! I'm free again!"

He was silent.

"Thaddaeus?"

"You said that we should do as our families wish," he finally replied. "You said we should accept the will of our fathers."

And what could she say? They had no choice but to accept their families' decisions. They had no choice at all. She felt the weight of her life, the weight of her village, the weight of the entire world pressing down on her, and all she could do was look at him.

Her beautiful Thaddaeus with the dreams of opening a shop in Jerusalem. Thaddaeus who had told her stories of faraway cities and different people . . . the man who had told her he loved her and held her hand behind the synagogue. The man who had exchanged glances with her in the market and talked to her in stolen moments . . . the man she loved.

"But I love you, Thaddaeus," she said, and she tasted tears on her lips without being aware that she was crying.

He didn't answer her. Instead he held out a pot. She looked at it in confusion.

"Your pot," he said. "You came for a pot."

Automatically taking it from his hands, she stared at it in misery. Her dreams and hopes were over. He would marry another.

And she would not.

Flinging the pot back at him, she turned and ran back down the path, her sobs wracking her body and her tears blinding her eyes. She heard the hollow clatter of the copper pot ringing against the rocky ground, and she raced blindly on.

And Thaddaeus stood miserably, looking at the copper pot at his feet, the polished metal reflecting an upside-down image of himself back at him.

"Thaddaeus!" his father called. "Come inside! We have much to discuss!"

What could he do but obey?

CHAPTER 26

I will lead the blind along ways they have not known,
along unfamiliar paths I will guide them.

—*Isaiah 42:16*

"Mariamne!"

The voice echoed through the halls, and the servants glanced at each other warily.

"Mariamne!"

The tone in the palace changed during the king's dark moods. It was as if heavy clouds settled down over the palace, seeping their cold fingers into every crevice and under ever tunic. Servants looked over their shoulders and scurried a little faster. Nobles tightened their robes a little closer. Herod's wives disappeared into the furthest parts of the palace.

In the king's chamber, amid a sea of purple silk and golden embroidery sparkling in the morning light, Herod sat on his bed and called out the name of his dead wife.

As he looked around, he frowned to himself. Where was she? Normally she came when he called. He knew, in a faraway part of his mind, that she was dead, but when he wished for her enough, reality seemed to evaporate, and he would be back in those happy days of early marriage. It was that happy state of mind that he clawed toward in the inner recesses of his tortured mind.

"Why do you call for Mariamne?"

Herod jumped, grabbing for a dagger under his pillow, and finding none there. He looked at the owner of the voice and saw a man standing casually beside his water basin. After dipping his hand in the water and letting it drip back into the golden bowl, he then looked up at Herod with an expression of curiosity on his smooth, ageless face.

"Who are you?" Herod choked. "How did you get inside? Guards!"

"They will not hear you," the man said simply.

"Guards!" the king bellowed, jerking back his sheets, still searching madly for the dagger he always slept with.

"You won't find that, either. We will talk, you and I."

"Get out! I am king! I will have your head for this blasphemy!"

Silently the man watched him with that same curious expression. Dread filled Herod's heart, and his stomach suddenly cramped to the point that he almost vomited where he sat. He would die, he thought. This man was an assassin sent by one of his children to kill him . . . The guards had been bought off . . . And he would be gutted like a fish right here in his chamber. The king stared in horror at the man before him.

"She is dead, you know."

Herod blinked, swallowing hard.

"Mariamne," the man qualified. "The wife you called for earlier. She is dead. You had her murdered for a crime that she did not commit."

"She is not," the king protested weakly. "She comes to me when I call her."

"She does not come. You dream it. You will her to come back to you, but it is only in your fevered mind that she still lives. The rest of the world has gone on without her for years."

"You came to tell me this?" Herod asked incredulously.

"This, and other things. I am sent from God, my friend. And you are not so incurably insane as your palace believes. You do not have to live in this fevered state. You can face reality, Herod. You can accept what you have done and ask God to forgive you."

"I have done nothing!" the king sputtered. "How dare you!"

"You have killed your children. You have murdered the only woman that you truly loved. You have ruled God's people with an iron fist. You sent out secret agents to root out rebels and had them crucified in front of their mothers. You killed anyone who opposed you. You are king of the Jews, yet you crush them. You have allowed your own fears to rule you. You have blasphemed Yahweh, the God whom you claim to serve."

"A king does what he must." Herod pulled the sheet up over his bare chest, gripping the soft fabric in his sweaty fists. "A king must keep control! You don't understand! Everyone wants my throne! They want me dead! The Jews hate me! My own children hate me!"

"You were an intelligent politician. You knew how to keep the good opinion of the emperor. You knew how to build cities into magnificent centers of commerce and trade. You knew how to manipulate the tensions around you. God gave you great intelligence and skill, but you did not choose to use it for His glory."

"I am still a king! I am still king of the Jews!"

"The world is about to change. And I am giving you prior warning of this. The Messiah will come, God's own Son in human form. The prophecies are about to be fulfilled."

"Prophecies!" Herod spat out. He licked at his lips and shuddered. "The Jews use those prophecies to declare that I will be overthrown!"

"The prophecies are at hand, Herod."

"And how do I forestall them? You warn me, but you give me no solution!"

"When God acts, who can reverse it?" the man asked, spreading his hands. "You cannot stop it. You cannot change it. And God did not put you in this position for you even to try. You have not become the man that He intended you to be. Instead, you have allowed Satan to rule you. You have let your own jealousy and fear control you."

"Then what should I do?"

"Look to God, Herod. Look to God once more. Beg His forgiveness, and allow Him to use you as His servant. Allow God to guide you and become part of His magnificent plan for His people."

Perplexed, Herod looked away. No one had ever spoken to him so directly before. No one had been so unafraid of his power. Staring at the embroidered sheet that lay across his lap, he picked at a golden thread that was coming loose. His mind was clearing, and his thoughts were coming together. And as his mind began to open, he felt the surge of guilt rush over him as if it would drown him in its heaving flood.

Terrified, he glanced up and saw that the man was gone. Quickly he scanned the room. Nothing had changed. The door was still barred from the inside.

Who was that strange visitor? A prophet?

But he did not want to think about it. All he desired was quiet and rest.

"Mariamne?" he called out tentatively. "Mariamne?"

But she did not come. And he somehow knew that she wouldn't. He was left alone with his thoughts.

Mary sat in the courtyard of her cousin Elizabeth's home, grinding flour with a millstone. The millstone was a flat, circular stone set in a stone base with a wooden handle near the very edge of the stone for better leverage to turn it. Spreading kernels of wheat underneath it, Mary rotated the stone to grind the grain into fine flour. She leaned as far forward as her expanding belly would allow, her strong arms moving the stone in its methodical tread.

"You seem sad, Mary," her cousin said. "What is bothering you?"

"I guess I'm homesick," Mary answered, looking up with a small smile. "I miss my parents and my sister and brothers . . . I miss Joseph . . ."

Elizabeth, also large with child, pushed herself to a kneeling position. Her lined and wrinkled face was clouded with her own thoughts. "Well, it won't be long now, I'm sure," the older woman said. "Don't worry yourself over it. They say that all things are in the hands of God except the fear of God."

Mary nodded.

"I don't mind admitting that I'm getting afraid," Elizabeth continued. "You're a young woman, dear, but I am considered elderly. You will give birth quite easily, I'm sure. But will I?"

"God did not provide you with a child without the ability to bring him into the world," Mary said.

Elizabeth let out a bark of a laugh. "True enough! True enough!"

"Will Joseph understand?" Mary asked even though she knew that her cousin had no answer for her.

"God only knows," Elizabeth murmured. She paused to pat her belly. "This little one is a fighter; I can feel it! He's constantly squirming. No patience at all!"

The younger woman laughed. "Don't we make a pair! First-time mothers, both of us, with no idea of how to bring a child into the world . . ." Mary lifted the stone with some difficulty and scooped the flour out with her cupped palm.

"Not so awkward for you," Elizabeth said with a throaty chuckle. "You can ask almost any woman older than yourself, and she will give you answers. I am an elder in this community. I am supposed to have the answers for the younger women, yet I go out in search of young mothers with my list of questions!"

"And how is Zechariah dealing with impending fatherhood?"

"He's excited. He keeps writing on his wax tablet how happy he is. The angel did not lie. We will indeed be parents, and my husband has not spoken a word since he was told the news in the Temple! If only he had believed the angel when he told him . . . Zechariah would not be mute right now! I'm reading better, though. If nothing else, I have become more literate now that my husband cannot communicate by speech anymore. He uses the opportunity to draw pictures and then write the script for them below. Leave it to him to turn this into an educational opportunity." She laughed again.

"Teaching a woman to read! Well, God is doing strange and miraculous things through us women! Maybe it is not so unbelievable that a woman should read after all . . . Was that horrible of me to say?"

"You will be mother to the Messiah, dear," Elizabeth said with a fond smile. "And I will be mother to a lesser prophet. God willed us to conceive, and we did. If God wills us to read, then we will read!"

Again Mary laughed and shook her head. Everything was different now. The world was different. Possibilities stretched out before her. The Messiah . . . the one they had waited for so long . . . the one they had prayed for in hard times . . . the one they dreamed about and longed for in politically difficult times . . . He was inside of her. It was hard to believe. He would be born in a matter of months. Would she see the new order in her lifetime? Would she see David's idyllic rule return? When she died, would she rest knowing that Israel was once more unified and now ruler of all?

As a baby goat tried to nibble at the grain on her millstone, she pushed its soft nose away.

"Was that a knock?" Elizabeth said. She pushed herself heavily to her feet and put one floury fist into the small of her back, pushing her large belly out in front of her. Then she pulled at her veil, tugging it up over her hair as she went, waddling toward the door that led into the front room of the house.

It still surprised Mary to see her aged cousin large with child. Even the villagers here would stand and stare at her with undiluted awe. They knew that something extraordinary was taking place. Although something physically impossible, yet clearly it was happening before them, defying all natural laws.

"One of my neighbors has a guest from Nazareth!" Elizabeth called, waving a scroll in front of her excitedly. "He's a friend of a friend . . . recommended by a mutual acquaintance to stay with them while he passes through our village. And he was kind enough to bring a letter!"

Feeling her breath catch in her throat, Mary heaved herself to her feet as quickly as she could, reaching out a hand toward the wall to steady herself as she rose.

"For whom?" Mary asked quickly. "A letter for Zechariah?"

She hoped not! Oh, how she hoped not! To wait until her cousin's husband returned would be too unbearable!

"For you!" Elizabeth said. "Simon!" She called out the name, and a few moments later the old scribe arrived.

"Yes, madam?" he said politely.

"Will you read this?"

The old man shuffled forward and took the scroll from her hands. He loosened the wax seal with one shaky hand, worming it free with careful attention. Then he unrolled the parchment and squinted, moving it first closer, then farther away. Finally he nodded.

"It says," he began in a high, reedy voice, "'To our Mary, our daughter and our joy. May God be with you and protect you.'" He bobbed his head in satisfaction.

Mary stood, holding her breath, as the old man savored the fine wording before he continued.

"'We ask you to return to us as quickly as possible . . .'"

"To return?" Elizabeth demanded. "Are you sure?"

"It says so right here!" Simon insisted. "It says: 'We ask you to return as quickly as possible with Nathan for your upcoming wedding.'"

"Wedding!" Mary gasped, her heart pounding in her chest. Dare she hope it? Did Joseph really understand?

"Wedding," Simon repeated, then paused. He turned the paper sideways, squinted once more, then nodded again. "Yes, wedding. It says: 'May God protect you. We long to see you. Pray for your affectionate parents.'"

"Wedding to whom?" Mary asked. The baby inside of her kicked suddenly, and she winced under the surprise of the blow. "To whom?"

Simon blinked back at her. Obviously he didn't think a reply was required of him.

"Joseph?" Mary turned her question to her cousin. "Am I to marry Joseph?"

Elizabeth looked back with an equally uncertain expression on her face. One of the baby goats came up close beside her, and the old woman patted its curiously probing nose away from her without looking down.

"I have to pack!" Mary said, her lips trembling with emotion. "Oh, Elizabeth, I'm going home!"

CHAPTER 27

"A time to keep and a time to throw away . . ."

—*Ecclesiastes* 3:6

"You!" Elias shook his head in disbelief. There, standing at his door, dressed in grubby goat-hair canvas and smelling like sheep, was the filthy shepherd he had encountered several weeks earlier. His head was bare and his hair was oiled as if it were some sort of celebration or special occasion, and his beard had been neatly combed. But no matter what a shepherd did to clean himself up, the fields were always evident in his manners, and in the very smell of him.

"God be with you," the shepherd said in a low voice. "My name is Amichai, and I am kinsman to the shepherd who dishonored you in your own home. I have come to try to make amends for his behavior."

"Sleeping in my stables is offensive, but keeping the brat away would have been enough," Elias snapped.

"Perhaps, but as a clan we must take responsibility. I have a proposal for you that you might find of interest."

"I doubt that," the innkeeper replied, and he put his weight against the door to close it.

"You think we are below you," Amichai said calmly, putting his foot against the door. Elias felt a surge of panic. Although he had been about to call one of his burlier servants, something in that quiet tone stopped him.

"You are. Get your foot out of my house."

"Orli is not as marriageable as you might hope. She is a good girl, and we see her favorably. However, she has already become part of our family in a significant way."

Instantly realizing what the man implied, Elias froze. "That is a strong accusation for a shepherd."

"It is the truth, sir. Please let me in to discuss this instead of doing so in the street in the hearing of anyone who passes by."

Elias opened the door and stepped back only enough to let Amichai squeeze into the inn. He eyed the shepherd levelly, letting his gaze flow over the grubby clothing and wrinkling his nose at the smell of him.

The inn was a courtyard surrounded by walls on two sides, and rooms on the other two. The primary stables were on the lower level, with rooms above for higher-ranking guests or caravan drivers to bed down. Some raised platforms allowed other people to sleep with the camels and other pack animals. The door on which Amichai had knocked was at the front of the inn, and it opened onto a receiving room next to the dining room for more distinguished guests. Straight out the back of the narrow receiving room was the enclosed courtyard, where the sound of disgruntled camels and aggravated goats mingled with the cursing of some angry caravan drivers.

"Perhaps we could speak somewhere . . . more private," Elias said irritably, then turned and saw a servant gawking. "Back to work, dog!" he ordered. "I don't pay you to stand around staring at your betters! Move!"

Elias heard the irony in his own speech. The shepherd was not better than very many people. Filthy and undistinguished, they were as low on the hierarchy of social status as were the weavers who did women's work or the tanners who stunk to high heaven from their disgusting trade. But it was the same tirade he gave all his servants, and the words flowed out of him as naturally as water from a jug.

"Come in here," he muttered, opening the door to the private room that he used for business that he did not want to advertise. Servants gossiped like old women, and caravans carried word as readily as they did goods to trade.

Settling himself in the rickety wooden chair, Elias steepled his fingers and looked at the shepherd with amusement.

"You made a very disgusting insinuation about my daughter," he commented in a mild voice. "But you did make a valid point. My daughter was seen in the company of a lowly shepherd." He spat out the word like a piece of food from his teeth. "Her reputation might be ruined by association. That might require a financial compensation for the loss I will likely sustain in her dowry, sir."

The shepherd was silent and looked at him with an unreadable expression. It was infuriating when such people decided to act as if they mattered! Elias looked up at his ceiling of brushwood branches that lay on top of the rafters, then sealed with clay. He could see a place where the last rainfall had begun to leak and had run a dirty rivulet down the wall behind the shepherd's head. It would have to be fixed.

"She is pregnant, sir," Amichai said after a moment of silence.

"Shut your mouth!" Elias hissed. "How dare you speak to me like that?"

"It is the truth. Call her in here and discover for yourself."

Thinking, Elias said nothing. Was it true? Had he missed the signs?

"Orli!" he roared. "Get in here, girl!"

Elias felt cold fear worming its way up through his rage and disgust. What would he find? Was his only daughter really pregnant by the likes of this filthy mongrel? What would he do? He'd beaten her almost weekly when he thought she was misbehaving. What good would one more beating do?

"I am offering marriage," Amichai continued. "We can discuss it more seriously once you see your daughter. But our clan is God-fearing, and we believe in standing by our own. The young man will marry her, with your consent, and the girl's child will be considered legitimate, as long as her pregnancy is not known before her betrothal becomes public."

"Married to a shepherd!" Elias hissed, and spat on the ground.

There was a tap at the door. Both men looked up, anxiety in their eyes.

"Come," Elias barked, and the door creaked open, Orli's ashen face appearing through the crack. She looked at the ground. "Get inside all the way and stand upright."

She did as told, her eyes flickering only once toward the shepherd sitting across from her father.

"Quit hunching!" Elias ordered. "Upright! Back straight!"

The girl unwillingly did as she was told, her eyes filling with tears as she did so. As she straightened to an erect posture, Elias could see the mound of her belly beneath her robes, and his head dropped.

Pregnant.

"Leave," he said icily.

Orli cast him one look of unbridled terror, opened her mouth, shut it again, then hunched her shoulders again and backed out of the room. Elias silently stared at the door that she had closed behind her.

"She would be married," Amichai said after a moment.

Elias was silent.

"And we would take good care of her."

Elias was still silent.

Pregnant. His little girl. Pregnant by a shepherd. A waste—of his money, honor, and good name! She'd wasted everything that he had put into her so that she could have a good marriage and bring a top dowry! A waste!

"You will not lose on her dowry," Amichai said, interpreting Elias' thoughts. "The clan will pay what she was worth before this."

"You'll pay more than that! You will pay for the loss of my daughter, as well! You will pay for the fall in the eyes of my community! You will pay for it all!"

"I see you are a man who respects a coin." Amichai leaned forward.

Elias flicked his eyes to the shepherd's serious face, suddenly paying attention. Here was a conversation he could find interesting. "Go on," he said coldly.

"If Orli comes to us in good condition, not beaten, not harmed, bruised, or neglected in any way—and our women will check thoroughly, believe me!—and healthier and more plump than she is now, there will be two gold coins and six quality sheepskins for you personally, besides the dowry that we negotiate."

"Make it six gold coins and a dozen sheepskins," Elias said, narrowing his eyes, "and you have a deal."

"Four coins and 10 sheepskins."

"Done."

Something inside of him squirmed as he wondered what Nona would say. But he was the man, was he not? He was lord of this house—master of his women! His word was law, and he had decided to marry his daughter to a shepherd. She deserved it, the little wretch. Nona would just have to keep quiet about it.

The journey had been long . . . and it had felt longer still because of Mary's swelling feet and waistline. Every bump of the donkey's walk had pounded through her, and the winter cold bothered her more than normal. The wind was moist and frigid, whipping down the wild scarps and blasting into her robes. But Nazareth wasn't far away now. They could see the flickering lights in the distance. The baby wiggled inside of her.

"Don't worry, little boy," she said, tenderly patting her belly. "We're almost home!"

And by home, she meant so many things that she could not express. They were almost at her birthplace, passing through familiar territory that she had seen every day of her childhood, approaching the village where she knew every face and every story behind them. Soon they would be at the house where her father and mother would be waiting for her, her mother's aromatic cooking waiting under clay bowls to stay warm . . .

But home was also fraught with feelings of misgiving. Home was where they knew her family, where they judged her, where they would regard her pregnancy as a slight against each one's personal honor. Home was where her betrothed was . . . but was her betrothed still Joseph, the man she had fallen in love with? Or had her father negotiated a different marriage for her—a marriage with someone less inclined to be picky? That was a frightening thought!

"Nathan," Mary said. Her fingers were cold, so that the reins in her hands felt sharp and clumsy.

"Yes, miss?"

The old man walked steadily at her side, his eyes alert and his walking stick ready if he needed to use it as a cudgel. He swatted the donkey's rump, for it seemed to slow, recognizing familiar territory.

"Not home yet," he muttered to the beast, his gravelly voice low and comforting.

"This is beautiful country," she said with a low laugh, and he nodded to her in agreement. It was his home, too. He had been away from his wife and grown children the past three months. And he had grandchildren who would have sprouted while he was away.

As they came up over a low hill, Mary could see her village below them, and her face broke into an involuntary smile. Home! But in the twilight and the flickering glow of the village cooking fires that were now burning down to coals, there was something wrong. She could hear the bark of a dog far away and the plaintive bleats of some household goats and could smell the acrid scent of smoke from dung fires. From further away drifted the laughter of some men still talking around a fire. But something wasn't right. She could feel it.

"Nathan," she said, her voice tight with fear.

The servant did not answer, but scanned the road ahead of them. And then Mary saw them. At first they were little more than shadows, but gradually they emerged from the forest along the side of the road, walking deliberately toward the travelers with measured steps. Mary wanted to scream, but her throat had closed, and she clutched at her stomach, feeling exposed and helpless.

"Declare yourselves!" Nathan ordered.

The men did not pause or alter their course. Mary could feel Nathan tugging at her leg, and slid down from the donkey's back, patting its rump as she sidled around it to use the animal as a barrier between herself and whatever it was the men had in mind.

"You shouldn't have come back!" one of them shouted.

Mary froze. She knew that voice. It was the blacksmith, wasn't it?

"You should have known we wouldn't tolerate a sinful woman like you in our midst!" another added.

The men were almost upon them, and in the darkness it was hard to make out the features of her fellow villagers, but she could feel their hatred coming at her in waves.

"O God," Nathan whispered, "protect us!"

The donkey nickered in fear and tossed its head, pulling the halter out of Mary's hands as it cantered away several paces. Mary stayed crouched on the ground, hunched over her belly protectively. The baby was responding to her fear, and she could feel him thrashing out. She tried to calm him by rubbing her stomach, but her breath came in short gasps.

"Move out of the way, old man," a voice said threateningly. "She's the one to be punished, not you!"

"You'll get through me first!" Nathan replied. "Men, you don't need to do this! She's only a girl! Wait till daylight, at least! This is ambush, not justice!"

A stone hurtled toward Mary, bouncing off a nearby rock, and she let out a scream of fear. They wanted to kill her! She'd be stoned right here on the road . . . before she had a chance to see her parents . . . or Joseph . . .

"Stop this!" Nathan demanded. "Leave her! Let her go to her father's house! You know where to find her!"

"He never should have sent for you, girl," someone sneered.

"Uncle?" she asked in confusion.

"He knew what to expect!" her uncle Reuben snapped. "You dishonored us all! You and your sin! We cannot stand for this."

Another stone whistled through the air, this time smashing against Nathan's side, and the old man grunted in pain. Mary thought she heard a crack, and tears filled her eyes.

"Step aside, old man," still another voice said. "You heard us."

"Please!" Mary sobbed. "Please, don't hurt him! Please!"

When a rock glanced painfully off her ankle, Mary cried out on shock.

"Stop now, you heathen swine!" Mary nearly sobbed as she recognized who had yelled it. "This is not lawful, and you know it! If it were, you wouldn't have done it during the night! She is my betrothed and my responsibility. I marry her tomorrow!"

Confusion began to break out among the angry men, and they began to argue. Joseph emerged from the shadows, walking tall with quick strides. He was at Mary's side before she knew it, and he lifted her carefully to her feet.

"Can you walk?" he asked, his voice low and tender.

"Yes," she answered, testing her weight on her injured ankle. "I'll be fine!"

"Simeon, is that you?" Joseph demanded. "And Bartholomew, hiding in the shadows like a jackal? Shan! I know you all! I've drunk with you at weddings and cried with you at funerals. I helped you bury your wife, Nathaniel! You helped me bury mine! And now you do this?"

Muttering, the men began to disappear back into the night.

"And Reuben!" Joseph said reproachfully. "I saved you from dishonor! You would take my betrothed?"

His hand firmly under Mary's elbow, Joseph escorted her down the dark road toward the village of Nazareth. She could hear the labored steps of Nathan behind them, and he was cursing quietly as he tried to coax the donkey back from the brush. The moon was high and the sweet smells of night flowed across the country on the cool evening wind.

"Are you all right?" Joseph asked gently.

Mary was silent as she tried to keep her composure . . . to keep the tears from flowing . . . to keep the strength of womanhood.

"How is our son?" Joseph stopped and turned her to face him. "Is the baby all right?"

Swallowing back the tears, she nodded mutely. Her ankle felt as if it was in flames, and she leaned more heavily on his strong, muscled arm.

"Had they come any closer, I'd have thrashed them with my staff!" Nathan was muttering. "Throwing rocks like children, the cowards! They'd have had a taste of old-fashioned oak if they'd cared to face me like men!"

Together they walked back to the village, Joseph supporting his young betrothed, and Mary rubbing her stomach to calm the baby, who had now settled on the side of her body closer to Joseph.

She was home.

CHAPTER 28

If you ever need a helping hand, you'll find one at the end of your arm.
—Ancient Jewish saying

The wedding of Joseph of Nazareth to Mary daughter of Ebenezer happened quickly. Joseph came one night to collect his bride, and took her to his home for the weeklong celebration. It was not a traditional one, because he would keep his physical distance until the birth of the baby. However, he took her home to care for her, not trusting her safety to anyone else. His love for her was one of the great loves of history.

Her parents were happy to see her married and properly in her own home as wife. Knowing that she had escaped with her life, they breathed a sigh of relief, and her mother resolved to visit her as often as possible to help her with her pregnancy.

"How is Naomi?" Mary asked, leaning her back against the cool wall.

"Not well," her mother replied. "She is angry and bitter. She wanted to marry some boy . . . the blacksmith's son. Said that she loved him. It sounds like stories of the Gentiles! And now Ashi's family no longer wants her—" Esther broke off uncomfortably.

"Because of me," Mary said softly.

"I'm afraid so. But looking through the water doesn't show what's under the rocks, girl. You remember that."

It was an old proverb. Mary's mother was full of old proverbs, brimming over with them like a foaming vat of fermenting wine.

"And she is unhappy?" Mary continued.

"Don't feel guilty about your own happiness. You did not cause her problem. Your sister has been unwise and too willful. Her misery is her own doing. If she would only listen to your father . . ."

"And Father? How is he?"

"Enraged by your sister!" Esther laughed. "But otherwise, he is just the same, I'm sure."

"The boys?"

Mary couldn't get enough news from her family. They lived in the same village, but not dwelling in the same house had distanced her in a way that she had not expected. The boys kept growing while her sister became more complicated. Her mother's days remained busy, and her father saw to business. Life went on for them, seemingly without her. But that was the change a married woman had to accustom herself to. She had a life of her own now. While her family would always be her greatest support in life, they would now be on the outside of her new home . . . the home that she shared with her husband and his family.

"And you!" her mother said. "How are you feeling? Very tired?"

"Oh, yes," Mary sighed. "But I don't mind. I didn't realize how much the tiredness would get to me . . . and I get so emotional that I don't understand myself."

"That's just the pregnancy," her mother said with a wave of her hand. "Think of other things . . ."

Mary was silent for a few moments.

"He is the Messiah," she said quietly, looking down at her stomach. "I still find it hard to believe."

"As do I!" Esther exclaimed.

"The laws . . . our laws from God . . . our laws of tradition . . . why did God not choose a married woman? Why did God not wait until after my wedding?"

Her face clouded, Esther did not answer. She clucked her tongue and turned back to some olives she was pickling in vinegar.

"We do not understand God," she said finally. "We only follow His commands!"

"But the laws!" her daughter insisted. "They are our culture. They are our identity! They are our faith . . ."

"They are tradition," her mother said firmly. "And God is so far above the earth, like a bird soaring in the heavens . . . God is so far above the earth that our laws do not touch Him."

"Are our laws not from God?"

"I am a woman!" her mother said. "You should be asking a rabbi this!"

"I cannot ask a rabbi!" Mary retorted. "I asked my mother!"

"Of course our laws are from God." Esther shook her head in confusion. "The religious teachers tell us so. They explain how to keep the laws to make God happy. The laws show us God's ways."

"Then why did an unmarried virgin conceive the Most High God? Why?"

"I don't know," Esther sighed.

"By law, I should have been stoned. I was not raped in the country. I have not been alone in the country. I should have been stoned by law, Mother. By law, this child is not legitimate."

"The Son of God? How can He not be legitimate?"

"By law."

Mary looked down at her belly and gave it a fond pat. She could feel her baby moving, and she wondered quietly what he would look like . . . who he would look like. Would he favor any family member at all? Not Joseph's family, of course. But would he favor her family in appearance? Would he have the nose of her grandfather or the laugh of her second cousin?

Would he look like his young, confused mother?

Amichai bent over a ram and held it still while he worked a burr from its wool. The creature bleated in irritation and clicked its front teeth. With a grunt Amichai pushed its head away from him.

"Tough, are you?" he muttered. "See how tough you are when the burr starts pulling out your wool!"

The sheep had been corralled now for two months, protected in their fold with stone walls surmounted with sharp rocks to keep out wild animals. It was not a time of rest for the shepherds, however. The sheep must still be tended, fed, and guarded. The winter months, when rain and cold wind swept over the plains, were not good for pasture. But spring was in the air, and the sheep were getting restless. It was time to mate—time to start another cycle of life . . .

It's cold. So wet. Why can't you dry my robes properly? Bring me coals for warmth! Do I have to ask for every bit of comfort due an old man?

It was a relief to get away from the confines of the clan's encampment and his father's irritable muttering. They had brought the sheep to the wilderness, further from pasture, but closer to the caves that sheltered them from rain. The sheep knew the way of the annual migration even better than the men did. But their stay away from the rainy weather would soon be over, and when the ground had soaked up all the moisture it could gulp, the tiny nubs of green plants would begin to push through the ground, braving taking root in the most barren areas. The moisture in the air was dissipating, and Amichai could smell the first signs of spring and hot weather to come.

"Is it all arranged then?" Shandy asked, forking hay over the gate that confined the sheep. Working methodically, he glanced up only to see his brother's face.

"The wedding?"

"What else is there?" Shandy said with a laugh. "Of course the wedding. A good wedding is just the thing this camp needs. An excuse to eat and drink and celebrate!"

"It's done. Everything was finalized with her father yesterday. The sooner we come for the girl, the better, he says."

"And Raold? Is he ready?"

Amichai laughed and shook his head. "He's been dragging his heels like a sheep to be sheared! While he'll not be ready, he will do as he is told."

"What kind of girl will she be like around camp?" Pausing for a moment, Shandy leaned on the hayfork. "I don't mind saying that I'm concerned. Not one with morals, that's for sure!"

"Don't speak of her that way. There is more to her than Raold's deception. She believed too easily. Her father is too harsh. Her mother is no help. She is . . ."

"Like us? A father who beats and with no mother to speak of?"

"A father who beats. But also one who likes a coin."

"And how will you convince the clan to pay more than her dowry?" Amichai's brother shook his head. "It was a clever way to get what you wanted, but where will the sheepskins and coins come from? You shouldn't have acted before speaking with the elders."

"I have the coins. And the skins."

"And what will you get out of impoverishing yourself?"

"Nothing."

"How will you ever pay a dowry with nothing?"

"I suppose I won't."

Shandy again shook his head and threw another pile of hay over the fence. "You're a fool, Amichai!"

His brother did not reply; he simply crossed his arms and looked over the flock.

"I'd better go tell Raold that he'll be getting his bride," Amichai stated when he at last broke his silence. Not waiting for an answer from his brother, he turned and walked away, leaving Shandy to continue the work. He knew where to find the boy, and his brother did not understand. Truth be told, Amichai didn't understand either. That was what a woman did to life—she confused everything.

But Amichai could not find Raold that night. Nor the next day. He was gone. No one had seen him. The tent he shared with some other young men was empty of his few scant belongings.

And unknown to any of his kin, a young man with unruly curls and angry eyes bargained for passage with a caravan heading east.

"I'll pay," he declared. "I'll work, too. I'm strong."

The caravan leader was shrewd. He saw that the boy had only a few pennies and some sheepskins. It was not enough. But he was young and handsome, and no one would miss him. If the young man's work did not please, he could always be sold as a slave to the Persians. It was not legal, but it was not unheard-of. And the caravan leader was not overly scrupulous.

Meanwhile, in a civic center in Nazareth, a Roman centurion leaned his hands against the table in front of him and shook his head. Although not a young man, he had aged well, and his muscles were still hard from his military training. His hair was an iron gray, cut short in the military style and combed forward to somewhat diminish his receding hair line. He looked at the soldier in front of him. "Killed, you say?"

"By his own people, commander. Always the same, these Jews. Stiff-necked and angry. Taxing them is harder than taxing stones! You never know what they've got."

"That is why we have one of their own appointed as tax collector," the centurion explained. "One of their own always knows!"

"And they kill their own for it," the soldier said. "He was found stabbed. His taxes were not missing, however. Lucky for them they didn't touch the money!"

"No proof of who did it, though." The centurion shrugged. "But he was no Roman citizen. His death does not concern us. The taxes do."

The soldier was silent, awaiting orders.

"We need another tax collector."

"Yes, sir."

"Any leads?"

"There is the son of a blacksmith offering to repair armor for the soldiers for a high fee. Does it on the sly, behind his father's back."

"Sympathizer?" The centurion's eyebrows raised.

"Maybe. Smart enough to know where the money is, anyway!"

The officer nodded, pursing his lips. "Send for him."

CHAPTER 29

Fear God and keep his commandments, for this is the whole duty of man.
—*Ecclesiastes 12:13*

Orli wiped the sweat from her forehead and straightened her back. She stood in the courtyard of the inn, a broom in hand. The sun was warm, heating up the urine-soaked hay into a fly's paradise. The camels always left a good deal of dung behind, and after it dried somewhat in the sun, Orli would sweep it with the broom reserved for outdoor use. Soiled hay and slopped water had the ammonia scent of animals that burned her nostrils. She sighed, looking at the work still needing to be done.

Her father and that shepherd were arranging a marriage, and she should be grateful. She knew it. And she was grateful. A pregnant, unwed mother had little hope. But she also knew that the young shepherd did not want her. That realization stung. Marriage to her was his punishment.

"O God," she prayed, "I've ruined my life. No number of sacrifices will bring back any happiness for me . . . It is my punishment, too."

Jeb . . . no, they said his name was not really Jeb. Raold, they claimed—Raold would not make a good husband. Irresponsible, he had lied. And he hated her. She'd seen him once during the negotiations. He had been slipping away unnoticed by anyone but her. And then—for the first time since saying his rushed goodbyes in the stable—he'd looked her in the face. His expression was filled with disgust, and she'd turned away so as not to see it anymore. This young man would be her husband.

Would he come home? Not likely often. Would he be kind? She didn't imagine so. Would his family respect her? Knowing what she had done, no! She would be the bottom of the lowest family, despised by the very shepherds who took her in. The women would talk about her. There would be no friendly visits or chats around the well—no nuggets of advice from those women . . .

"Orli, it won't be so bad," her mother said, startling the girl out of her reverie. "You'll be married at least."

"Married but hated," the daughter replied, her voice low and sad.

"You brought this on yourself, you thankless girl!" Nona snapped. "You shouldn't dream of anything better!"

"I know." Orli turned to give her mother a sad smile. "And I will gratefully marry the father of my child. I don't want to be a burden on my father for a day longer than I have to."

And she didn't want to look at her father for a day longer than she had to.

"The boy won't always resent you," her mother went on. "He'll come around after he tastes your cooking and sees his son—God willing it's a boy and not a girl! He'll come around . . ."

Orli looked at her mother doubtfully. Her cooking had never been her strong point.

"Just let him have his fun." The older woman shrugged. "Let him have a girl here and there, and don't nag him. Don't get jealous. Just be glad for what he gives you. Let him be, and he'll settle into a routine with you."

It was sound advice for a girl who couldn't expect anything more. After all, she'd be married and have at least one child.

"Finish up," Nona said curtly. "You have some scrubbing to do inside."

No longer dragging her feet the way that she used to only a couple months ago, Orli did not complain or do the job halfway. Nor did she mutter under her breath.

She realized that she needed to be strong, because her father's position and his money would not get her anything anymore. Orli had come to understand that life would keep coming at her with the force of a hammer, and that she would have to bear up under it.

God make me into a better woman, she prayed. *God give me strength to face my punishment.*

And her punishment, she knew, would last a lifetime.

The synagogue was a busy establishment in any town. It was the center of Jewish life, the place of scholarship, debate, and intellectual prowess as well as politics and potential advancement. It was also a courtroom and a meeting hall. But most of all it was where the community worshipped. Because all wisdom began with the fear of God.

People met in the central hall for worship and gatherings on Sabbath, and the side hall served as the school for boys and a place where the more senior students debated with each other.

"The Mishnah tells us that there are 39 principal acts of labor that are forbidden on the Sabbath," the rabbi said. "What are they?"

"They are as follows," Ashi said, his mind flowing easily along the familiar paths. "Sowing, plowing, reaping, binding into sheaves, threshing, winnowing, fruit cleaning, grinding, sifting, kneading, baking, wool shearing, bleaching, combing, dyeing, spinning, warping, making two spindle trees, weaving two threads, separating two threads in the warp, tying a knot, untying a knot, sewing on with two stitches, tearing in order to sew together with two stitches, hunting deer, slaughtering the same, skinning them, salting them, preparing the hide, scraping the hair off, cutting it, writing two single characters, erasing in order to write two characters, building, demolishing in order to rebuild, kindling, extinguishing fire, hammering, transferring from one place into another."

"And why are the principal acts of labor delineated so precisely?"

"Because if a man were to labor throughout the Sabbath, he must offer a sin offering for each infraction."

"And if the man broke all 39?" the rabbi continued.

"Then he must offer 39 sin offerings."

"How many sin offerings for mowing clover hay?"

"Two, one for mowing and one for sowing, because the seed is shed at time of mowing."

"And if he mows two crops, but not crops that shed their seed?"

"One sin offering for the infraction of mowing," Ashi replied.

"And if the man, who had broken all 39 infractions, cannot afford to offer all of the offerings and feed his family as well?"

"He must remember how many offerings he owes. But Rabbi, I have a question. What if the man offered 39 offerings appropriate for a poor man, a total of 78 pigeons?"

"Is the man a poor man?"

"Let us say he is not."

"Then does he dishonor God by giving the offering of poverty even though he is wealthy?"

"Would God not be further dishonored if the man cannot properly care for his family?" Ashi questioned.

"If a man eats a clove of garlic," the rabbi said, "his breath then becomes foul. Does his breath improve by eating more garlic? I say no. More evil does not create good."

"And if the man commits the infractions through ignorance?"

"There is an honored rabbi who claims that ignorance is an excuse," Ashi's teacher explained. "But does ignorance negate the sin? If the heathen do not know that sacrificing their children is detestable, does the act become less repulsive to God?"

"On the other hand," Ashi countered, "if a man does what is right, but for selfish reasons, is this credited to him as righteousness?"

The debate was part of the education. A rabbi must be able to answer questions and to find answers in the Torah as well as the Mishnah, the oral law passed down through generations of debate and scholarship. A Pharisee rabbi must also be able to debate with his rivals—the Essenes and the Sadducees—and come out victorious. Once named a rabbi, a man held the responsibility of guiding the uneducated populace in the law of God so that they might please the Almighty and gain His blessing. He must also champion his theological stance—for a man who did not stay solid in his beliefs was nothing.

"The fear of God is a great responsibility," the rabbi said. "It stands between life and death, blessing and curses."

"Yes," the younger man replied. "It is a great responsibility."

The problem for Ashi was that while he knew the correct answers, and he knew how to argue in the style he had been taught, his heart did not always agree with his mouth.

Serving God, according to the scholars, was the greatest responsibility. But it was also the greatest burden. The more a person knew, the more they were responsible for, and the more they realized that they were incapable of fulfilling every stroke of the law. It was an exercise that could never be perfected.

Was it wrong to feel hopeless? Was it wicked to feel incapable? Was it a sin to wish he could stop trying?

Lydia and Shali stood outside the latter's house, Lydia having stopped on her way home from running some errands for her mother. A small, flat-roofed dwelling roofed with brush and sticks, Shali's house was built into the side of a hill, causing the back of the house to be lower to the ground as a result, making the roof an easy hop for the household goat. It stood, chewing noisily on some twigs, looking down at the two girls whose heads were together in conversation.

"He was found stabbed!" Shali whispered. "Dead and cold with a dagger in his chest! They say that if a dead man's eyes look at you, you're cursed!" She shivered.

"I wonder who killed him," Lydia mused. "I can't imagine anyone in our village murdering someone! Even someone as vile and loathsome as that tax collector."

"Can't you? You'd be surprised what people will do! I'm never surprised anymore, and neither should you be. Your father wanted to have your cousin killed."

"That was lawful!" Lydia protested.

"But she'd be dead! And what if her dead eyes looked at you?"

"Oh, stop it!" Lydia slapped her friend's arm in anger. "She's married to Joseph now, and I don't want to hear about her!"

It wasn't in defense of her cousin that Lydia didn't want to hear about the situation anymore. Rather, it was jealousy, mainly, for her cousin's happiness despite her pregnancy before the marriage was finalized. And defense of her father, who had shocked Lydia a great deal when she saw the most brutal side to his character—but, after all, he was still her father.

"Fine," Shali bit off, obviously wounded.

"So who will replace that vile tax collector now?" Lydia continued. "The Romans always have someone to do their evil work for them!"

"That is the strangest news of all," Shali said, lowering her voice. "Nothing is confirmed yet, of course, but it has been said that the blacksmith's son will be next!"

"Thaddaeus?" Lydia demanded with a laugh. "Not a chance!"

"You just think he's handsome," Shali said, giving her friend a wise look. "But I can tell you that a handsome face guarantees nothing."

"He's betrothed to Leah, though," Lydia observed. "And Leah's family is very pious. They would never stand for a son-in-law in league with the Romans!"

"Well, we'll have to see! But I've personally seen him talking to the Roman soldiers, and he wasn't one of those who threw rocks at them, either. So he might be more sympathetic to them that you'd think!"

"That would be traitorous to his own people!" Lydia protested. "Who ever heard of someone wanting to be tax collector? The Romans only want a spy to tell them how much people have!"

"Well, there is always someone willing, isn't there?" Shali asked meaningfully. "There is one in every town, betraying his own people!"

"But Thaddaeus!"

"And I saw him working on a Roman breastplate once," Shali continued.

"You did not!"

"I did!"

"You would have told me if you had!"

"Well, I didn't realize what it was then. But now that I think back, I realize what it was that I saw! And I'm telling you, it was a Roman breastplate!"

"How could you not recognize such an ugly thing as that?"

"He had it covered up with a cloth. And when he saw me coming with my mother, he pushed it aside. But I'm telling you what I saw!"

"You just never know," Lydia said sadly. "A handsome boy like that, and you just never know!"

"Well, he'll be rich enough when he starts collecting taxes," Shali said with a sniff. "They collect what they want, which is far above what Rome has agreed on! He'll be living off the fat of his own neighbors!"

"I'll believe it when I see it," she said in a final, feeble protest.

But she did believe it. And she wondered if Naomi knew. Or had she known all along? The thought made her raise her eyebrows and purse her lips.

"What?" Shali demanded when she saw her friend's expression.

"Just a suspicion!" She pecked Shali on the cheek and turned back to her own home.

Yes, her cousins might be prettier, and at least in Mary's case, more lucky in marriage. But the ugly truth about them was coming out! First a pregnancy before the marriage celebration, and now this. Lydia wouldn't be surprised if Naomi had known about Thaddaeus's wicked betraying heart the whole time!

CHAPTER 30

But you, Bethlehem . . . , though you are small . . . , out of you will come for me one who will be ruler over Israel, whose origins are from old, from ancient times.

—Micah 5:2

The past several weeks had been bliss for Joseph. Not only was Mary his wife, but she was safe under his roof instead of somewhere unknown. He could care for and protect her. Now he could see her sleeping next to him and watch the soft flutter of her eyelashes as she dreamed.

Mary pulled the blanket up over her rounded belly and murmured something in her sleep.

"What's that, love?" he asked softly.

"H'mm?" she sighed.

Touching her cheek with one finger, he smiled to himself. She was beautiful. But more than that, she was gentle, kind, sweet, intelligent . . . everything that he'd ever dreamed of both as a boy and as a man. And she was now his very own!

"You're awake?" she murmured.

"Yes, I'm awake."

"It isn't dawn yet."

"No, not yet."

She shifted her position to look up at him, then turned her head to glance at the small strip of sky in the high window, gauging the time of morning.

"You can't sleep?" she asked.

"No. I've been thinking. But you sleep. You need your rest . . ."

"I'm awake now," she said, sliding one hand across her belly. She looked down, absorbed in the miracle within for a moment. "He isn't yet, though . . ."

Joseph also put his hand beside hers. For once, there seemed to be very little movement. Lately the baby had been as active as a village market, sending ripples across the smooth, tight skin of her stomach. The time was nearing. Sometime soon she would give birth, and it worried him.

"There will be a new tax collector," Mary said.

"I heard. The Romans find any way to wring every last penny from us. It wouldn't be so bad if they didn't use our own against us . . ."

"In our lifetime we may see the end to the Roman rule," Mary said thoughtfully.

"They have ordered a census," Joseph commented quietly.

Mary turned her attention back to her husband's face, frowning. "Where?"

"My people come from Bethlehem," he said with a sigh. "I have no choice. If we are caught avoiding an official decree, the punishment will be severe."

"It's all right. How long is the journey?"

"Five days, I'd say. I'd be back in two weeks. I'm sure your parents would be glad to help you all they can while I'm away . . . God willing the baby won't be born until I return."

"That's just silly."

"I've spoken to your father already," he went on, frowning.

"Well, I would rather not go to be with my parents."

"Wife," Joseph continued more sternly, "the circumstances are not ideal, but I have no choice but to go to Bethlehem. I don't want to leave you alone in this condition. You could give birth at any time! You need people with you to take care of you, and I believe that your father has a more sensitive appreciation for your safety than my son's wife would. I don't want your uncle to get any ideas while I'm away . . . I should not have to explain myself."

"You are very kind, Joseph. I know I should obey. But I don't want to be left without you. I want to come to Bethlehem. You are my husband. I should be with you. I don't feel safe being without you, even in my father's house. He has been sick lately, and my uncle is a devious man."

"A five-day journey on the back of a donkey will not be comfortable," he said uncertainly. "Even if I had the money to hire a wagon, the jolting would be torture for you, especially now!"

Mary pushed herself to a sitting position and looked around the room. "I should bake some bread to bring. Some cakes of raisins . . ."

Seeing the obstinate set to her face, Joseph repressed a smile. So this was what marriage would be like with a woman who held him by the heart!

She glanced at him with a little smile.

"All right," he sighed. "I don't think it is in your best interest, my dear wife, but if you are so insistent . . ."

"Thank you, Joseph," she said, that sparkling smile of hers breaking over her face.

"I don't mind saying that I . . . I didn't want to go without you . . ."

"Of course not ,"she said with a wink. "We are one, aren't we? We face life together, whether that be the strange birth of a miracle boy or the jolting trip to Bethlehem for a census."

Standing, she pulled her robe around her, over her white tunic. The fabric stretched as far as it could to cover her belly, and she reached for a wooden comb to comb her long, straight black hair, her back to him.

"I've never seen Bethlehem," Mary said after a moment.

"It is close to Jerusalem."

"I've never been to Jerusalem, either."

"We'll go every year!" he promised. "Passover is extraordinary in Jerusalem at the Temple. You'll love it!"

And he felt such a wave of love for his beautiful young wife that he had to hold himself back from taking her in his arms. She was turning out to be stubborn and strong-willed . . . And he realized, with a wry smile, that he wouldn't have her any other way.

Herod stretched out his arm and watched as the servant smoothed lavender-scented oil over the king's skin with firm, practiced hands. The servant massaged, one hand over the other, pulling his strong fingers along Herod's muscles. Another servant was buffing and polishing his toenails. Closing his eyes, Herod willed his body to relax. Beauty was not something that occurred naturally in nature very often. Yes, there were sunrises and flowers, but people tended to be calloused, dirty, and dry-skinned. Feet were cracked, hands gnarled, and faces lined beyond all recognition. Teeth were rotten and missing. Humanity in its basest form was hideous. An individual was beautiful when he or she knew how to care for their beauty. And Herod knew how.

Yet even as he inhaled the delicate scents of oils and creams . . . even as he felt the skilled hands of his servants and could feel the softness and luxurious shine returning to his skin, he could not fully relax. Still, Herod remembered the strange visitor who had told him things that he did not want to hear.

Gingerly he felt in the back of his mind for Mariamne. She was there . . . the memories of her . . . the fantasies of her . . . comforting him. He loved her. Why would anyone want to take her away? Some things about her life were best forgotten . . . others better left alone. What was wrong with keeping the best of her alive? What was wrong with letting her comfort him and hold him and bring him some happiness? Did he not deserve happiness?

The plan . . . the man had spoken of a bigger plan that Herod was a part of. The thought was not pleasant. After all, Herod had his own plans!

"Stop that!" Herod snapped, snatching his hand away from the servant buffing his fingernails. "That's enough."

The servant backed away, head down. Yes, just what Herod liked to see! Worship! The honor shown to a god! The Romans had a very seductive life. Their leaders were gods . . . adored like gods, pampered like gods. And Herod, in his palace, was no exception. He liked to see the servants grovel, their eyes roll about in their heads from fear. Their bent backs and murmured apologies delighted him. Sometimes he would stop them in their work, just to see this display of his power.

Herod looked down at his fingernails. They were not finished. He shook his head in exasperation. "You!" he barked, gesturing toward another servant. When the king fluttered his fingers in the young man's direction, the youth hurried forward to finish the buffing.

"Call the master of construction!" Herod said. Someone slipped out to do as he had ordered.

Yes, Herod had plans. He more plans to build. Caesarea was spectacular—a port city of rare beauty and modern advancement. The king had ordered the construction of a harbor, a 50-acre basin, with gates to allow ships entry and with breakwaters to keep it calm and safe. Sebastos, he had named it. The walls around the harbor prevented silt and sand from washing close to the land, ruining the deep anchorage needed for large merchant ships. The gardens of the city were magnificent. The buildings were majestic. As with all Roman-style cities, the streets were straight and plotted in a grid for easy navigation. The city was walled and patrolled, protected from military attack on all sides. Outside the main walls were still more civic buildings, such as a hippodrome and an amphitheater. Caesarea was a rare feat of architectural genius, and Herod knew it. But he was not dead yet. There was still more building to be done . . . still more achievements to make people remember his name.

Rome would remember him. He would be revered for what he gave back to those who had elevated him to kingship. The Jews should have remembered him for the Temple that he built them, but they were a stubborn and prideful people, and still looked to heaven and prayed for his downfall. But he was one of them! Perhaps his mother was not Jewish, but his father was! What did a few minor laws in the Torah matter? They were his people, and he was their king! Why would they not love him?

"Your Majesty . . ."

The master of construction had arrived, and he bowed low, one knee bent and the other stretched out behind him.

"Rise," Herod said, flicking one finger.

The man did, and regarded his ruler with proper deference. "How may I be of service, Your Majesty?"

"I want to build!" Herod declared. "I have plans. I have big plans! I have plans that God Himself cannot overthrow!"

Herod let out a deep laugh. Plans—was that not what that strange man had said? God had a plan, and Herod had been put in this position for a purpose? The very thought brought bile to his throat. God's plans! What about Herod's plans? He was king! No one should ever dare use him! The Roman senate pushed him around far too much, and now some strange magician would invade his palace and claim that God had a plan bigger than he? That Herod the Great was simply a pawn in some infinite pattern? The king tried to control the rage welling up within him. No, he would not be a pawn to anyone . . . He would be king! He would control! He would maintain power!

"Do you think I am insane?" Herod unexpectedly asked, turning on the official with sudden intensity.

The man blinked, swallowing quickly.

"Well?" Herod demanded.

"Your Majesty, you are a genius and a leader of unrivaled skill and sensitivity. How could you be mad and have created such beauty around you?"

"Indeed! I have created magnificent cities!"

"Think of the Herodium," the official went on. "I worked with you on that edifice, and I was stunned by your brilliance! It is something to behold."

"It is impregnable. One entrance—a staircase of hewn stone! It is a mountain with steep sides, and a palace within . . ."

"Not only that, it is part of a military strategy of outposts, all within signal distance of each other to guard the farthest reaches of your land."

"But inside!" Herod's eyes glowed. "While battle rages without, I . . . and whomever I please to take with me, will be safe. Bathing in scented pools, hosting banquets, commanding royal entertainment . . ."

"I found the gardens to be most luxurious," the master of construction chattered, desperate to distract the king. "Most beautifully designed with foot paths and pools . . ."

Smiling serenely to himself, Herod sighed. Yes, he had created wonders that would not be quickly forgotten! And he would create more!

The plan . . . a bigger plan . . . a plan that was in motion in spite of Herod's best-laid schemes . . . what was it? A threat to his throne? Another ruler to rise? What plan had he just been warned of by the strange, disappearing man?

His heart pounding, Herod scanned the servants in the room with him, searching faces for secret knowledge. If there was a plot afoot, there would be people conspiring together, and they would seek to get into the deepest recesses of the palace—into the king's dressing room if possible!

And then Herod saw him . . . the secret visitor of the night before! His arms crossed and his eyes fixed sadly on Herod's face, he stood in the doorway, leaning casually against its frame, head cocked slightly to one side with an expression of pity. All at once all of the rage and terror that Herod had been so carefully controlling came welling up inside of him like an overflowing sewer.

"Guards!" he roared. "Seize that man!"

And then, right before his eyes, the visitor vanished into thin air. The guards came running into the room, armor clattering and swords swishing out of their sheaths in one fluid movement. They stood where the strange visitor had been, their gaze darting around the room, searching for the person that Herod had commanded them to capture.

"He's gone!" the king shrieked. "He's left! Search the palace! He is young, with curling black hair. He is calm, like a cat, and walks like a king! Kill him! I want his head! I'll give a city to the man who brings me his head!"

And as the soldiers rushed off, Herod sighed. "Mariamne," he whispered. "Oh, Mariamne . . . Come to me . . ."

CHAPTER 31

From the lips of children and infants you have ordained praise.

—Psalm 8:2

Amichai pulled his fingers through his mop of unruly hair and sighed. How could this have happened? How could he have missed it?

"Tell me again," he said, his voice tired.

"He said not to tell anyone," the boy replied, his lip trembling. "He said he'd be back in a few days, and if I kept quiet he'd bring me something foreign!"

"And this was when?"

"Two days before Sabbath. When he comes back, you can't tell him I told you!"

"Two days before Sabbath . . ." That made it five days ago that Raold had been seen joining a caravan going west. Five days of travel, the Sabbath included—Raold was as good as gone. Unless . . . unless the blasted boy had been telling the truth, and really did intend to return! The Amichai mentally chastised himself for his own naïveté. Raold had no intention of doing so.

"You did well to tell me." Amichai put a reassuring hand on the lad's shoulder. "Secrets are never right, remember that."

The boy nodded in despair, and, hunching his shoulders, headed toward his tent, where his mother was watching with a look on her face that said she would bridle no nonsense if her son didn't tell her exactly what was going on. Arms crossed over her chest and lips pursed, she watched her son amble toward the tent. Amichai couldn't help smiling. A father may be law, but until a boy was a man, his mother enforced that law, and this young lad was about to experience a little enforcing.

"Gone!" Amichai's father blurted out later that afternoon. "I don't know why you ever stuck your neck out for that good-for-nothing brat . . ."

"He has no father," Amichai said in a low voice.

"And you have no son!" his father bleated out with a reedy laugh. "Why pretend you have a family when you don't? You put your hairy face near the coals, and now you smell the smoke!"

"He deserved a chance to act like a man!" Amichai's voice had begun to rise. "He deserved that chance. Treat him like a child, and he'll never grow up!"

"Like you?"

"What do you mean?" Amichai regretted the question as soon as it was out of his mouth.

"You think I never gave you a chance to act like a man?" his father demanded, pushing himself up on his bed and squinting his watery eyes. "Is that what you think, boy?"

"I would not criticize you, Father," Amichai said woodenly.

"No? Well, I'd criticize you! You were weak and spineless from the day you were born! Pathetic, mewling thing, you were. You always wanted your mother and would howl like a wounded dog if you weren't latched onto her. It never changed. Even when she died, you acted like that mewling baby. I tried to beat some sense into you, and that never worked. I tried to tell you some sense, but you'd just turn blank like an idiot . . . and you think that I didn't give you a chance to be a man? I'd have been proud if you'd had the guts to go find you a girl or two! But you never even showed the interest . . . might as well have been a castrated ram!"

"Proud?" his son exploded. "Proud if I'd dishonored the family? Proud if I'd ruined some girl and gotten her stoned at her father's door?"

"At least you would have had some manly fire!" Jonah muttered.

"Fire? I had fire, Father! I had passion! I had desire and honor and strength. But you beat me with no notice. You beat me with no excuse. The things you said to me . . ."

Amichai was shaking now.

"The truth was hard to hear?" His Father laughed.

"Truth?" Clenching his fists, Amichai tried to control the shaking. "It turned into the truth, didn't it? Did you ever tell me you were proud of anything I did? Did you ever see what I did right? You kept after me until I was afraid to do anything! Until I was so afraid of you that I'd cower rather than take a firm step! And look at me now! I'm exactly what you said I'd be, aren't I?"

"At least you recognize it," the old man said, turning his face away.

"I let life go by me," Amichai said, his voice quivering. "I let it pass me by because every time I thought of some step to take, I'd hear your grating voice in the back of my mind. Did you ever give me a blessing? Did you ever encourage me and show me how to be a man?"

"A little late for you now. No dowry left. Nothing to give. So why cry over it like a little boy? What's done is done! You've got your lot. Even now you can't face it like a man!"

"It isn't too late for Raold," Amichai replied icily. "There is a boy who doesn't have to throw away his future. There is a boy who can benefit from having no father!"

The old man looked up in stunned silence, his mouth slack and his eyes wide. "You would speak to your father like that?" he whispered. "Breaking God's law?"

His mind still reeling with the things he'd said, with the things he'd felt for the past 30 years but had never dared speak, Amichai did not answer. But when he looked down at his father, instead of seeing the heavily muscled brute who had terrorized him throughout his childhood, he saw the flabby, weak old man in front of him. He smelled the odor of old flesh and moist, sour breath.

"I curse you!" the old man hissed. "I curse you! I ask God to ruin you . . . to tear you down and break you apart! I call down the curse of God on you for your flagrant disrespect of your own father!"

The words should have chilled him, but somehow they didn't. Instead Amichai gave his father a sad smile. "You cursed me a long time ago, Father. And I live with that curse today."

Then he turned and walked from the tent.

"I'm cold!" the old man whimpered.

Picking up a sheepskin in one hand, his son threw it across the tent. It landed solidly on his father's lap. Amichai did not speak, but his eyes locked with his father's for one moment.

"I'll be back to cook you supper, Father," the son said, his voice strong and low. And even to his own ears, his voice sounded different. He would cook for the old man. Jonah was his father. Children cared for their aging parents, no matter what kind of people they had been in their youth. It was duty ... it was law. But something had tangibly changed.

As Amichai walked away from the tent, his mind focused on the work ahead of him. He had a young man to find. The wedding arrangements were final. All that was left was for Raold to come for his bride . . . his bride who carried his child.

And if Amichai failed? The thought wriggled its way into his resolve. If he failed? Then a girl would be stoned, no doubt. Mother and child would die. And something inside of Raold would die, too.

"The dreams," Simak said. "They have been coming nightly now. I dream of the child that is born king of the Jews."

Several Magi from other provinces sat together on pillows and rugs in a private chamber, golden goblets by their sides, and servants in attendance with large feathered fans. The servants, all young boys, had facial expressions of stone. If they listened at all to the discussion, they did not betray it by a flicker of their eyes. They knew the law. If they ever revealed a word of something said by their masters in private, their lives would be forfeited. No amount of gold or promises of riches could erase the memory of the public beheadings they had witnessed.

"My dreams are more vivid now," Deepak said. A tall man with a long, flowing beard, his robes were embroidered in crimson, and his dark eyes were small and direct. "And as I offer sacrifices to Ahura Mazda, the dreams flash back to me in greater intensity still. Could it be that the great Ahura Mazda, Creator of all, is speaking to us?"

"In the past Ahura has always used signs in the heavens," Lian added. "Why does He now change His way of speaking to us?"

"The dreams foretell of a star to appear," Simak observed thoughtfully.

"True," another Magian agreed. "And we all have the same dreams, which cannot be ignored. This is truly a monumental event."

"And Judea!" Deepak exclaimed. "Persia is the center of the world, is it not? Why does this baby (king or not), in Judea, of all places, merit such attention?"

No one answered.

"Jewish prophecies point to this event as well," Simak said, breaking the silence.

"Yes," Lian agreed. "But why does our God care about the king of the Jews?"

"Things of the gods are not in the realm of men," Simak answered.

"But the gods do deal with the lives of men!" Deepak shook his head. "We are told of the rise and fall of our own kings and rulers . . . the gods work in Persia to bring themselves glory!"

"Perhaps our understanding of the concerns of the gods is not complete," Simak suggested. "Because somehow, each of us, a Magian from a difference province, has been given the same dreams heralding the birth of a Judean king. Somehow this matters in Persia."

"What are we expected to do?" Lian asked. "Just simply to know? To record the appearance of the star when it appears in the night sky, to measure it and study it? To realize that an upstart of a nation now has a ruler to be reckoned with?"

"Perhaps this is a diplomatic opportunity," Simak mused. "Perhaps we are to welcome this new king . . . to give him honor. Perhaps a political allegiance with this new ruler will be beneficial to our nation in the years to come."

"Do you think this is political?" Deepak questioned.

"No," Simak decided after a moment's thought. "But I don't know how to make sense out of it in any other way."

"It should be noted," Lian said, "that we are all rulers of our provinces, are we not?"

A murmur of agreement.

"We are also all of the Magian caste, priests of Ahura Mazda," Lian went on. "Kings outside of our caste have not received these dreams. Magi who are not rulers have also no share in this strange phenomenon."

"What does it mean?" Deepak asked.

Again silence. Everyone sat looking thoughtfully at each other across the leopard-skin rugs and ivory tiles. Ornately embroidered, their cloaks were each distinctive of the province that they governed. Their turbans had been wrapped with precision, and jewels sparkled from the coils of silk that rose above their heads. And their expressions were contemplative as each looked inward, remembering the dreams that stayed with them so vividly.

"It is not entirely true," Simak said, finally.

All eyes turned to him, and he looked down thoughtfully.

"Not true?" another king, Mina, inquired, his high voice entering the conversation for the first time.

"There is a child," Simak explained. "A child who shows promise in our arts. I have taken special interest in this boy and have tutored him personally."

"Your illegitimate son?" Deepak asked.

"No," Simak replied with a shake of his head. "He is not mine. But he is gifted and intelligent. And he too has had dreams."

"The same as ours?" Mina questioned.

"Yes, but with some difference. I suggest that you hear it from the child's own lips."

A murmur of agreement spread through the group, and Simak looked up at Nadr, giving him an imperceptible nod. The servant swung open the heavy door, and a small, pale boy slowly entered. His hair was dark, his eyes wide with fear, and he licked his lips, swallowing hard.

"Come inside, Anoush," Simak ordered.

The boy took two tentative steps forward, his hands clutching anxiously at his short tunic.

"Come," Simak repeated, softening his voice. "You know me. I will not hurt you, will I?"

Seeming to rally his courage, Anoush picked up his pace and walked to Simak's side, his large almond eyes fixed on the man's face as if he were pleading for his life.

"I want you to tell these men what you told me. Your dreams are of great interest to us."

Anoush opened his mouth, but nothing came out. He closed it again, looking pleadingly at Simak.

"Perhaps you would tell Nadr about your dreams . . ."

When Anoush glanced hopefully back toward the door, Nadr nodded and came forward, kneeling down in front of the boy.

"Please do tell me, Anoush. I would so much like to hear it."

"Well," the child said, his voice barely above a whisper, "I have these dreams at night about a star."

"A star?" Nadr encouraged. "What kind? Have you studied about that type of star?"

"No, Nadr. It is a star that appears one day, and no one knows where it comes from! But when it appears, it is because a little king has been born."

"What king?" Nadr urged. "A king in your province?"

"Oh no." The boy shook his head. "It's a king from a faraway land. It's a king of the Jews!"

"How do you know it?"

"I just do, somehow. And I know he is from far away, because everyone starts to travel in order to see him. And they all put on clothes . . . clothes . . ."

"What kind?"

"Like yours," Anoush whispered. "White tunics. Without robes and all the beautiful embroidery and things . . ."

"And what do the people do?"

"They are going to find the new king!"

"Why?"

"Because he is a king!"

"But why should Persians care about a king in Judah?"

"Because Ahura Mazda cares."

A few murmurs greeted the child's frank logic. The boy glanced behind him at the men, suddenly looking afraid again.

"That is a good reason for Persians to care!" Nadr encouraged, pulling the boy's attention back to him. "And what do the people do when they find the baby king?"

"They give him gifts."

"Did you see this in your dream?"

"I wanted to bring a gift," Anoush said, his eyes clouding with tears. "But I did not have a gift for a king. I'm not a prince. I have nothing special enough."

"So what did you do?"

"I prayed to Ahura Mazda in my dream. I prayed that Ahura Mazda would show me what a poor, small boy could bring the new king."

"And what did Ahura Mazda say?"

"A voice told me to bring myself."

"And who was that voice?"

"Well, I asked that, too!" the boy replied with a proud smile coming to his lips. "I asked who it was who spoke!"

"And who was it?"

"The voice said, 'I Am, who created all.' I don't know what it meant, but I felt that it must be Ahura Mazda, because it is Ahura Mazda who created everything, isn't it?"

"Yes, that was sound judgment. And was that the end of the dream?"

"No, not quite. I asked, 'If I brought myself, what would I do?'"

"And?"

"And the voice said, 'Little one, you must worship Him!'"

More surprised murmurs swept the room, but this time Anoush didn't look frightened. A big smile filled his face.

"Why is that?" Nadr continued, keeping his voice low and calm.

"Because the baby King is the Son of the Voice!"

A stunned silence greeted his words. Never before had Ahura Mazda sent his seed to earth. It was unheard-of, unprecedented! Why would the Creator of all lower Himself so?

"Anoush," Simak said gently. "What would you say that we must do?"

"Teacher," the boy began, then cleared his throat and amended himself. "Your Majesty, we must worship Him!"

CHAPTER 32

Therefore the Lord himself will give you a sign: The virgin will be with child and will give birth to a son, and will call him Immanuel.

—Isaiah 7:14

Aha!" Ebenezer shouted, clapping his hands and laughing out loud. Esther emerged from the courtyard where she had been cooking and looked at her husband, her eyebrows raised questioningly. She stood with her hands held out in front of her so as not to dirty her robes, and her veil draped across her shoulders, leaving her gray hair bare. The large bulk of her filled up the doorway, blocking out the sunlight.

"Praise God!" he said, snatching a cloth from his wife's waist and holding it in front of him, bending low to dance. She watched him in bewildered silence as he kicked out his heels and flicked the cloth to an unheard rhythm.

"Husband," she said finally. "You are not a young man. Doesn't that hurt?"

"And what if it does, woman?" he asked with a chuckle, stopping his dance. "Will you dance with me?"

"I will not!" she retorted. "I know what my body will endure, and what it will not!"

"Esther, our worries are over," he announced, leaning over and kissing her cheek with a loud smacking sound. "Over completely! God has answered our prayers!"

"How?" she asked, a smile coming to her face in expectation of the news. "What happened?"

"Naomi will be married!" he replied, standing back to observe her face fully. "Married to the family we chose!"

"How did this happen?"

"I just met with Ashi's father. Since Mary is safely married to Joseph and gossip has died down, he feels that union with our family is still desirable!"

"I had heard, husband," Esther said quietly, "that it is not so guaranteed that the young Ashi will be a rabbi."

"I know it," he said with a wave of his hand. "Does this bother you?"

"Not me." Esther took the cloth back and tied it around her broad waist. "He's a good boy, and hardworking. The family is respectable and God-fearing. I couldn't ask for more!"

"I have one concern . . ." Ebenezer said slowly. "What about Naomi?"

"What of her? Thankless girl, we've got! She'll survive it. I did, didn't I?"

"What's this?" he retorted. "Was I such a trial?"

"Oh, husband!" Esther laughed. "All I meant was that I had never met you before we married, and I was scared out of my mind!"

"You said she thinks she loves that son of the blacksmith." He spat out the words in disgust. Esther watched him in surprise.

"He was not our choice, husband. But I did not know you disliked the boy so much!"

"That boy! No, woman, there are things best not repeated before women . . ."

"I've heard the rumors that he sympathizes with the Romans, but I thought that was just talk. You know how rumors start from some sort of jealousy . . ."

"He may, he may not . . . That is one more reason to distrust him, I'll give you that. But no, my reasons are much more solid than passing rumor, woman."

"Would you tell me? It might help Naomi to know the truth of the boy. It might break her infatuation."

"The boy has been seen frequenting prostitutes." Her husband's face darkened with disgust. "He gambles, and he has no respect for his father or the business the man has built up for his entire lifetime!"

"How do you know this?" she demanded in shock.

"Men talk, my dear. You women always mutter about the idle gossip of men, don't you? Well, I've never put much stock in what men will say around a pot of stew, but when I saw the boy myself slipping off with some filthy harlot . . ."

"And you were sure it was him?"

"I'm sure." Ebenezer shook his head. "To think that our girl spent any time at all talking to that boy after I ordered her not to!"

"Well . . ." Esther suddenly found herself speechless.

"Now, Ashi," Ebenezer beamed, "he is a different story! He's been raised to be gentle and good. Intelligent—almost a rabbi, you know, and he'll make it yet, too. Just a little too idealistic at the moment, but marriage and babies have a way of straightening out a young man's perspective!"

"Handsome, too. Naomi will like that!"

"She'll like the respect of being the wife of a rabbi!" he retorted. "A God-fearing man., he respects his parents. And he follows God's laws. After all, he's a Pharisee!"

"A Pharisee rabbi . . ." Esther sighed from happiness.

"My son-in-law, the rabbi, said . . ." Ebenezer stated with a wink. "You know, my son-in-law, the rabbi, was mentioning that just the other day!"

"Really?" Esther's eyes widened with pretended surprise. "My son-in-law, the rabbi, just loves my garlic cucumbers. He always says that no one can make them quite like me!"

"Well, if the rabbi says it . . ." Ebenezer reached out to pat his wife's cheek affectionately.

"Father?"

Ebenezer and Esther both blushed and turned to look at their daughter, standing in the doorway. She was pale, and she pressed her lips together in a firm line, her eyes anxious.

"Naomi!" Ebenezer said, pulling her into a hug. "I have good news, my girl! You are to be married!"

"Married?" A mixture of emotions flew across her face. "To whom, Father?"

"Ashi! It's come through after all!"

"Ashi!" Naomi gasped, her face crumbling. "But, I thought . . . I thought . . ."

"They reconsidered." Ebenezer frowned at his daughter's response. "You are a lucky girl, Naomi. You'll be wife of a rabbi! You should be thanking me!"

"Thank your father," Esther commanded.

"Oh!" Naomi sobbed, pulling her veil over her face, then turning to dash back into the courtyard. They could hear her sobs quite clearly through the door.

"Don't worry about that," Esther said, waving her hand dismissively.

"Don't worry?" her husband demanded, fury replacing his earlier joy. "What kind of bride will she be acting like a paid mourner?"

His wife shrugged. "She'll have her cry, and she'll accept it."

"I'll tell you something!" Ebenezer said, looking darkly past his wife and out into the courtyard after his hysterical daughter. "The rabbi will have to take her firmly in hand! That's the truth of it! He'll have to take her firmly in hand!"

Esther shook her head with an unexpectedly broad smile on her face.

"What is so amusing?" he demanded.

"My son-in-law the rabbi will have a wife as sweet as he could hope for!" Then her smile became grim. "Hand me the wooden spoon, husband. I need exactly 20 minutes with no interruptions."

And Ebenezer watched his wife walk resolutely back into the courtyard an expression of dazed respect spread across his face. His wife was an amazing woman . . . to that think he'd ever questioned his parents' choice!

Mary and Joseph stood on the road that led through Bethlehem, travelers slowly wending their way past them. The census brought people from far and wide, and they all moved with the same exhausted plodding, their tempers short and exhaustion on their faces. The roads were damp from rain, and the animals flung up muck with their hooves. Roman roads were straight and slightly higher in the center to help rain drain into the ditches along the sides, but with so many travelers, road conditions had deteriorated considerably. There didn't seem to be anyone who wasn't mud-splattered from the knees down, Mary noted tiredly. The donkey's back was a lumpy, bumpy place to be seated, and from time to time, she would slide down to the ground and walk a little ways. But her energy was growing thin, and the pains in her belly were getting stronger. She didn't want to mention it. It wasn't something that one talked about to men, even to a husband!

"How are you feeling?" Joseph asked. "You look pale."

"I'm fine." She forced a smile. "Are there any other inns?"

"One more. There has to be room somewhere."

Mary grimaced as another contraction seized her, and she steadied herself against the donkey's neck, sliding down to a standing position to try to ease the pain. She gripped the donkey's mane and squeezed her eyes shut.

"Mary?"

Swallowing hard against nausea, she tried to breathe through the pain.

"Mary? Has it started? Mary?"

"It hurts," she whispered.

"Where?"

Blushing, she gave him a peevish look. He cleared his throat and had the decency to appear contrite.

"Mary, I've been married before," he reminded her gently. "I have five children . . ."

"Well, I haven't!" Tears sprang to her eyes.

"I'm sorry," he murmured. "The inn is just ahead. We'll get inside, and then you can rest. Everything will be all right, love."

The pain started to subside, and it felt safer, somehow to be leaning against his strong arm. She tried to pick up her pace, working her way carefully through the crowded street, and she felt a wave of relief as they approached the front of the inn.

To the side was a camel's gate, closed and barred, but ready to be opened to allow animals and luggage through. She eyed it longingly, hoping for some soft straw and a place to lay down away from the animals and prying eyes.

"Yes?" the innkeeper barked, opening the door a crack.

"Please, sir," Joseph said, "we need a room."

"No room left," the man said, thumping the door shut.

Joseph pounded again, and the door repeated the same grudging crack.

"Anything, sir," Joseph pleaded. "My wife is at her time! We are desperate!"

Voices rumbled behind the door, and Mary strained to hear.

". . . the upper room . . ." a woman's voice was saying. ". . . poor thing . . . we could make room . . ."

"No, Nona!" the man barked. "Why do you question me, woman? That room is reserved for the honorable gentleman who is arranging for us."

"He'd understand, I'm sure."

"And you would take that chance with your daughter's dowry?"

Mary glanced uncomfortably up at Joseph. It was embarrassing to hear private family squabbles, even at a time like this.

The door jarred again, a little wider this time, and the man appeared irritable and sour. His beard was scraggly, and his belly pushed his tunic out in a display of obvious wealth to be able to eat so much. Behind him a woman, plump with a longish nose and slightly protruding front teeth, stood watching her husband with an unreadable expression on her face. A girl, obviously pregnant, was watching warily as well.

"The stables . . ." the man said. "Best I can do. You pay first."

While the men arranged the money matters—and to Mary's ear, the innkeeper was taking more than a small advantage—she let her eyes stray toward the women. At a time like this, it was the company of women that she craved. They would know what to do. They would know what was needed and would rally together for a birth . . . at least if she were at home in her village. But this was Bethlehem, and no one knew her here.

The girl seemed more sympathetic than her mother. The older woman observed the exchange of money with an eagle's eye, and she gave the distinct impression of a bird of prey as she stared at the coins, her teeth pushed out like a beak. The girl, however, offered Mary a sympathetic smile and then looked anxiously toward her father.

"Out back," the man said finally.

"Through the gate?" Mary asked hopefully. At least being inside the enclosed compound would be safer.

"No, filled up," he muttered. "Around back there are some stables. There are some goats in there, a donkey and a cow. If you push the cow over, you should have room . . ."

Joseph looked at Mary in misery.

"It will be fine, thank you," she said. She could feel another contraction coming on, and the more time they argued with this sour man, the longer she had to stand in the street.

Taking the donkey's reins, Joseph led it around the back of the walled courtyard. Mary did her best to keep up, clutching his arm, trying to draw strength from his reassuring presence.

But what about women? Who would deliver her baby? Certainly

not Joseph! He hadn't even taken any husbandly liberties with her yet . . . To have him see her . . . to have him see this! The thought brought frustrated tears to her eyes.

"Mistress?" a soft voice called behind her. Mary turned to see the pregnant girl lumbering toward her as quickly as she could move.

"Yes?" Mary tried to keep the waver out of her voice.

"I'll help you," she said, pushing some swaddling cloths into Mary's hands. "I'll bring water and more cloths and some food that my father won't miss . . ."

"Oh!" Mary said, tears springing to her eyes. "Thank you!"

"I'm Orli." The girl suddenly looked shy and uncomfortable. "I don't know much, but I'll do my best! I'll be back . . ."

Then she hurried off with the same lumbering gate that Mary knew she used herself, being so large with child. Joseph led the way into the stable, searching carefully for any signs of danger.

Mary wrinkled her nose at the strong smell of animal urine and moist hay. The cow lowed a quiet greeting as they entered the dark confines of the cave. Joseph set to work immediately, moving animals and fetching fresh hay. And as Mary lay down on the bed he had created for her, trying to breathe through another contraction, she looked up into the soft, moist eyes of a goat.

"O, God!" she whispered. "Help me!"

CHAPTER 33

Glory to God in the highest, and on earth peace to men on whom his favor rests.
—Luke 2:14

Amichai rubbed the fat into the leather of his sling, the leather strap moving through his fingers in a slow, sleepy rhythm. Around him he could hear the sound of the sheep chewing, blissfully eating the first tender grass of spring. He didn't blame them for relishing it so much. As for himself, he loved the smell of spring—the scent of fresh growth and sweet, moist air. The crackling fire served more to warn off wild animals than it was for warmth. Sighing in contentment, he looked over the white and brown shapes of the sheep in the field, all his worries feeling, at least for the moment, very, very far away.

Raold had vanished, it seemed. And someone would have to tell the father of the girl. That thought nagged the back of his mind, destroying his complete calm. The boy was gone, and Amichai very much doubted that he would reappear at all. Searches had been fruitless. Several more people had seen the boy with the caravan, and it was by this time too far away to be able to catch up with. If Raold had a father desperate to find him, perhaps a group of men would have tried, but the result would not have been favorable. They would have made the attempt solely for the father's sake.

And somehow, surprisingly, life had gone on. The sheep still grazed, mated, and gave birth to their young. They still needed to be cropped and defended against wild animals. Life with the sheep didn't stop because a man decided to run away from marriage. Nor would it stop when Amichai would be forced to give the news to the girl's father. No, life with the sheep just went on with the regularity of the seasons . . . the moon . . . the feast times.

"He says he's doing all the building for us Jews," one shepherd was saying. "Herod insists that he's one of us! But when he builds, he uses our men as brute labor. When he gives us a gift, he offers us a graven image to set up in our city!"

"He's no Jew," another shepherd muttered. "Gentile as they come! His mother was Gentile!"

"Rome rules over us and claims that we govern ourselves!"

"When the Messiah comes . . ."

". . . we'll be free!"

"We'll have a king like David—good and moral, keeping God's laws. A man after God's own heart!"

"Not this Gentile pig!"

Amichai ignored their conversation. It was always the same. Men would complain about the Romans and wish for the Messiah. Amichai wished for the Messiah too, but tonight, sitting out on the hills with the sheep, even politics seemed very far away.

None of them had any warning. When he looked back on this moment, as he would every day for the rest of his life, he would not be able to recall any kind of prelude or buildup. Suddenly an intensely bright light flooded the night. And for a moment Amichai thought of lightning, except that the light stayed and did not flicker, illuminating the hills like broad noon, the sheep standing out like lumpy rocks. He covered his face, his eyes searing from the shock of the light, his heart pounding in his chest.

"Don't be afraid!"

The voice seemed to come out of nowhere and from everywhere at once. It was a booming, melodious sound, and Amichai tried to look through the gaps between his fingers. The light was blinding, but he could make out the outline of a form, like a man's, except much taller and broader.

"I bring good news of celebration and joy for all people . . . For all mankind . . . For Jews and Gentiles alike! Today, in Bethlehem, the Messiah has been born for you. He is the Christ. He is Lord!"

The shepherds were still hunched, trying to peek at the source of that voice. Amichai could sense the sheep frozen in shock, and he wondered irrationally if this would affect their stomachs. By nature the animals were finicky eaters, and upset stomachs could kill them. Slowly, though, his mind wrapped itself around the words, and he felt himself grow heavy with the weight of them. The Messiah! He had come!

But why were they being told? Dirty shepherds? Social outcasts? Men whose word could not be trusted to the point that the law would not let them testify in court?

"This is how you will know Him," the being went on. "You will find

Him in a manger, wrapped in swaddling cloths . . . in a stable with animals."

A manger? How could that be? The Messiah was in a barn? And the announcement made to shepherds? Who were they? They were nothing! They were lowest of the low, stinking from their work.

And then the light grew brighter still—so intense that Amichai felt as if he could see it through his eyelids, through his hands, through his robe that he held up to his face. A song burst out, so beautiful that Amichai felt himself wanting to sob in pure joy. The tune was one that he would never forget, and never fully remember. But he felt so overwhelmed in love that he wondered how he had ever felt alive before this moment.

"Glory to God in the highest of heavens!" the angels sang. "And on the earth, let there be peace and goodness . . ."

Then the song died away, the light dimmed, and the shepherds found themselves staggering to their feet with their hands stretched out in momentary blindness. None of them spoke as they tried to understand what had just happened to them, and then all at once they began to jabber.

"The Messiah!"

"Born! He's come!"

"Where was it? Where do we find Him?"

"Bethlehem! It's not far!"

"In a manger? Is that what he said?"

"Yes, I heard it too! A manger! A stable somewhere . . ."

And all at once, Amichai had an image in his mind of a stable . . . a cave behind an inn in Bethlehem, where he had stood, listening to Raold say his goodbyes to the girl he planned to abandon . . .

"I know where it is!" Amichai shouted. "I know it!"

And they left the sheep—in fact, they did not even think to have anyone watch them. The fire still burning and the sheep bleating in confusion, they forgot about everything else and raced into the night. They pulled up their robes and ran, their legs shining in the moonlight as they jumped over rocks and sheep alike. As they sped toward Bethlehem they shouted to each other, repeating the news, trying to make it sound more real to their ears. Their hearts pounding in their throats from the sheer effort, they laughed out loud.

The Messiah!

Simak smoothed his hands over the leather map of the heavens, uncurling the edges and frowning as he studied it. He turned back to the sky to verify the position of the star.

"Nadr. A star has definitely appeared."

His servant, always the mask of proper decorum, looked up at the star and then down at the map, and in uncharacteristic familiarity, he nudged his master gently out of the way so that he could see.

"The star!" Nadr exclaimed, his voice filled with excitement. "This is it!"

"It moves, however. I've been watching it for two hours now, and it has shifted perceptively. It used to be here, close to the edge of the sword of the warrior, and now it's farther away from the edge . . ."

"A comet?"

"I thought of that. But it has no tail, and the course is not characteristic."

"It shines in a peculiar way—different from the other stars."

"It is much different," Simak assured him. "It is exactly the star that I saw in my dream, Nadr. I have no doubt about it."

"What is to be done, Your Majesty?" The servant looked at him expectantly.

"I don't know . . . but it moves steadily westward, and as it does, it grows a little dimmer. If we followed the star, perhaps it will lead us somewhere. Nadr, is this crazy of me to suggest?"

"No, Your Majesty. You are a Magian ruler. You make worship of Ahura Mazda your life's goal. You make the stars and their courses your education. This star, sent by the one and only Creator of all, is meant for the very men who will understand its import. You are one of the few mortals, Your Majesty, with enough knowledge to put the pieces together."

Simak heard the flattering words, but he did not believe them. He knew that good, honest Nadr meant them with every fiber of his being, but Simak recognized his limitations better than his servant did. No, he did not understand the heavens. He had just studied what other men had studied, absorbing theories and calculating distances and measuring celestial courses. Yes, he knew what the other priests had taught him about predicting the future through the stars, but he also knew that such predictions did not always come true. Long experience had taught him the limitations of their knowledge. The sky was much vaster than they were, and he knew that they could never fully understand it.

"I am not worthy of this, Nadr," Simak said softly.

"But regardless, you were chosen, Your Majesty."

"The Son of Ahura Mazda," Simak repeated. "If the child Anoush is right, and I suspect that he will be the most powerful Magian ever to be born in Persia—if he is right, then this is the Son of the Creator, touching the earth and bringing us up into the realms of the stars . . ."

"And we must worship Him."

"The king of the Jews?" Simak said with a frown.

"Perhaps it is how the Jews will know Him."

"Is not the Creator the Creator of all?" Simak asked. "He did not create only Persia, but the entire world. He did not create stars to cover our nation only, but the entire expanse of the earth. And His Son does not govern only Persia, but the Jews, Rome, India, and China . . . May Ahura Mazda live forever!"

And what if Judea did not recognize Him? What if those backward people did not know the Creator of all when He was born in their midst?

"We must follow the star!" Simak decided. "Send messengers to the other Magi! We must ride tonight!"

In a smaller house, within sight of the palace, a little boy stood outside, looking up into the night sky.

"Come back to bed, Anoush," his mother called him. "You have a busy day tomorrow."

"But the star! Mother, come see the star!"

"Yes, sugar date, I have seen it. It is wonderful! But a boy still must sleep."

"The King has been born, Mother."

She came out to stand next to him and put her hand on his soft, curly hair.

"Is that what it means?" she asked after a moment. "That a king was born?"

"The King of the Jews," Anoush nodded with certainty. "And we must go worship Him!"

"The wise Magi will know what to do, sweet. You are a boy and must sleep."

"But they will go find Him! It was the dream that I had, remember? They will search for Him! And I want to go too!"

"Oh, Anoush," his mother said tenderly. "You can't go. You are too small. If you were a man, you would go with them. But you are still a little boy and need your mother. Who will feed you and hug you? Who will make you sweet goat's milk the way you like it?"

"How will He know that I wanted to go?" Anoush asked, his voice quivering with tears. "I had the dreams, and if I do not go to Him . . ."

"He will know, dearest," she said softly, leading him back toward the house. "He will know . . ."

"But how?"

"Because the Magi will bring Him gifts fit for a king! And you will give Him the most precious gift of all, right here at home.

"What is it?"

"The heart of a small boy."

"How do you know it is most precious?"

"I didn't know it always," she said, bringing him back to his sleeping mat. "I only knew it when you were born. And when I looked down at you, so tiny and so perfect, I knew right then that the most precious thing in this entire world was the love of a small boy."

Anoush lay back down on his mat and his mother kissed his forehead and let her cool fingers linger on his cheek for just a moment.

"Mother?"

"Yes, Anoush?"

"When I am big, I'm going to find Him!"

"He has already found you, my sweet. He has already found you . . ."

And Anoush closed his eyes and thought about the star until sleep came over his tired little frame and he slipped into soft, dark folds of oblivion . . .

Afterward Salma stood in the garden behind her house, staring up into the night sky, the sugary scent of flowers mingling with the smell of sleeping animals. As she looked at the star, her heart went out to an unknown mother. Because if Anoush was right, and somehow she did not doubt it—if Anoush was right, then somewhere in Judea there was a mother looking down at her tiny son realizing with startling clarity the same thing that Salma had discovered when her own son had been born . . . that her heart would never be free of him . . . that her life would always be about him . . . that his love was the most precious gift the Creator had ever given.

"My people hate me," Herod sulked. "They despise me! They refuse to accept me as one of them!"

"Perhaps another city in their honor," his adviser suggested.

"I build for them, and they still hate me! I gave them a Temple! I built a Temple to rival Solomon's, superior in every way! Did they thank me? No, they still distrust me!"

Herod took a piece of fruit from a silver dish and bit into its crisp, sweet flesh. Frowning, he looked thoughtfully into the dish. Yes, he would survive! He would rule! They would love him in spite of themselves.

"I have it!" he said. "I have read the Torah and the prophets. There are prophecies there about a king to rule over them. If we can make them believe that I am the fulfillment of those prophecies . . ."

"I'm afraid, Your Majesty, that the prophecies are too specific."

"Specific?" Herod laughed. "They are prophecies—vague and mysterious by nature! You are telling me that we cannot twist them? What about their king that they await so breathlessly? Find me the parts of prophecy about this king . . ."

"Your Majesty." Fear edged the man's words. "The prophecies clearly state that the king will come from the lineage of David."

"David!" Herod spat. "A roving bandit, he was! A wandering leader of thugs! And this is the king they look back on with such warmth?"

"The prophecies are very clear," the man continued weakly. "Perhaps there is another way we might discover . . ."

"Get out! Get out!"

Herod staggered up from his seat, his purple robes falling down the throne beside him. The man scurried from his presence as the king sought to control his rage. Finally, exhausted, Herod sank back down onto his throne.

The king to rule over Judah was from the line of David . . . The thought chilled him to the bone. From the line of David! He did not belong to the line of David. The prophecies would not be thwarted . . . Or would they?

He was Herod the Great! Magnificent and powerful, he made his own destiny! This so-called Messiah . . . this king to be born of David's line . . . he would be a man, would he not? And men bled. Men died. Men were vulnerable. Herod knew how to frighten them, to search out their plots—through torture if need be—and he knew how to snuff the life from their bodies.

This Messiah. If He were born in Herod's lifetime, Herod would ensure that their self-proclaimed "king" would not survive.

A deep sense of terror gripped Herod's belly. They wanted his throne! They all wanted his throne!

"Mariamne!" he called desperately. "Mariamne!"

And his voice echoed through the throne room and out into the halls. The servants shivered. The nobles looked away from the insane king of Judea. The soldiers shifted position, ever so slightly, making their armor creak.

CHAPTER 34

She wrapped him in cloths and placed him in a manger, because there was no room for them in the inn.

—*Luke 2:7*

He was so tiny that Mary could hardly believe that he was really here in her arms, his pinched little face and thatch of black hair standing straight up. His fingers and toes—she'd counted them four times—were so little and perfect, and she hadn't the heart to bind him up in the swaddling cloths yet. She wasn't finished looking at him!

"He's ours!" Joseph said quietly, putting a finger down for the baby to grasp. Mary smiled up at him. Although she still hurt all over from the ordeal of giving birth, now that she held this little squirming bundle in her arms, the pain no longer mattered. As long as the little one was safe . . . as long as he was fed and happy . . .

"Are you all right?"

Joseph had asked the question 10 times already. Hearing her screaming out in pain couldn't have been easy for him, she knew. A man had no part in the birth—he could only endure breathlessly as he waited, praying for the best. The girl, Orli, had been more helpful than Mary had hoped. Quick-thinking and able-handed, she'd brushed Joseph quite successfully out of the way with the authority that only a woman assisting a birth seemed to wield. And when it was over, she'd covered Mary carefully and let Joseph come to her while she bathed the baby and cleaned him.

"I'm fine," Mary answered softly.

"The pain?" he pressed.

"No worse than our mothers felt," she said with a wry smile.

Joseph looked pale and spent. His hand was shaking as he touched her cheek, and it was only then that she truly grasped how difficult it was for the man to stand by and helplessly wait.

The baby opened his mouth in a hiccupy wail, and Mary made soft noises, kissing his tiny face.

"The angel said to call him Jesus," Joseph explained.

"The Messiah . . . Can you believe that this tiny little baby is the Messiah come at last?"

Just then they heard the sound of a scuffle outside. Voices called out to each other, and Mary instinctively pulled her son closer to her breast. She felt vulnerable—so sore and unable to stand up on her own, with her tiny son depending on his mother.

"This is it!" a rough voice insisted.

"This? Are you sure?"

"This is—I'd swear to it. It's the place, all right."

"We can't just go in."

"But He's there!"

"Still—there is propriety!"

"Maybe if one of us went first . . ."

Mary looked wide-eyed at Joseph. He put a reassuring hand on her shoulder. Two oil lamps flickered inside the stable, and he picked up one of them and stepped to the entrance of the cave, holding the lamp high and peering out into the darkness. Joseph exchanged some words that Mary could not make out with someone outside. After slipping her veil up around her head, she pulled the swaddling cloths up over Jesus' little shock of black hair, her breath quickening.

Then Joseph came back into the cave, looked to make sure that Mary was covered, and made a gesture behind him.

"Joseph?" she asked uncertainly.

"The Messiah!"

"Is that His mother? Oh, mistress, you are blessed!"

"Could we see Him?"

"Just a little look?"

"The angels told us about him, you see . . . out in the field . . ."

"The light was brighter than lightning at noon! And the voices . . ."

". . . songs like you've never heard, praising God for the Messiah!"

"And this is Him?"

Trailing after Joseph was the strangest group of visitors that Mary could have imagined. They were rough-looking shepherds, walking as gingerly as tanners in a palace. One, an older man, was rubbing his grubby hands on the front of his rough robes. Another, about 30 by the looks of him, and the shyest of the lot, peered down at the baby in her arms with a look of such gentle reverence.

"We came as quickly as we heard, missus," the shy shepherd said quietly. "And I didn't think till now that we've brought nothing to give Him . . ."

"It's all right," Mary said reassuringly. "You don't have to . . ."

"I would have wanted to," the shepherd said. "He is our Messiah . . . our deliverer sent from God!"

"I've brought more water!" Orli announced as she burst in, then she stopped abruptly, reddened, and murmured some hasty apologies.

Mary glanced at the shy shepherd and was surprised to see his eyes locked on the pregnant girl quite intently. It was as if he no longer heard the chattering of his companions all pressed into the small space together, and he stared at the pregnant girl with a strange, direct earnestness. It took a few moments for Orli to notice his attention, and when she did, she reddened further.

"Sirs," she said awkwardly. "Tonight is such a busy night, but my father will be happy that you have come!"

Happy? For shepherds? Somehow Mary had trouble imagining that self-important innkeeper being anything but disgusted by this group of shepherds. But there was obviously something unspoken passing between the shy one and this pregnant girl. It was funny how a woman's observation never seemed to stop!

Mary looked back down at her child, and he was opening his little mouth in a tiny circle the size of a grape. Could he be hungry again? She looked uncertainly toward the men who were pressed into the stables, gazing down at her in amazed wonder.

"Oh!" one of them gasped.

"I think, Amichai . . ."

"I think perhaps the mother needs some time . . ."

"We've come and seen, men. Let's not be in the way . . ."

"Praise God!"

"The Messiah! Missus, you are a blessed woman indeed!"

"Thank you for letting us see Him . . ."

"We'll just . . ."

". . . be out there . . . somewhere . . ."

And they backed out of the stable, casting awe-filled glances backward toward Mary and the baby in her arms. All the while Joseph stood, nodding his goodbyes and standing solidly and protectively in front of her.

Elias looked out the window at the starry sky and back at his daughter in disbelief.

"Now?" he demanded.

"They are here! I saw them when I took some things to the woman who gave birth!" Orli insisted. "They are here!"

"To take you now? We hadn't finalized everything . . . well, not exactly . . . I was under the distinct impression that there would be one more meeting before they came for you."

Elias clamped his mouth shut irritably, realizing that he was explaining himself to his own daughter. She stood in front of him, her belly pushing out her robes and her eyes open in a look of anxious surprise.

". . . but Jeb . . . the young man I'm to marry . . . Raold, I suppose they call him . . ."

"What about him?" her father snapped. He'd like a better look at the little pig that had dishonored his daughter! Forced Elias into this . . .

"He's not here," Orli finished.

"Then why come in the middle of the night?" Elias shook his head, trying to keep his voice down. "If it isn't to take you to his tent, then why?"

Orli was silent.

Her father grunted something obscene and brushed past his daughter, heading toward the front door of the inn. There he unbolted the door and looked uneasily outside. Nighttime was dangerous in any town, and Bethlehem was no different. He felt the hair stand up on his neck as he thought about the possibilities if they had meant to rob him.

But there they were, this strange group of shepherds drifting away from the stable and toward him.

"Sirs!" Elias called. "Come inside!"

They approached, and he beckoned hurriedly.

"Quickly, quickly! Inside!"

Elias looked up the street, glaring at a neighbor who put his head out a window in curiosity. This was the last moment he wanted to be spied on by the neighbors! When the shepherds were ushered inside, Elias barked out for some wine and dipped his head in polite greeting.

"So good of you to come, sirs. The time is surprising, of course, but I am still delighted."

A half smile on his lips as he glanced from man to man, he waited expectantly. They weren't about to change their minds, were they? Not after they'd already good as made it binding! He'd never drag a shepherd to court, not in front of his peers, and demand him to marry his daughter! But he'd hoped to do this quietly . . . get rid of the girl without too much fuss . . . then make up a story to circulate.

"I would have come alone for this, sir," Amichai began, coming forward. "I'm afraid I have some news that will be difficult to hear. It is embarrassing for us, no less . . ."

And Elias' mouth went dry, and his smile dropped from his lips.

Orli crouched next to the door, tears of disappointment filling her eyes as she heard the words. Something was wrong! She'd been stupid to hope for anything else! Stupid to think they'd want her—a common tramp, pregnant and unmarried. Why should they?

". . . he's disappeared, I'm afraid . . ." the shy shepherd was saying, his voice strong and apologetic. "He's a disgrace, and we can't tell you how sorry we are for his actions. The family does not support his actions, I can assure you. If he comes back . . ."

Jeb—Raold—whatever his name, had run away . . . the humiliation was complete! She'd been willing to marry the boy, knowing how foolish she had been, and how sinful. Even knowing that he would be a poor husband, she still had been willing to marry him. Orli had been willing to submit to him and bring him as much honor as she could, even though she knew that he would despise her. Yes, she had been willing, because she deserved this . . . deserved it for the sin that she had committed—dishonoring her father and demeaning herself.

"Gone?" her father repeated. The girl recognized his barely concealed rage. "Gone, you say? And what of my daughter? What now?"

There was an awkward silence.

"Oh, God," she whispered. "What will become of me?"

"There was a baby born in your stable last night," Amichai said surprisingly. Orli pressed closer, holding her breath to hear his subdued voice.

"What of it?" her father demanded.

"A tiny baby, fresh in this world. He will be someone extraordinary!"

"Or some peasant," the innkeeper snapped. "What is your point?"

"Something changed inside of me when I saw that baby."

Orli knew that her father would barely be controlling himself at this point. In fact, if his rage had been directed at her, he'd have begun the beating already! But then it might not be far behind, she realized with a shudder, and she eyed the back door hesitatingly.

"My kinsman did not act honorably," Amichai continued. "He tricked your daughter and sinned against you and God. Now, he has done worse by abandoning his family's direct order to marry her."

"We have established that!"

"For the past few days I have been thinking of how to break this news to you. I knew it would be a disappointment, but you must know that Raold would never have been a good husband to your girl. We would have watched him like a hawk, mind you, but . . ."

Silence. Orli held her breath. What was the shepherd getting at?

"I don't know if you would accept a different husband in his place . . ."

A different husband? Her heart hammering her throat, Orli tried to hear better. Was it a cruel joke? Would they produce a sheep?

"What sort of man?" her father asked carefully.

"I am a poor shepherd," Amichai continued. "I have not lived my life to the fullest, for my own reasons. I regret this. I have no dowry to offer . . . not much, at least. Just a few pieces of gold."

"And the child?"

"I'd raise it as my own."

"Why?" Elias sounded shocked beyond belief, echoing Orli's own sentiments.

"I don't know," Amichai said slowly. "Because while I don't deserve another chance at the life I refused to live, I want it. And I believe that Orli wants another chance to live hers . . . and that the baby inside of her would want a chance at honor . . . The boy is my kinsman. I can take his place, and the child will not be considered illegitimate if we marry soon."

"Orli!" her father roared.

His daughter shakily stood to her feet, her hands trembling as she pushed the door open and came into the room.

As Amichai looked at her, his eyes were so gentle and nervous that it melted her heart. The man wasn't angry ... or mocking. He was terrified too!

"Then take her!" Elias ordered. "And the sooner the better! I don't want any more holdups!"

At that moment Orli glanced at her father, his grizzled beard, his receding hair, his sharp, squinting eyes. As she did she saw a tired old man with too many burdens and too many fears. Tears welled up in his eyes, and for the first time in her life she realized that her father loved her.

Then she turned toward the man who would be her husband, shyly looking up at him, too grateful to trust herself to say a word. He wanted her—wanted to give her a life to give her baby a life!

"Orli . . ." Amichai began, watching her gently. "I'm not young anymore . . . I'm not handsome . . . But I'll be good to you. I swear, I'll be good to you!"

The girl dipped her head in respect, as much to hide the tears in her eyes. And outside she could hear the soft cry of a baby, a new and tiny baby, just born in a stable outside her home . . .

There was nothing for Orli to say. The deal was struck. And outside, the soft cry of the new baby gave her the unexplainable, overwhelming feeling that she was forgiven.

EPILOGUE

And so Jesus, who was called the Christ, was born in the city of Bethlehem. For reasons unknown to scholars, Joseph and Mary remained in Bethlehem instead of returning to live in Nazareth, their hometown. Perhaps they decided to relocate to the city of Joseph's ancestry to get away from the constant rumors and antagonism of a village that refused to forget.

Regardless, they stayed in Bethlehem, and that was where the Magi found them when they finally finished their journey following that strange star. It has been suggested that the star was, in fact, the angels themselves singing out their song of joy in the cosmos, guiding the Magian kings from the East to the newborn King of the Jews.

Herod remained true to his reputation. When the Magian kings asked him where to find the newborn king, he tried to deceive them and told them to find Him and send him word. God, or Ahura Mazda in their understanding, warned them in a dream to go home by a different route. In a frenzy of terror and insanity Herod ordered the murder of all baby boys under the age of 2 in Bethlehem. He would not take a chance on anyone overthrowing him. Interestingly, Josephus, a historian of the day, failed to mention this episode. Perhaps it was because Josephus was a Roman sympathizer. Or perhaps 20 to 30 peasant children did not rank high enough on the scales of history to be recorded. Regardless, Joseph took Mary and their little son to Egypt, as an angel directed in a dream, escaping the king's murderous plot.

Herod died a little while later. Josephus records the drama surrounding Herod the Great's death. He had a horrible disease that caused tremendous amounts of pain in his colon and throughout his entire body. It was said that worms were eating him from the inside out. In fact, he was in so much pain that he tried to kill himself with a knife used to peel an apple. If his cousin had not restrained him, he would have succeeded. His son believed that his father had indeed died in his suicide attempt, and began to make his own adjustments in the kingdom. When Herod heard this, he ordered his son's execution. Five days after the son's death, Herod himself died.

History would remember Herod for both his political genius and his evil cruelty. Yet despite his constant attempts to keep his throne, he was not able to stop the birth of the Promised One . . . the Messiah . . . the Mighty Counselor . . . the Prince of Peace.

A Baby born in a stable who would change the world.

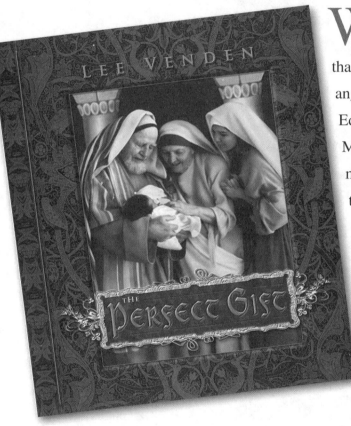

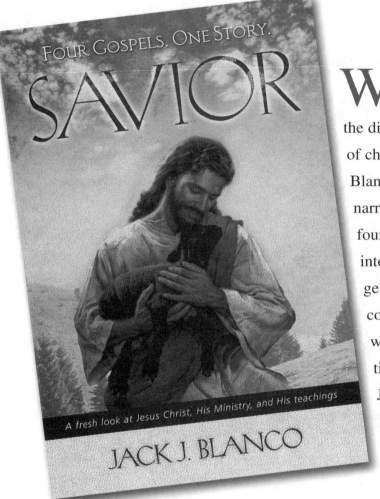

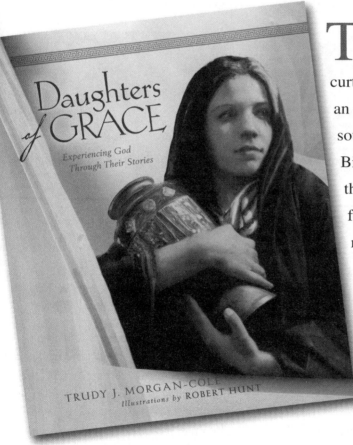

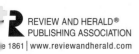

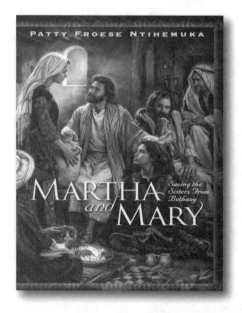

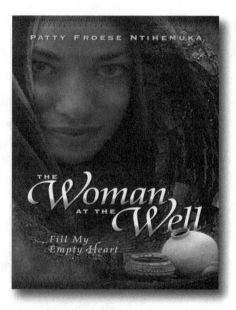

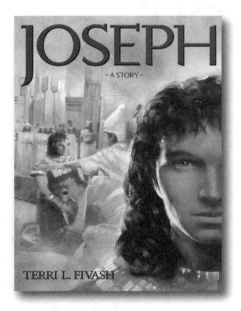

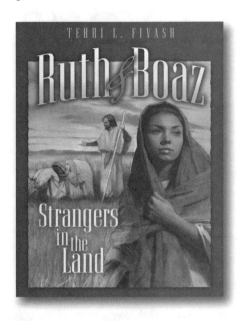

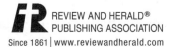